BOOK TWO OF THE ∅IGIL SAGA

SOVEREIGN

HUMANITY NEEDS AN UPGRADE

P.B. OBENG

ASCENDANCE PUBLISHING

Published by

ASCENDANCE PUBLISHING

ISBN: 978-0-9998186-5-7

Cover illustration: Eric Leon Westray

Cover design & interior formatting: Mark Thomas / Coverness.com

*I dedicate this novel to my wonderful wife Eunice and my family.
I especially want to thank my older brother Kofi for exposing me to the world of
superheroes which directly inspired me to create Vigil.*

PREFACE

To sum up my journey in creating this novel: "Rewrites, rewrite, rewrites!" After completing the first novel, Vigil, I had to figure out where to go next. Originally, I envisioned the Vigil Series as a five-book series. In fact, Face the Nations, the now third planned book in the series, was originally supposed to be the second book in the series. But as I saw the expansion of artificial intelligence into every aspect of our lives, both its potential harm and benefit, I knew that I had to write on this. The Vigil series was always meant to be topical, and the issue of data privacy, the power of big tech and how it affects almost every area of our lives, I felt called to write on this. We have seen the power of large tech corporations in every aspect of our lives. Tech executives have been called up to Capitol Hill to address their outsized influence over every aspect of our lives. We are discovering how some corporations intentionally turning a blind eye to the harmful content they allow to flow through their servers and on to our screens. And with the Internet of Things becoming a real thing I knew that this was fertile ground for a great story.

Going back to my earlier summation about the whole writing process—I was seriously stuck on how to make this story work within the framework of what I was trying to say about the influence of tech in our lives along with the broader overarching storyline. So, it was a task. I struggled with how I could incorporate plot threads from the first book into this one without confusing a new reader. I completed the original manuscript at the end of 2019, and it was over 90,000 words---yeah, a real whopper. After going through several edits and receiving feedback from my developmental editor, I was able to cut a considerable amount of fat. Mind you, some of that fat was actually good!

For example, there was a subplot of Agent Fighting Bull going undercover at a Chinese tech firm but upon my revisions decided it did not serve the greater story. I hope to incorporate that subplot in a novella in the near future.

Anyway, after multiple false starts (thanks to my book designer for his patience with me with this process) I was able to get the manuscript to where I feel it's at its best. I was able to incorporate threads of the first book without distracting from the present storyline. I hope that you enjoy the final product. And to all of my Vigilants out there, thank you so much for your support.

All the best,
P.B. Obeng

"You may live to see man-made horrors beyond your comprehension."
-Nikola Tesla

(1856-1943)

PART ONE

VIR EX MACHINA

(DAME-DAME: ADINKRA SYMBOL OF INTELLIGENCE)

PROLOGUE ONE

December 5th
Shibuya District
Tokyo, Japan

Raindrops pelted Kaori Fujihara's smooth, oval face as she squeezed her way through the evening throng of people walking across Shibuya Scramble Crossing. Her thumping heartbeat drowned out the screams of her pursuers calling on her to halt. Five men adorned in light, hooded jackets with grey, camouflaged BDU pants with combat boots, followed quickly behind her. The gap between them shrunk to a hair's width. Rain mixed with the tears streamed down her face as she felt them gaining on her. She cut her eyes to the subway station entrance. Her pace quickened as she darted in the direction of what she hoped would be her salvation.

Her pursuers barreled past pedestrians with little regard for their wellbeing. One of the men with a buzzcut and tattoos at the base of his neck, shoved a small, five-year-old girl into the path of an oncoming transit bus. The bus driver violently yanked the steering wheel to the right. As Kaori ran through the subway entrance, she glanced back to see the young girl, feet away from losing her life. Kaori's pupils emitted a cool, azure glow. The bus's electrical braking system activated, bringing the vehicle to an immediate stop. The forward momentum of the vehicle jostled the bus's occupants out of their seats, but they were none the worse for wear. The little girl stared in amazement as her parents quickly collected her from the middle of the intersection. Without breaking her stride, Fujihara continued through the subway entrance.

She pressed her way through the congested escalator. A gloved hand latched on to the back of her thin, right wrist like a vice grip. Kaori swiveled her head around to see the man with the buzzcut's firm hand grasping her own. She frantically wriggled her wrist backward and forward but to no avail. Kaori's eyes traced down to a bulge in the man's right thigh pocket. Sparks exploded from his BDU pants as an azure glow beamed from her pupils. The man screamed in anguish as he collapsed to the ground. Seizing the opportunity, Kaori yanked her right arm away as the man released his grip to tend to his injured thigh. She moved with alacrity to the subway platform at the base of the escalator, slipping lithely through the bustling crowd.

"Dammit, I told Jenkins to leave his phone behind," shouted one of the wounded man's fellow compatriots who followed close behind. He reached for a plastic, archaic looking walkie-talkie in the side compartment of his jacket. "Stiles, this Shepherd. The target is headed toward the Hachiko exit."

"Copy that. So, five grown men couldn't catch a twenty-three-year-old girl?"

"Now's not the time for your crap Stiles," the man spat back through the walkie-talkie receiver.

Stiles snickered, "I'm on it."

Kaori slipped through the gleaming, metallic sliding doors leading to Hachiko square. She was welcomed by the unrelenting rain as she exited the station. A crowd of people surrounded the statue of the loyal Akita dog that was the square's namesake. She slowed her pace, trying to mix in with the group. A person in the crowd offered her their dome-shaped umbrella to share as they walked toward Adores Game Center. Kaori obliged, taking shelter under it. The pursuing men followed closely behind. They pushed aside many of those in the crowd as they furtively looked for the young woman. An on-duty policeman noticed the commotion and accosted one of the men.

Another pursuer with a silky, black mohawk pulled out a taser from his thigh pocket. He firmly thrust the end of the weapon into the policeman's chest. 50,000 volts coursed through the hapless officer. He convulsed violently and began foaming at the mouth before slumping to the ground. Bystanders looked on in disbelief at what they were witnessing.

Kaori used the momentary distraction to break away from the crowd to make a beeline to Adores Gaming Center. Her red, Adidas tennis shoes sloshed heavily against the pavement as the Gaming Center's entrance came into view. Her mind drifted back to when she was a little girl; her father brought her there as a reward for her good grades at the end of each school semester. She frequented the Center so often she virtually knew it like the back of her hand. The rain-soaked pursuers, now whittled down to four, split off as they entered Adores Gaming Center. Two broke to the opposite sides of the Center with the remaining two following directly behind Kaori.

Fear quickened her thinking. She made her way between two unattended crane games she saw in the corner of her eye. Kaori shivered as the cold from her drenched clothes seeped into her body. With her heart beating a thousand times a minute, she tried to calm herself. Fujihara used a technique that helped quell her pre-game jitters before high school soccer matches. Thoughts of how her younger brother made her laugh before family dinners by plugging his nose with noodles, and how her father's warm embrace made her feel before she left for her first year of university flooded her mind. Her heart rate started to steadily come down.

Two of the flanking pursuers fanned the crowd looking for her. One of them grabbed his walkie talkie. As he clenched the device, his sleeve receded back to accentuate a tattoo of an eagle grasping lightening and a rifle in each talon.

"This is Cane. I have no sign of her," the man said. "Duval and Shepherd what do you see?"

"Me and Shep have got nothing," the bearded pursuer responded. "Faulk, you got eyes on her?"

Faulk scanned the crowd like a hawk, noting every facial detail, mannerism, and movement of those around him. He took his time before responding. "Nothing yet." He reached for the holstered 9 mm M9 Beretta on his right hip, sliding back the holstering strap. Faulk turned the corner to the cluster of crane games hiding Fujihara. Hearing the lurch of his footsteps drawing nearer, she lets out a small gasp. He immediately drew his weapon. The barrel of his gun led his advance.

As Faulk turned the corner around a *Pokémon*-themed crane game, its glass casing shattered in his face. He fell to the ground with a face marred with glass shards. He yelled in pain as the errant crane claw retracted back from where it shattered the glass. Immediately, Kaori shot out of the cluster of games and through the crowd of people gathered at the latest *Dance Dance Revolution* game.

Picking out the bloody shards from his face, Faulk radioed his teammates, "The target's on the move." Through blood-streaked vision he saw Kaori making her escape. "She's headed for the north side exit."

"How'd she get past you?" Shepherd asked.

"She activated one of the games on me. Threw me for a loop with a face full of glass."

"You ok?"

"Better than that bitch will be in a few seconds."

Fujihara looked back to see she'd shaken off her pursuers. A sense of calm fell over her as she slowed her pace. The crowd in front of her thinned out the closer she got to her exit. Her feet barely made it through the exit doors when she was met with a stiff, clothesline strike to her throat. The force from the strike laid her flat on her back. Her shoulder-length hair flopped in the air as her occiput slammed hard into the drenched pavement. She gasped, as she struggled to catch her breath.

Kaori tasted a faint hint of iron on her lips as she wiped the blood coming out of her left nostril. An overwhelming shadow hovered over her. Glancing up, she saw Stiles leaning over her with the barrel of a Heckler and Koch P30 pistol pointed squarely in her face. Stiles struck an imposing figure, standing over five-feet-ten inches in height with shadows obscuring most of her facial features. The spikey black hair and her spiraling dragon tattoo around her neck sent chills down Kaori's spine. Reacting instinctively, Kaori's eyes began to glow. Stiles' left arm started to spasm violently, causing the pistol to jerk out of her hand. Before Kaori's eyes reached full luminescence, Stiles delivered a quick karate-chop blow to Kaori's right temple—knocking her unconscious.

Kneeling over Fujihara's body, Stiles grabbed her gun from the ground, returning the weapon to the right shoulder holster hidden underneath her hooded jacket. She winced slightly as she grabbed her left arm and looked back down at Fujihara before reaching for the walkie talkie hooked on her back waistband.

"Target neutralized," Stiles said, as she spoke into the device.

PROLOGUE TWO

December 10th
Four Seasons Hotel
Palo Alto, California

"Results people, I need results," Bridgette Huntley said. Standing six-foot-one in height, her confident stature loomed much larger in the eyes of her subordinates, Finn McCullough and Lachelle Pitts.

Loosening his tie, McCullough tried to ease the tightening feeling around his neck. His thin cheeks became flush as he glanced up in Huntley's direction. He could feel her silver-hued eyes boring into him. Huntley leaned over the conference table with fists firmly planted. A piece of hair that was tucked behind her ear floated in front her face and she gently tucked the errant lock of her auburn hair behind her right ear as she looked down at McCullough.

"We-we're a go, Ms. Huntley," McCullough responded as his voice cracked. He quickly retrieved a small tablet computer from his leather shoulder-strapped bag. McCullough tapped the center of the screen. The glass covered circular aperture at the top of the tablet emitted a bright light. Suddenly, a holographic display of an elaborate array of satellites, cellphone towers, cars, laptops, and aircraft came into full view.

"The integrated A.I. system received federal approval," McCullough said. "Thanks so much for your help on this Ms. Huntley."

Huntley eased off the table and winked in McCullough's direction. "That's what I'm here for. Thankfully, we have connections with people in high places.

The Tessellation satellites look amazing by the way."

"Thank you, ma'am," McCullough replied as he smoothed over his tousled hair.

Huntley lightly tapped the top of the table. "Lachelle, what have you got for me?"

The young network engineer eased back in her chair and smiled.

"Everything you want to hear."

Pitts leaned over to the seat next to her to pull a small, chrome-colored laptop from her briefcase. She tapped a few digits on the keyboard and a holographic image emitted from the laptop's backscreen. Within clear view of the trio was an image of a white plastic cased cylinder approximately twelve inches in length.

"That's our next generation millimeter wave access point," Pitt said, pointing her left index finger at the image.

Huntley nodded approvingly as she looked back at her, "Pretty sleek looking model. Good work on the design Lachelle."

She bowed her head slightly. "Thank you, ma'am."

"And those will be able to run the CYBRA program?"

"Faster than 5000 gigs a millisecond," Pitts said smiling.

"And it's carrier wave potential?"

"Virtually infinite."

"And their coatings are impregnated?"

"Yes."

"Good," Huntley said. "We'll need it." Her eyes tracked over to McCullough. "What about the beta testers?"

"We've collated the Personal Digital Records of our target cohort. They're being recruited as we speak."

Abruptly, Huntley's cellphone ringer played the tune to Kanye West's *Stronger*. She immediately reached into her purse perched on the chair next to her.

"Yes sir." Huntley's spine straightened as she answered her phone. She nodded her head as she continued to listen. "That is correct sir, Stiles' team acquired the Asset. We are a go."

* * *

December 20th
Capitol Hill
Washington, DC

Senator Matrice Malveux shuddered as a small swarm of surveillance drones buzzed by her as she walked the steps of the Capitol building. Her eyes glared at the metallic devices as they ascended above the dome of the Capitol Building.

"I wonder how many FAA regulations that violated," Max Golding, Senator Malveux's senior aid, said as he handed her a binder-clipped document.

"Tell me about it," Malveux said as she grabbed the document.

"Have you talked to her about this?"

Malveux shook her head. "She hasn't taken my calls in months. Since she's taken the name 'Vigil' more literally she's been a ghost."

"I understand, Senator, but it's concerning how far they've expanded their surveillance apparatus. Not to mention their orbital drone deployment system."

"I know. I swear my god daughter is becoming a mini-autocrat," Malveux replied as she flipped through the heavy document. "This is the final draft of Digital Emancipation and Privacy Act?"

"Yes, Senator."

"We'll see how this goes. I've noticed that we've been getting some push back on this from Royce and her people."

"Well, we know AlphA.I.'s funded a lot of their campaigns."

"It gives me some solace that at least we'll get their COO up on the Hill soon to testify about their New Road Initiative."

"Yeah," Golding said. "Almost like pulling teeth to ger her testify."

"It's just amazing to me they were able to get this whole thing approved,"

Malveux replied. "Max, I mean this one company's got the green light to create an integrated artificial intelligence system for the entire nation."

"I'm with you, Senator. The project is already set for nationwide completion early next year."

"Damn, how are they able to get turnaround so fast?"

"They utilized Variant employees with the skillsets for the job."

Malveux shook her head. "I guess that's why they've invested in the VERGE academies, right?"

Golding shrugged his shoulders. "Exactly. They've basically created their workforce pipeline."

Malveux crossed her arms and said, "I'm worried Max. This has the potential to amass the control of our national tech infrastructure in the hands of one entity. And that terrifies me."

CHAPTER ONE

UNFINISHED BUSINESS

Nine months later
Tokyo Institute of Technology
Minato City
Tokyo, Japan

Automated beeps emanated from the metallic entryway into the geological research lab as it slid open. A female lab assistant outfitted with thin-rimmed glasses and a hip-length baby blue lab coat entered. She scanned the expanse of the lab as she entered its inner sub-chamber.

The young woman carefully placed a sleek cell phone sized device against the casing system's glass exterior. Red lights on the side of the device lit up sequentially. A slight hissing sound—like a pressure release valve—was heard as the glass casing slid back. The smell of fresh leather filled her nostrils as she pulled her gloves on. She reached into the glass casing, carefully pulling the tectonic module and agitator from their clamps. Her hands quivered slightly as she placed the device into her duffle bag.

The light steps from her flat-soled shoes were barely heard as she left the lab and walked down the long hallway. She quickly made her way through the labyrinth of winding halls and corridors. As she exited the building, she brushed past a thin man wearing sunglasses, and a bespoke pinstriped suit. She gently passed the duffle bag over the man without breaking her stride.

The man in the tailored suit carefully slid the duffle bag over his right shoulder. He eventually walked down a cobble-stoned winding path through a crowd of bystanders, toward the ornate temple of Zojo-ji in Shiba Park. Sweat beaded up on the back of his neck as the afternoon sun began to break through the clouds. He walked up behind two women—one with a pixie-cut and the other with shoulder-length hair.

"Madame Harada, we have the device," the man said.

The woman with shoulder-length hair turned to glance up at him.

"Very good work, Seiji," Codai Harada replied, as she lowered her Dolce and Gabana shades.

The freckle-faced Yakuza boss looked spritely considering she survived the collapse of the Network just over a year ago.

Seiji passed the duffle bag to the Harada's assistant with the pixie-cut. Her assistant carefully pulled the zipper back. With gloved hands she placed the devices into a large foam lined, carbon-fiber reinforced suitcase.

"Should I meet you at the rendezvous point?" Seiji asked.

"Yes." Harada said as they began walking toward the stretch limousine waiting for her just outside of the temple. As her assistant stretched her hand to open the door for her, the hairs on Harada's neck went erect. She quickly turned around.

"Is there something wrong, Madame?" her assistant asked.

"Give me your weapon."

Her assistant nodded and pulled a Ruger SR9C pistol from her shoulder holster and handed it to Harada. After placing the weapon in her coat pocket, Harada quickly made herself comfortable on the limousine's plush, leather seating.

Unbeknownst to Harada, Captain Alicia Conrad observed everything below. She used her high-powered binoculars to zero in on Harada's limousine from the Top Deck of the Tokyo Tower. Standing at approximately 1,093 feet, it served as the perfect perch for Conrad. Harada's limousine was flanked by four leather jacket-clad men on all black Suzuki Hayabusa motorcycles.

Conrad pulled out a rifle that bore a slight resemblance to an AR-15 from her tactical bag. She firmly planted the butt-end of the weapon against her right shoulder. Conrad brushed back the few thin dreadlocks as she looked down her rifle's laser scope. She pulled the trigger. The rifle hardly made a sound as she fired the tracer disc directly at the limousine's rear bumper. Harada's entourage didn't even notice the device as it assimilated to the shape and color of the vehicle.

"Got it," Conrad said over her earpiece radio link.

"Don't be so cocky Alicia, just 'cause you made the shot," Lieutenant Aaron Blankenchip retorted. His dark brown hair peppered with gray was illuminated by the noonday sun coming through the windshield of his Silver Dodge Charger. He shifted gears from park to drive as he moved in behind Harada's caravan.

"You know I've always been a better shot than you, Aaron," Conrad responded with a roguish smile.

"Get the hell out of here! I coulda hit that shot with my eyes closed and right hand behind my back!"

"I need you all to focus," Agent Cynthia Fighting Bull interrupted, with a schoolteacher-like tone. "We've been tracking Harada for the past year. This is the best chance we've had. Outside of Weiping Pei, she's the last Network Principal still on the run."

"I thought keeping the team on task was my job, Cynthia?" Conrad said.

"I guess you're rubbing off on me, Alicia."

"Isn't that a good thing?"

"Depends on who you ask," Fighting Bull said.

"You all set at Shinagawa train station?"

Fighting Bull shook her head and smiled. "Come on now. Don't forget who you're talking to here."

Conrad smiled at her remark as she packed the rifle in her tactical bag. and carefully slid her legs into her sturdy, leather lined rappelling harness and rappelled down the Tower's steel girded elevator shaft. Conrad made it to the ground floor and sprinted to the Harley Davidson Livewire motorcycle stowed away a block south of the tower.

Meanwhile, Blankenchip maintained a distance of three car-lengths behind Harada's entourage while Conrad's tracker signal displayed on the screen of his center console. Appling light pressure to the accelerator, he moved closer to Harada. Several car lengths ahead, a fender-bender brought traffic to a standstill.

Blankenchip patiently kept his distance. After a few minutes, the traffic began to lighten. He continued to follow behind Harada—tucking himself behind a bluish Nissan and a small Corolla.

One of the four motorcyclists that flanked Harada's limousine saw the out-of- place Charger in his rear-view mirror. He tapped his helmet and nodded to his partner. Immediately, the entourage split off in three directions—two motorcyclists headed east, another two to the west, while Harada's limousine continued south.

"Dammit, I think they spotted me," Blankenchip shouted within earshot of the team's communication line.

"I see what's happened," Conrad said as she saw the real-time satellite images on her motorcycle's display screen. "Stay with Harada, I'll tail the Gijo Hei going east."

The motorcyclists that accompanied Harada were her elite Honor Guard, or Gijo-Hei. These men were Harada's specially trained bodyguards, as deadly as any Navy Seal or Army Special Forces operative.

"Copy that, Alicia."

The Charger's Hemi engine rumbled as Blankenchip stepped on the gas in pursuit of Harada's limousine. Forty, then thirty, then twenty feet separated him from his target. Blankenchip's heartrate sped up, almost matching his car's acceleration as he drew nearer. As the distance narrowed to ten feet, his rear tire blew out.

The exploding tire sent the Charger careening headfirst into a nearby light pole on a crowded street. The Charger's front windshield and passenger windows shattered into multiple pieces. Many people scattered the scene. Blankenchip suffered whiplash from his neck bouncing off the exploding airbag, aggravating an old injury he incurred in the field many years ago. The airbag's impact cracked the bridge of Blankenchip's nose, leaving him bloodied. Blankenchip looked out of the cracked driver's side window to see Harada's motor cycled Gijo Hei shoving clips into their weapons.

"Careless, Aaron!" Blankenchip thought to himself, as blood flowed from his nose and mouth. He struggled to reach for his left wristband tucked under his sleeve---or more like a forearm bracelet (although he Blankenchip was too macho to call it that) to activate his exoskeletal suit. The bands covered the lengths of his wrists and forearms.

After they dismounted from their vehicles, they crept toward Blankenchip's damaged vehicle. They methodically screwed on silencer tips to their Sig Sauer pistols. They stood just feet outside of Blankenchip's damaged passenger door. Aiming their weapons in his direction they unleashed multiple rounds on the Dodge Charger with little regard to injuring any bystanders. Shell-casings of the spent ammunition littered the ground beneath the gunmen as they emptied their clips on the vehicle. They left the remnants of the vehicle resembling Swiss Cheese.

One of the gunmen inched closer to the destroyed Charger. As he reached for the driver's side door handle, the door flew opened explosively. The gunman fell backward, landing hard on his mid-back. After he briefly gathered himself, he looked up. Blankenchip, in his black hexagonal patterned exoskeletal armor, stood over him with the barrel of his modified H&K MP7 submachine gun pointed squarely at him. Being the wiser, the man raised his hands up.

"Put your hands behind your head!" Blankenchip shouted down to the man in Japanese—finally utilizing the translator suggestion that Conrad suggested over a year ago.

The assailed Gijo-Hei complied and clasped his fingers behind his head. Blankenchip tapped the side of his right thigh and an interlocking sliding panel opened, revealing a holstered H&K SFP9 M pistol. He plunged his hand into the thigh compartment, removed the weapon and pointed it at the second Gijo Hei who was about to fire on him.

"Get on the ground!" he screamed to the second one. Just as Blankenchip was briefly distracted, the first downed Gijo Hei opened his mouth. His vocal cords vibrated and unleashed a sonic scream that rocketed Blankenchip off his feet. He was slammed him back into his destroyed Charger. He shook his head before tapping the side of his feline-looking helmet to activate his armor's onboard countermeasures analysis. It was intended to automatically activate on his own, but it still had a few bugs to work out. Blankenchip's heads up display went crazy with streams of data that scrolled across his field of vision. Data about his assailants' abilities and vital statistics popped up.

"So, we have an Augment and a cyborg," Blankenchip said. Blankenchip's HUD immediately ran counter-measure protocols; none too soon as the sonic screaming Gijo-Hei got up from the ground and unleashed another sonic blast. Immediately, Blankenchip leaped out of the way, landing on his right side. As he tried to recover, he bumped into a young man trying to escape the havoc. Blankenchip pushed him out of the way just before he was walloped by an uppercut punch from the second cybernetically enhanced Gijo-Hei. The blow lifted Blankenchip diagonally off his feet and slammed him through the wall of an adjacent pharmacy. Blankenchip winced as his lumbar spine slammed against the wall. He grabbed the area where his old surgical scar was. As he looked through his helmet's cracked view screen, his HUD spat out gibberish.

"Aw hell, let's do it old school." Blankenchip ripped off his helmet and fired two rounds into the ground, just past the charging cybernetically enhanced Gijo Hei. The bullets ricocheted off the ground and struck the sonic screaming Gijo Hei in the torso and right thigh—severing his femoral artery. As blood gushed from his leg, he let out a sonic scream. The ensuing sonic scream blasted the advancing cybernetically enhanced one off balance and in Blankenchip's direction.

Dread came upon the Gijo Hei's face as he bowled toward Blankenchip's pointed weapon. Three bullets ripped through his midsection and another through his right shoulder, taking him down for good.

As he leaned over the dead Gijo Hei, Blankenchip noticed exposed wiring and metallic plating underneath his right shoulder. He used his armor's enhanced strength to rip off a piece of the metallic plating underneath the Gijo Hei's skin. He observed the intricate circuitry and silicon wafers. Flipping over one of the wafers, he saw a Japanese name etched on its surface.

Blankenchip crept toward the wounded sonic screaming Gijo Hei. He pressed his right knee into the Gijo Hei's wounded thigh while creating a seal over his mouth with his left hand. Blankenchip then firmly planted the barrel of his weapon in the center of the Gijo Hei's chest.

"You even dare let off a sonic scream and I swear I will leave a crater in your chest."

The Gijo Hei's eyes widened as sweat beaded up on his furrowed brow. Blankenchip released the tight seal over the man's mouth. Blankenchip lifted the silicon wafer to within an inch of the Gijo Hei's face.

"Tell me where you got these enhancements."

As he felt the firm thrust of Blankenchip's weapon in his chest, his eyes looked down worriedly at the barrel and then up to Blankenchip's menacing face.

"Saisentan."

"Thanks."

Blankenchip struck him in the face, with a forceful enough blow to knock him unconscious. He radioed Conrad.

"Alicia, watch your ass. Harada's upgraded her personal bodyguards."

"Yeah, I see that," Conrad responded as she swerved to dodge a bio-electric pulse blast from one of the motorcycled Gijo Hei. The blast seared through the front grill of the black Toyota Land Cruiser behind her. The downward impact flipped the vehicle over in mid-air, right above Conrad's head. As the vehicle somersaulted over her, Conrad glimpsed the occupants of the SUV through the vehicle's windshield. They were barely older than her siblings.

The male driver and female passenger were thrown about inside the vehicle's cabin. As their world became a jumbled mess, the driver didn't notice the windshield shattered. Suddenly, he felt his seatbelt release as Conrad cut it. Conrad stabilized him with a scissor leg hold while she reached for the other passenger. With a speed that defied comprehension, the passenger side seatbelt was quickly cut by Conrad's Night Force knife. Conrad attached a metallic disc with numerous drilled holes on the young woman while the SUV was still airborne. The disc released a grayish-colored microencapsulated polymer that encased the woman in an expanding foam composite. It made the woman resemble something like a human puffer fish. She was thrusted through the passenger side door as the protective foam casing rapidly expanded. Her composite encased body bounced lightly into traffic as many drivers veered out of the way to avoid her. Some couldn't avoid her but she ping-ponged from some of those cars without any harm to herself or the other passengers.

Conrad pressed the center button of her tactical belt which released thin metal filaments from the belt's side compartments, entangling the man close to Conrad. She pulled a grappling gun from her thigh pocket and fired a high tensile strength grappling line through the shattered windshield. The electrostatic grappling hook latched on to one of the light poles that aligned the freeway.

Conrad and the driver were immediately yanked away out of the tumbling SUV. As they retracted out of harm's way, she pulled another metallic disc from her harness and threw it in the direction of the tumbling vehicle. The damaged SUV was suddenly encapsulated in a foam composite as well, keeping the vehicle from causing more damage to the other oncoming vehicles on the freeway.

Conrad and the SUV driver came down from the light pole on the freeway shoulder. Emergency service vehicle sirens suddenly immersed the area. She unstrapped the driver. A quick visual observation showed some minor cuts on his face from the broken windshield glass but no other major wounds.

She asked the passenger if he was ok, trying her best in broken Japanese. He acknowledged he was fine. An ambulance quickly pulled up just feet beside them. As the paramedics brought out their stretcher, Conrad looked up to see Harada's Gijo Hei had already sped off.

* * *

Fifteen Minutes Later
Shinagawa Train Station
Tokyo, Japan

Harada was quickly ushered out of her limousine through the train station's Konan entrance by her four Gijo Hei bodyguards who were in the limousine with her. Their way was impeded by the mob of shoppers. As they pushed aside bystanders, they caught the attention of onlookers as well as an observant transit police officer.

"Stop. Put your hands up!" the transit officer screamed.

Harada and her entourage momentarily paused at the command. Within moments, a squad of five more transit police officers converged on Harada's location. Three of the officers formed a perimeter around Harada and her Gijo Hei, which blocked them from ascending to the first-floor JR platform.

Harada looked in the direction of a member of her Gijo-Hei who wore a brown leather jacket, shades, and gloves. He nodded in her direction and removed his shades---behind them were glowing eyes crackling with power. A pulsating circle of red energy began to form in the palms of his hands. He raised his hands to unleash a bright red bioelectric blast as the three officers returned fire.

Meanwhile, on the upper platform, Fighting Bull heard the cacophony on the floor below her. She checked the shoulder holster underneath her fitted beige trench coat to make sure that her Sig Sauer P365 and glasses were in place. Fighting Bull ran toward the first-floor platform. She leaped over turnstiles and in between screaming crowds fleeing the scene. As soon as her feet touched the ground, she saw the fire fight.

Bullets buzzed back and forth between the transit police and the Gijo-Hei. One transit officer wounded the super-powered Gijo Hei. As he fell, he emitted an errant energy blast that hit a horizontal fluorescent light fixture. The fixture descended upon a large crowd of civilians below. A little girl with an incredibly over-sized *Hello Kitty* backpack was left behind as the crowd scattered. Fighting Bull's heart raced as she moved swiftly to move the child out of harm's way. As she grabbed the girl, she pulled the child close to her chest and tumbled forward in a front roll. Fighting Bull let out a slight grunt as her back slammed against the platform handrails.

After they recovered, the girl's parents quickly ran to gather her. With the girl safe with her parents, Fighting Bull immediately morphed into one of the transit police. She aimed her Sig Sauer P365 pistol on her target. Her aim was fixed on the Gijo Hei who fired his Beretta. She let off three shots. They hit their mark and pierced his chest wall and neck. Since the Lemalian war, she honed her action-shooting skills to almost, but not completely, rival that of Conrad's.

Another Gijo Hei saw his comrade felled by the flurry of Fighting Bull's bullets. He then trained his pistol on Fighting Bull, firing errantly. She took cover behind a news stand as she morphed into Agent John Arrowhawk's form. She immediately erected a broad band energy shield to deflect the bullets that were being fired up on her. Due to recent upgrades to her uniform, she was able to store the abilities of the people who she morphed into for a 15-minute window—something the tech division called "tactile memory."

As Fighting Bull defended herself, Harada rushed up the escalator to platform 23, for the Shinkansen train to Kyoto. Noticing Harada making her escape, Fighting Bull directed a broad bright blue energy blast from her left hand that knocked the gunman out. She quickly morphed back to her natural form as she raced up the escalator behind Harada. As soon as she hit the platform, Fighting Bull saw Harada slide into one of the forward train cars. She swiftly made her way through the sliding doors of the train car immediately behind Harada.

Fighting Bull put on the dark-tinted glasses with metallic black frames that she had previously tucked away. Thankfully, those weren't affected by her multiple metamorphoses. The glasses provided her with heads-up display-like schematics on everyone on the train. She scanned the train car intently. As she looked around, every detail popped up on the lens of her glasses—everything from height, age, and gender were laid bare for Fighting Bull to see. She walked down the nicely carpeted aisle to make her way through multiple train cars until she got to the Gran Class, or high-class section of the train.

Around the fifth row from the train car entrance a matched heat signature popped up. With her target acquired, Fighting Bull folded the glasses and put them back in her coat pocket. As she made her way toward Harada, her original face melted back to reveal the face of a young Japanese woman. Fighting Bull took a seat in the luxury chair across from Harada. To her right was a port window. She saw Harada with her leg crossed and the suitcase with the tectonic agitator. Harada had placed her coat over the edge of her armrest, to give herself some breathing room. Fighting Bull looked unassumingly at Harada, eliciting a small smile.

"Nice weather today isn't it?" Fighting Bull asked in Japanese.

Harada nodded, trying not to look too frazzled, "Yes, it is."

"Too bad they say a heavy storm is coming this evening."

"What was that?" Harada asked.

"A storm is supposed to be coming," Fighting Bull said, with an intonation that was slightly off, something Harada clearly picked up on. Fighting Bull may have looked like a native-born Japanese woman, but she didn't sound like one.

Harada gently uncrossed her legs as they continued speaking. She abruptly got up from her chair and grabbed her coat and suitcase. Fighting Bull reached out to grab Harada's right wrist. Harada in turn, plunged her free hand into her coat pocket and pulled out the Ruger SR9C compact 9 mm semi-automatic pistol. She trained her weapon on Fighting Bull—hitting her squarely in the chest with three rounds. The impact of the bullets laid Fighting Bull flat on the ground. Other civilians in the train car immediately ran for cover at the sound of the gunshots. Harada quickly grabbed the suitcase and rushed in the opposite direction.

Struggling to get up, Fighting Bull winced in pain. Thankfully, even though her uniform morphed with her, it still retained its protective and impact-absorptive properties. The intrinsic mesh of biosteel and Duritium held. She turned to see the deformed bullets from the Ruger pistol laid on either side of her. Thankfully her glasses weren't damaged by the gunfire, so she placed them on the bridge of her nose and tapped the right rim of the glasses. A schematic of the train cars popped up on her lenses. Within seconds, Harada's location was triangulated two train cars down.

As Harada ran rapidly between cars, she looked back to see Fighting Bull just a few feet behind her. Her Ruger was still in her hand and she made good use of it as she fired wildly in Fighting Bull's direction, hitting a side panel and a handrail. Fighting Bull ducked out of the way of the bullets. Running at her current stride, she wouldn't have dared return fire with her Sig Sauer for fear of hitting civilians.

Harada hurried to the next train car. As she slid the door open, a transit officer came into clear view. The transit officer cautioned her to stop. She fired one bullet straight through his chest. The Yakuza boss barely broke her stride before one of the civilians, ducked under their seat, extended her right foot into the aisleway. Tumbling forward Harada lost the suitcase with the tectonic agitator. As Harada tried to pull herself from off the ground, she heard Fighting Bull's voice.

"Don't move."

Harada's eyes darted around the floor looking for her gun.

"Looking for this?" Fighting Bull said with her foot on the suitcase. She pointed the Ruger and Sig Sauer in Harada's direction.

Harada cautiously rolled around from her prone position with her hands up.

CHAPTER TWO

ALLUVION

Cox's Bazar
Chittagong Division, Bangladesh

FBI Agent John Arrowhawk heard the screams of Rohingya refugees who were trapped in their makeshift mud houses, or kuchtas, as a voracious cascading mudslide swept away swaths of homes and property. His mind drifted back to the battle of Kalaran in Lemalia; their screams echoed those of the Lemalian soldiers who died around him on the battlefield.

The unrelenting rain made his task all the more difficult. Adorned in a fitted black and gold tapered raincoat, Arrowhawk focused on keeping the falling refugees from being swept away. Bluish energy crackled from the palms of his hands as he created an interweaving energy net to form a firm energy barrier. He wrangled the energy barrier to keep a quartet of kuchtas from tumbling down one of the Chittagong Hill Tracts mountains. From his vantage point, perched upon an adjacent hillside, he could see the barrier holding, but barely. Arrowhawk strained under the pressure of the deluge of mud and debris collapsing on the barrier.

"I'll be damned if I let these people die like in Kalaran," Arrowhawk said to himself.

Although it had been over a year since the Lemalian war, which catapulted Vigil into the public eye, it seemed like yesterday to him. He suddenly heard team pilot, Regent Chiu, in his earpiece.

"John, you need an assist?" the Marine pilot said. Chiu had joined the team as their pilot four months ago. Even without superhuman abilities, his piloting skills were near flawless.

"No, I can handle this. Just make sure you help Karen get into position."

"Got it," Chiu said, hovering over Arrowhawk from 10,000 feet in the air.

As he lowered the energy barrier down to agent Terrell Morrison and the UN emergency relief team located the secure part of the mountainside, Arrowhawk thought back to the events that led up to their intervention. Intercepts from Vigil's Satellite Defense System picked up an early warning alarm from the Geological Survey of Bangladesh. The GSB was specifically designed to forecast rainfall induced landslides in the Chittagong Division. It was calibrated such that when rainfall thresholds exceeded the automatic rain gauges, they immediately sent SMS messages to the mobile phones of the first responder organizations. In this case, the Vigil SDS picked up on this signal and relayed this to the team.

Arrowhawk's energy barrier opened to form a solid-state energy bridge to the emergency rescuers below. Tapping his earpiece, he talks to Morrison below.

"You able to get those people to the shelters, Terrell?"

"Easy work John," Morrison responded as he wiped away the rain from his face. His uniform, similar to Fighting Bull's and the rest of the team's, was an intrinsic mesh of biosteel and Duritium. Not only did it absorb virtually all form of weapons fire and blunt force, but its new design was also rain repellant. This was something Morrison was very thankful for, particularly at that moment.

Arrowhawk smiled. "How do you think Alicia and the rest of the gang are doing in Japan?"

"Probably have Harada in the bag."

"Her splitting us into two teams might have been a stroke of genius."

"Yeah, I'll give Alicia that. To be honest, I'd rather be rescuing these refugees than going after Harada."

"I'm with you on that, Terrell," Arrowhawk responded as he motioned his right hand around to reinforce the energy bridge to safety. He felt a slight tweak in his mid-arm as he made the motion—a reminder from the Lemalian war.

The Rohingya refugees made their way across the energy bridge to makeshift encampment staffed by members of the UN and Bangladeshi emergency services. Something struck Morrison's heart as he eyed the despair in their faces as they passed by.

A collapsing portion of the side of a kutcha started to hurtle down toward the crossing refugees. Quickly, Morrison switched his six-foot-eight molecular density to titanium. He immediately rushed to their aid. Streams of mud, wood, and rusted metal bombarded Morrison's body as he shielded the refugees. After the worst had passed, he checked on the refugees hunkered down closest to him.

"Are you all right?" Morrison asked. They stared at him with confused looks. He reached into his uniform's left upper shoulder compartment to remove his transdermal language translator. He slapped it on to his neck.

"Are you ok?" he asked again, now in a language that they could understand. They nodded their heads to the affirmative.

Morrison looked up to see the remainder of the refugees made their way safely to the encampment site. Linette Paulson, the field director of the UN emergency relief team, ran from the staging ground up to Morrison.

"Are you alright, Mr. Morrison?"

He wasn't used to being asked how he was doing. Usually, he was the one checking on the safety of others.

"I'm fine," he replied as he removed the translator.

Morrison noticed the UN peace keeping troops working with the relief team as they aided the refugees to their shelters. He nodded in their direction. "How are they doing?"

Paulson glanced over to the soldiers. "They are doing well. They've been stretched lately, having to rotate in and out from Lemalia and other hot spots."

"I see," Morrison said, looking intently at Paulson. "Have all of the refugee's been accounted for?"

"Yes, we have all of the people based on the local data."

Morrison tapped his piece. "Regent, what have you got on SDS feed?"

Chiu lightly tapped on the plane's telemetry screen with his right forefinger. Instantly, the Vigil SDS video and thermal feeds popped up.

"She's right, Terrell, the coast is clear."

"Great. You're clear to head out to the Bay."

"Copy that, Terrell."

Morrison pressed his earpiece again. "Karen, are you ready?"

"As ready as I'll ever be," she responded. She brushed aside her gray-streaked red hair off her shoulders. This twenty-year Navy officer was never one to shy away from a challenge.

The Avian's engines began to roar as it zoomed toward the Bay of Bengal. A strong gale force wind slammed into the plane's fuselage, throwing it into a dizzying tailspin. Chiu struggled with the controls as the plane started to lose altitude. Bledsoe hung on to the ceiling hand grips that led to the aircraft's hatch. As Chiu gathered his bearings, he stabilized the plane.

The epicenter of the storm gradually came into sight. Chiu looked over the Avian's telemetry to confirm they were in fact right above the eye of the storm. More and more the Avian rumbled around in the storm. The newly installed aeronautic stabilizers were working overtime to keep the ship from ripping apart.

"This is as close as I can get you, Karen," Chiu said, turning back to look at her from the cockpit.

Bledsoe glanced at him and nodded. "That's good enough."

The Avian's rear hatch opened up to the chaos of the storm. Bledsoe hurled herself out of the aircraft. She was immediately enveloped in the crashing winds and rain. As she descended, the housing pores in her arms and hands emitted super-charged, silver, iodide particles into the clouds. Twisting and turning, she created a localized wind current to buoy herself within the storm.

Bledsoe closed her eyes to focus on the task set before her. Within moments, the clouds around her began to reverse course.

As she cracked her eyes open, a whitish glow emanated from her pupils. Bledsoe stretched out her hands to emit a current of wind. The clouds unleashed a sheet of rain. Chiu observed this from high above, aboard the Avian. He could clearly see the counter-storm Bledsoe created within the original storm. The raging monsoon met the full might of Bledsoe's own storm. As the countering weather pattern intensified it reached a peak where both storms began to cancel each other out. The original monsoon began to recede, almost as if being eaten from the inside out, thanks to Bledsoe's actions

CHAPTER THREE

TECHNOCRACY

September 21st
Halcyon Studios
New York, New York

"My name is Pat Tanaka, and I am the host of Flash Point," the young, thirty-one-year-old news anchor said.

Her eyes focused in on the teleprompter. "Artificial Intelligence, it's all around us, from virtual assistants on our phones, on-line banking, to chatbots. But what is it? And does our increasing reliance put us at risk of becoming slaves to the machines?" Tanaka stared directly at the camera and continued, "I am joined by a roundtable of experts."

Tanaka gestured to each individual as she mentioned their names. "Mr. Dennis Stroud, founder and CEO of tech conglomerate AlphA.I. Corporation, Doug Lawson, futurist and ethicist with the thinktank Hexagon; and Elijah West, president of ColourCoded, a non-profit foundation advocating for more people of color in the tech industry."

The men waved as the camera panned to each of them.

"Mr. Stroud," Tanaka said as she turned in his direction, "first off, can you define what artificial intelligence is?"

Stroud leaned back in his chair and crossed his legs that were draped in lightly faded Levi's jeans. "Good evening, Pat," he began to say in a melodious voice. "Thanks for asking. In the simplest of terms, artificial intelligence is software or computer programming that learns."

Tanaka leaned into Stroud's direction. "So, essentially thinking machines."

"Not just that, Pat," he said as he smoothed his khaki vest against his buttoned-down shirt. "It's the ability of machines and computers to learn without being explicitly programmed. We've gotten to the point where we have programming that can solve problems once thought to be too complex for the human brain."

"Are you referring to deep learning?"

"Exactly, Pat," Stroud said with a hint of glee. "It allows for the use of neural networks which are layered to recognize complex relationships and patterns in data. Mimicking how our own brains work."

"That brings so many images of a crazy futuristic movie gone wrong," Tanaka smiled as she leaned back in her chair.

Stroud smiled back confidently. "No, Pat it's not some crazy, dystopian future. It's life right now. Look we have chatbots which help us make purchases online, intelligent digital assistants that help us find the best pizza shop and searchbots to help us purchase vehicles. Artificial intelligence is nothing to fear, it's something to be embraced."

"It'll be a cold, suffocating, embrace if we aren't careful," Lawson retorted as he scratched his graying beard.

Tanaka redirected her attention to him. "Ok, Mr. Lawson, let's dig into that. What do you mean by this 'cold embrace'?"

"Too often we allow machines to take total control." He tussled his thinning, sandy brown hair which was peppered with streaks of gray. Lawson shifted his overweight body in Tanaka's direction. "It's gotten to the point where we've even outsourced our thinking to machines. Look, Dennis mentioned we use AI to help us decide where to buy a pizza. What kind of nonsense is that?" Lawson gestured his arms in Stroud's direction. "There was a time we got a phone book and looked that up, or better yet actually asked someone about a good pizza joint…"

"We also don't hunt by bow and arrow anymore, Mr. Lawson," Tanaka interjected.

"I am not a Luddite, Pat," Lawson responded. "I used to be the COO of *Google*. I understand technology has its place, but there are limits." Lawson pointed to his temple, "We have come to the point where we're relying on these machines and A.I. constructs as our 'external brains.' It's getting where these devices are quickly morphing from just knowing about us through algorithms, to representing us, and ultimately becoming us."

"Your thoughts on this, Mr. Stroud?" Tanaka said, looking in his direction.

"Is that such a bad thing?" Stroud said coolly. "With the help of AI, we've been able to prevent natural disasters, reduce crime, and improve our economic productivity."

"But at what cost, Dennis?" Lawson fired back. "We've been so married to our devices we no longer know how to act. How often, when you get on a train or plane, do you see nothing but people buried in their phones. We've lost connection to each other. And frankly, that scares me."

Stroud raised his right hand in protest. "That is a gross fallacy, Pat!"

"How so?" Tanaka said as she motioned to Stroud with her pen.

"Web connectivity and social media have revolutionized how we communicate with each other," Stroud said as he leaned forward in his chair. "Now, anyone can keep in touch with whomever across the world. Decades ago, that was closed to impossible."

Lawson gave a loud grunt. "Hah! What are you talking about Dennis? You mean the 500 or so Facebook 'friends' that each of us have that we truly don't know? I would argue social media has made us less social. It creates a false sense of community, where people remain in their echo chambers without having their beliefs challenged."

Stroud's brow furrowed; his right fist clenched slightly. "So, you'd rather we go back to the ancient Greek times where only the Sophists could engage in discourse in the arena?

"Please, Dennis," Lawson said as he threw up his hands. "Now, you're making a false equivalence."

"No, I am not," Stroud fired back as he leaned forward in his chair and thrusted his right forefinger into the glass table in front of him. The impact of his forefinger left behind a slight crack in the table. "Advances in technology have done nothing but equalize the playing field for those who have been traditionally left behind. And artificial intelligence that will move humanity forward."

Tanaka tapped her pen against her chin as she peered down at her notes. She pointed the end of her pen in Elijah West's direction.

"Mr. Stroud just made the assertion that technological advancement has leveled the playing field for those who have been left behind. Do you believe this to be true?"

West adjusted his tie and realigned the frame of his glasses atop the bridge of his nose. His kinky, but neat, jet-black hair was haloed by the stage lights behind him. "It's not as simple as Mr. Stroud has stated. It's true technological advancement has improved communication and has helped coalition building among people of color, but it also has kept many people of color, specifically African Americans, behind."

West reached into the right breast pocket of his grey suit to pull out his cell phone. "Are you familiar with the term 'digital divide'?"

Tanaka nodded.

"Well, that divide between underrepresented people of color and the majority culture continues to grow. Additionally, the increasing use of automation and A.I. has slowly been moving black people and other people of color out of jobs as well as opportunities."

"What do you mean by that?" Tanaka said.

"Now, robots and automated systems are supplanting low-skilled workers; a vast majority of which are people of color."

Tanaka propped up her notes as she leaned in her chair, "Let's go with that. What do you think is the biggest challenge facing people of color with society's increasing automation?"

"I think the biggest challenge is the algorithmizing of society. Machines adopting the biases of the developers and programmers that create them." West leaned back slightly in his chair. "For example, years ago there was an A.I. program called COMPAS. The criminal justice system used it to determine which defendants posed the greatest recidivism risks. Unfortunately, it was racially biased and disproportionally predicted black defendants as having a higher rate of recidivism than other groups."

"There have been other examples of racial bias in A.I. in the past, right?" Tanaka responded. "Like, facial recognition programs that have been ineffective in darker skinned people."

West pointed back at Tanaka. "Exactly. Those very same algorithms that run facial recognition programs led to many Black people being misidentified as suspects, when in fact they were innocent."

"You have all have made some excellent points but let me switch things up a little bit," Tanaka said. "What about the haves and have nots? It seems like these advances in technology tend to benefit the wealthy. How do we keep, as Mr. West mentioned, the digital divide from growing?"

Stroud raised his hand to respond. Tanaka nodded in his direction.

"That's where AlphA.I. is trying to make a difference. Our charitable organization, A.I. Stars has gone out to under-represented and under-served communities to promote tech education among students. We also invested millions of dollars in a job retraining programs to prepare people for the jobs of the future."

"That's not enough," Lawson vehemently protested. "There has to be an intrinsic change in the system." He looked in Stroud's direction. "Even AlphA.I.'s takeover of our transportation and telecommunications infrastructure is concerning. We have to have strict checks and balances to keep these tech advances from overtaking our very humanity."

"Mr. West?" Tanaka said as she looked in his direction.

"I think there is hope. But we need to make sure everyone is included in this new technological frontier."

Tanaka's producer cued her through her earpiece.

"Well, I'm being told I have to wrap things up. Lastly…" Tanaka said as she shuffled through her notes, "and this is the big question, 'what does artificial intelligence mean in the era of the superhuman?' As you know, we live in a superhuman era. What place does all this, A.I., automation, smart cars, mean in a world where people can level buildings with a simple look or soar into the stratosphere?"

"That's a great question, Pat," Stroud began, "I'm from St. Paul Minnesota and my home, and a lot of my loved ones were devastated by the Minneapolis Event several years ago."

"I am so sorry to hear that," Tanaka responded.

He nodded in acknowledgement. "Thank you, Pat, I appreciate your sentiment. Look, the superhuman population represents both a boon and an existential threat. I am one who believes you have to be prepared either way."

"That's true, as we've seen that you've utilized superhumans heavily in your business."

Stroud nodded then rolled up his right shirt sleeve and grasped the distal part of his right wrist. "I was born with a condition called phocomelia, where children are born with malformed shortened limbs. As you can imagine my life was hard living essentially as a crippled child." As he said this, he peeled back his forearm skin to reveal circuitry and gleaming steel underneath. "It was the advances in prostho-cybernetics that allowed me to have a somewhat normal life."

Tanaka gasped as Stroud exposed his cybernetic forearm for everyone at the roundtable as well as the world to see. Lawson recoiled slightly as West clenched the seat of his chair.

"If I didn't have these enhancements there is no way I would be where I am today. And I think that improvements in tech can enhance us as humans, so that there will no longer just be a select class of 'superhumans.'" He paused to look in Lawson's direction, "We will all be superhuman."

"Now, Dennis, you sound like a futurist gone rogue," Lawson said. "I understand what you went through as a child but we as people don't need enhancement. We were never meant to be fused with tech to make our lives more meaningful. It's incumbent on us rather to become better humans. Not better cyborgs."

Stroud gave a slight smirk as he rolled his right sleeve down and carefully buttoned its cuff.

"How about you, Mr. West? Any thoughts?" Tanaka asked.

"I think there has to be understanding between superhumans and normal humans alike. If African Americans and other people of color aren't shut out of technological advancement, nor unduly targeted by the superhuman community, I believe we have a bright future ahead of us."

Tanaka placed her pen on the table and motioned with opened hands in the direction of her guests. "I would like to once again thank Dennis Stroud, Doug Lawson, and Elijah West for being my guests today."

Each man nodded in the direction of the camera as their names were called.

"This has been Flash Point," Tanaka said, concluding the session. After the studio lights dimmed, production assistants quickly gathered microphones from the panelists. As Stroud's mic was unpinned from his vest, his eyes tracked over to Lawson. His gait was initially slow as he got up from his chair.

"When I get back to San Fran, I am definitely going to upgrade these," Stroud thought to himself as he took a second to get going.

"Doug, can I talk with you for a second?" Stroud said as he motioned in Lawson's direction.

"Sure, Dennis, what is it?"

"I just wanted to say it was good seeing you again." Stroud said as he extended his right hand.

"Same here, Dennis," Lawson said as he grasped Stroud's hand. "It has been a while since our days at DARPA."

"I know, working on SHARP was something else. I was kind of surprised to see you were so anti-tech, considering your history," Stroud said, as he looked at Lawson with haunting, silver-gray eyes.

"Let's just say I evolved." He pointed to Stroud's right arm. "Much like you I see. All these years and I never knew about your condition."

"My condition?" Stroud responded curtly.

Lawson put up his hands apologetically. "I'm sorry, I didn't mean it that way."

"Most people don't." Stroud raised up his right hand and glanced at it briefly. "It's not something I freely share. After I designed these enhancements, things changed." He then stared back at Lawson. "So, I guess I'm one of those better cyborgs you were talking about."

"Not what I meant by that."

"I know, I'm just kidding," Stroud said with a crooked smile. He brushed back a wisp of his thinning, light brown hair from his face. "Well, it was good seeing you." Once again, he reached to shake Lawson's hand. Stroud then turned around to head to the exit before pausing for a moment. He glanced back in Lawson's direction.

"By the way, Doug, are you going to make it to the AlphA.I. Con next week?"

"Where it's rumored you're going to debut your new super-secret project? Yeah, I wouldn't miss it—just to make sure it doesn't go rogue," Lawson replied with a belly jiggling laugh.

Stroud's crooked smile once again re-emerged. "Great. I can't wait to see you there." Stroud then walked off to meet with his assistant. As they made their way briskly out of the studio, he asked the assistant to give him his phone. She handed him a gleaming steel-colored touchscreen phone. Stroud pulled the phone up to his face. A bright, blue light washed over his face. Once his facial scan was complete, a calming female voice emanated from the device.

"Yes, Mr. Stroud. What can I do for you?"

"Get me Huntley, please."

CHAPTER FOUR

OVERWATCH

September 22nd

Sublevel Two

The Pentagon

Arlington, Virginia

Mark Pendleton walked purposefully down the gleaming hallway that led to the briefing room. His black, Clark's, dress shoes barely made a sound as he got closer to his destination. He checked his brown bowtie and noticed it was cocked sideways and straightened it.

Metallic automatic sliding doors opened as soon as the motion sensors detected Pendleton as he walked up the briefing room's entryway. He entered a room filled with the team members as well as support staff. It was lined with multiple LCD screens. Numerous data raced across these screens. At the center of the room was an oval shaped table with a woodgrain finish. The table was embedded with multiple touchscreen keyboard panels.

Conrad sat at the head of the table, wearing the skirted version of her Class A green service uniform. Seated to her left was Blankenchip, who tightened the sport coat of his Class B green service uniform. Across from him was Fighting Bull, whose light brown hair had grown to her mid-back over the past year or so. To her right were Arrowhawk and Morrison. The pair of men wore crisp designer suits from Sean John and Kenneth Cole, respectively. The two new faces of Karen Bledsoe, with her red hair pulled back with a hairclip, wearing her formal naval uniform; and Regent Chiu who looked sharp in his dress blues, rounded out the attendants at the table.

"Good morning, everyone," Pendleton said as he pulled a chair up next to Conrad. A blue uniformed officer handed him a tablet computer. He tapped on the screen and an immersive holographic display of Minato City and Codai Harada engulfed the room.

"Thanks to you all, we've pretty much captured or prosecuted every Network Principal," Pendleton said appreciatively. "The only one that's left is Weiping Pei," Suddenly, a holographic image of a middle-aged bespectacled Chinese man with thinning hair popped up. "Being that he is the sitting director of the Chinese Ministry of State Security he's hands off."

"That's ridiculous!" Arrowhawk protested as he slammed his open hand down on the table. "We have clear evidence he committed war crimes against the Lemalian people."

"Sorry, John, no dice," Pendleton responded as he leaned his forearms against the table. "China's not a signatory to the International Criminal Court. They can't touch him."

"And they can't touch as either," Conrad said.

Leaning back in his chair, Pendleton sat dumbfounded. He eased himself around to scan the faces of the rest of the team. "True, but that's why we have laws. So we don't just trample on statutes that have been put in place."

Conrad leaned forward on to the table with clasped hands. "But the rules are getting in the way, Mark. You see it yourself; these people escape under the cloak of diplomatic immunity."

Morrison cringed.

Fighting Bull saw this and glanced over to see red creeping up Pendleton's face. "Mark, so we know we can't touch Pei," she said, as she tried to cut the tension, "but we can still track him, right?"

"Of course." Swiftly, the holographic images switched to a view of deep space filled with the dozens of satellites that encompassed the Vigil Satellite

Defense System. "We have a full surveillance suite on Pei."

"Onsite drone recon as well?" Blankenchip asked.

"Without question, Aaron."

"Well, it's good to know we have Pei under tight surveillance," Fighting Bull replied. She pulled her cellphone from her right, sport coat pocket. After tapping the screen, an image of the tectonic agitator popped up in full view. "Now, I'm curious as to how Harada was aware of the tectonic agitator and who her potential buyer was."

Pendleton tapped his tablet computer. "Harada had an inside man in the PSIA, a guy named Shinzo Takayasu." A holographic image of Takayasu's head, along with his vital statistics filled the room. "He was a former director of the PSIA's First Intelligence Division, and I say former because thanks to you he's been taken into custody. He fed her intel on the Tokyo Institute's research which of course made things easier for her to intercept the agitator."

Pendleton pointed to Takayasu's image. "Harada planned on putting the agitator up on the black market. She had a couple of suitors, Al- Shabab, the National Freedom Alliance, ISIS, and Hezbollah, to name a few."

"The market's good for a super device that sets off earthquakes I guess," Arrowhawk said with a slight smile. The young FBI agent folded his hands and gently placed them on his lap. Part of the barbed wire tattoo that wrapped around his forearm and down his hand was evident as he placed his hands in his lap.

"Exactly," Pendleton responded.

"Is that in anyway linked to the events in Bangladesh?" Morrison asked.

"Not so far as we can tell, Terrell. That was an absolute random act," Pendleton responded. "The problem is Harada has so many connections within the Japanese Intelligence Community, that it's hard to tell how deep this goes. We've given the PSIA all of the pertinent information so we will leave it up to them."

Morrison nodded in acknowledgement.

Blankenchip thrusted his right hand in the air. "Why is no one asking how in the hell Harada's security detail got cybernetic tech?"

"We are looking into that," Pendleton said as he swiveled his chair in Blankenchip's direction. "In your report you mentioned the circuitry in the Gijo Hei had a branded label?"

"Yeah, a company called Saisentan."

Pendleton tapped on one of the table's embedded touch screens. "Interesting, Saisentan is a Japanese cybernetics company, founded by Michiko Hirohito. They're on the cutting edge of cybernetic enhancements. But their focus is mainly on kids with birth defects and amputees."

"Any info on illegal cybernetic enhancements?" Blankenchip asked.

"Nothing concrete so far."

Conrad angled herself to face the rest of the team. "We also don't have intel on how she either enhanced or recruited superhuman bodyguards."

"Probably through her contacts in the PSIA, they had their own version of the SHARP program years ago," Pendleton responded.

Looking ponderously at the holographic images, Arrowhawk reached into the breast pocket of his tan sport coat and pulled out his cell phone. He typed three digits into the screen. Sliding his right thumb across the screen he came across an image that widened his eyes. "I know this program," he said as he motioned his right finger at the hologram. "PERSD."

"What's that?" Bledsoe asked.

"The Power Enhancement Research and Superhuman Development program. I want to look into this because we liaised with PSIA a few years ago regarding the case of a PERSD subject who went rogue. I was on the case because of my unique situation."

Fighting Bull nudged his elbow slightly, "Just say it John, they used you because you're a Variant."

He reluctantly nodded as he bit the inside of his cheek.

Conrad chimed in, "You have the go-ahead to check in on them, John." She shifted her eyes in Fighting Bull's direction. "Cynthia, you'll back him up on this."

Fighting Bull glanced over at Arrowhawk before looking back at Conrad. "Understood."

"Anything we can find on illegal cybernetics programs I want to know," Conrad said as she looked at them both.

"Gotcha Cap," Arrowhawk responded.

Conrad's eyes locked on Pendleton. "What else do we have on the agenda?"

The immersive holographic images that filled the room receded back to images of the Vigil Satellite Defense System.

"We've pretty much completed the drone deployment upgrade on the Vigil SDS," Pendleton said. "When everything's done, we'll have a full complement of surveillance and tactical drones that can deploy anytime from geostationary orbit."

"Nice," Blankenchip stated. "And they're heat-shielded, too?"

"Yes." Pendleton then scanned the faces of the Vigil team members. "I wanted to get some feedback from you guys, about the tech upgrades. What are your thoughts?"

"Good, but not great," Blankenchip responded gruffly. "My nanosuit upgrade was useful but I think it can be improved on, especially if I'm going to go up against the crap we just encountered."

"I like them," Fighting Bull chimed in. "And being able to access everyone's powers without immediate tactile input is a Godsend."

Pendleton nodded. "Since we lost a good chunk of our original tech team after Ramsey's ouster, I wanted to make sure we replaced them with top notch people." He looked down on his tablet computer again. "We are going to continually enhance our tech. In fact, we're looking at a contract bid, with AlphA.I. to upgrade the Avian, and if that works out we'll expand to other areas."

"I saw that clown Stroud on Flash Point the other day, "Arrowhawk said. "Thinks he is the love child of Steve Jobs and Alan Turing."

Blankenchip leaned forward in his chair. "But he has some good points though."

"You serious? The guy pretty much thinks you can solve everything with an algorithm and a hard drive."

"Please," Blankenchip said as he leaned back with folded arms. "We're all headed toward an evolved humanity. Some of us weren't lucky enough to be born special." His eyes traced over Arrowhawk and Fighting Bull, respectively.

"What the hell do you mean born special?" Arrowhawk spat back as he pointed at Blankenchip.

"You know what I mean John, some people weren't born with fancy powers."

"Can we say 'Variant-hate'?"

"No. I'm saying he's just trying to create the connection between people and tech seamless. Ultimately making a better humanity."

Arrowhawk shook his head. "Karen, I think you have some competition 'cause I think Aaron wants to marry Stroud."

"Get the fuck outta here," Blankenchip said as he waved Arrowhawk off.

"In regard to the preliminary negotiations," Pendleton interjected, trying to keep things on track. "So far, everything checks out, but you can never be too sure."

Looking at his teammates around the table, Blankenchip responded knowingly with a slight smirk, "Believe me, we all know this."

Pendleton peered in Morrison's direction. "Terrell, I believe you're up next for the Lemalia security oversight?"

"That's right," Morrison said as he stroked his goatee. "I'm heading out tomorrow morning."

"The rest of you guys are free for R&R. Any other questions?" Pendleton asked as he glanced around the table. No response was elicited. "Then we're done here."

Blankenchip firmly clasped Bledsoe's right hand after getting up from the table. "You still good to make the trip to New York to see Jack with me?

"You know I wouldn't miss it honey," Bledsoe said with a gleaming smile as the pair walked out.

"Alicia, you got a minute?" Pendleton asked.

Conrad slowly turned in Pendleton's direction.

"Yeah."

"We have to talk about the Mirador construction budget."

Conrad lifted her right hand. "Believe me it's under control."

Pendleton shook his head slightly. "Are you sure? Because Congress slashed our budget."

"I know, Mark, we're fine."

He folded his arms across his chest. "The building's construction was based on a budget incorporating Network dollars."

"Like I said, Mark, it's fine."

"Look, when you asked me to take over after Ramsey's arrest I was honored. Plus, how could I say no to my friend's daughter, but I can't cover for you anymore." He turned his head away from her then looked back. "From what I hear in the beltway, there've even been talks of cutting you guys off completely."

"I've planned for this Mark. Everything is under control. The funding will be there."

Pendleton cocked his head to the side. "What's going on?"

"Believe me, there is not enough time in the day," she said with a half-smile.

Pendleton lightly touched her shoulder. "Have you heard from him?"

"Hanahan?"

"When did he become 'Hanahan'? I remember when he was 'Uncle Chuck,'" Pendleton said with some brightness in his face.

"Hah, he lost that right after he killed a sitting president."

"When's he getting out?"

Conrad's eyes traced downward. "I don't know. He's still dealing with a boatload of charges."

"You going to see him?"

"Maybe. There're still some things he owes me," Conrad said with a clenched jaw.

Pendleton glanced down to see her tightening her fist.

"How are the twins?" he asked, as he cleared his throat.

"I don't know."

"When is the last time you heard from them?" he asked as he sensed a hollowness in her voice.

"They've kept me from reaching out to them."

"But we know that Ramsey's people fabricated that photo."

"I know, but the county still placed an injunction on me communicating with the twins."

"Ok, let me know what I can do," he said, as his voice softened.

"Sure, Mark, I will."

Conrad swiftly turned and exited the room.

CHAPTER FIVE

WILLFUL NEGLECT

September 24th
Ben's Kosher Delicatessen
209 West 38th Street
Manhattan, New York

"Salami and cheese were always your favorite," Blankenchip said as he observed his son downing his meal with reckless abandon.

"I didn't think you'd remember," Jack said cutting his eyes up to his father.

"I always remember, Jack."

Jack looked down at his plate. He sopped up some ketchup with a handful of fries before continuing, "Would've been nice to have seen you more back then."

Blankenchip looked away. "Well, that's what life dealt me. I had to manage."

"You weren't the only one managing, Dad. Me and Charity had to deal with a lot of crap when you weren't around," Jack said as he pointed in Blankenchip's direction.

Blankenchip's nose crinkled. "It's not like my life was a walk in the park either. I was in the field, damn near getting killed every day."

"That was your choice, Dad! But we had to deal with the consequences!"

"I know you and your sister had a hard time," Bledsoe broke in, as she tried to ease the situation. "Despite all that, I'm impressed with how much you've accomplished."

"Thanks," Jack responded appreciatively.

"My son is in high school right now and I'm trying to get him to focus. What's your secret?"

"Hunger."

Bledsoe looked down at his plate.

Jack laughed. "That's not what I meant. I just mean I want to be better and do more than my parents."

"Well, you've had an amazing start, graduating top of your undergrad class, and working on your MBA. I'm curious, what's your endgame, Jack?" she asked as she leaned forward toward him.

"Start my own consulting firm. I figured I'd get my feet wet interning with Venturepointe."

Bledsoe's ears perked up. "Do you feel like you're getting that experience so far?"

He took a drink from his bottle of root beer, before answering. "Oh, hell yeah! I'm assistant to the senior MIC in the M&A division. I'm getting exposure to things I never would have."

"MIC?" Bledsoe asked, with eyes raised.

"Sorry. I'm using business-speak. Merger and Integration Consultant."

"Wow. So, what have been some of your biggest contracts?"

"I can't spill all the beans. But I will tell you we're working on something big."

Blankenchip folded his hands and leaned in on the table to look closely at his son. "You know I have access to the most sophisticated intelligence network in the world. So, you can spill the beans now or I can find out later."

Jack laughed. "I'm still not telling you, Dad."

Bledsoe looked at both men and interjected, "How about a subtle hint then? I'll say a company and you can tap a finger on the table if I'm right. Sound like a plan?"

Jack nodded his head as he took another swig of his root beer.

"Celedane?"

Jack continued eating his sandwich.

"Binary Technologies?"

He shoved a few more fries into his mouth. Bledsoe looked in Blankenchip's direction, who shrugged. Bledsoe looked back in Jack's direction.

"AlphA.I.?"

Jack put down his drink and tapped his right forefinger on the table.

"Really?" Bledsoe asked, as she perked up a bit. "They're the hottest thing in tech right now. What's your company doing with them?"

"Like I said, I can't divulge company details," Jack said as he tried to tamp down Bledsoe's enthusiasm. "But I can invite you to an event they're having in Cali."

"You talking about AlphA.I. Con?" Blankenchip said.

Jack looked at his father and smiled, "I can get you both in. VIP status."

Bledsoe looked in Blankenchip's direction with a huge ear-to-ear grin. He shot a look back of slight disinterest.

"What?" Blankenchip asked, feigning surprise.

"Don't tell me a big tech-head like you isn't salivating over the opportunity to go?"

Blankenchip's disinterested expression slowly transformed into a broad smile. "You're damn right I am."

CHAPTER SIX

BETAS

UCLA Campus
Los Angeles, California

Twelve college students gathered in the basement of an on-campus Marriott hotel. They were ushered by five burly men, who looked to be in their late-twenties, into a medium-sized meeting room with three large rectangular metal tables. On the tables were twelve electronic devices---six smart phones and six tablet computers. The students were directed by their ushers to the refreshments in the back of the room. Many took advantage of the free oatmeal cookies and flavored waters. They failed to notice the camera and black speaker perched in the upper corner of the room as they reached for the food. At the front of the room stood a smiling young woman wearing a fitted vintage t-shirt with slightly faded dark-blue jeans paired with white throwback Chuck Taylor Converse tennis shoes.

As the students made their way to the hard-plastic seats that surrounded the tables, their host welcomed them. The woman took a brief glance at the mirror across the room.

"Hi guys, my name is Joyce," she said as she motioned to herself with her right hand. As one followed her hand upward, they could see a smartwatch with a rectangular shaped face.

"We appreciate you guys coming out to beta test our new app, Cinq." She lifted one of the tablets, pressed the start button and the screen came alive with an icon of the letter 'C' in bold bright red. She slid her finger across the screen and the image transformed into a sign-on screen.

"Cinq is an app that helps you integrate all of your technologies in one spot," she tapped the tablet screen again. "For example, if you want to control your smart speaker remotely, you can do it through Cinq."

A student with dark, wavy hair spoke up, "You mean we can control our devices all with just this app?"

"Precisely. Let's say you're away on a trip and you want to turn on your Alexa smart assistant as well as the dishwasher, you can do that on this app. It seamlessly controls all of your tech from one spot, eliminating the need to fumble with a hundred devices."

Another student raised her hand, "But how is this any different from smart hub devices we've seen in the past, like Google home? Virtual Assistants have been around for years. How's this any different?"

Joyce glanced at the mirror across the room again then back at the person who asked the question. "What's your name ma'am?"

"Coryn. Coryn Baisden."

"Well, Coryn, it's because Cinq is designed to interface with whatever hardware or software it comes in contact with through proximity-linking."

She typed on the tablet's screen. "Once Cinq has been downloaded you can link to all of your devices even without any internet connectivity." Wu walked up to the close-cropped haircut student and calmly picked up her cellphone and tapped it against the tablet. Baisden's cellphone screen lit up with the same bright red 'C' logo as that of the tablet's screen.

The other students looked on in awe.

"Go on, try it for yourself," Joyce said.

The students gladly turned on the devices in front of them. As they operated the app, live video of their smart devices came on screen.

"How are you able to get video on my Google home hub? It's in my basement." Baisden blurted out as she looked on the tablet's screen.

Wu didn't respond, but calmly put on thick black sunglasses. The other five male ushers placed their glasses on as well. Immediately, the screens of both the smart phones and tablets emitted a bright white flash, temporarily blinding the students. As the students recovered, thin metallic circuit-like tendrils started flowing from the devices in the students' hands. Metallic tendrils rapidly ate away at their skin and flesh, leaving behind metallic paneling and circuitry in its wake. One of the students tried to fling his tablet against the mirror, but it was fused to his body. Tears welled up in his eyes as he witnessed his flesh being eaten away by a metallic cascade of circuitry.

Wu and her men stood idly by as the students screamed for help. One student raced to the door as her leg was eaten away by metallic tendrils. She was blocked by one of the burley ushers, who delivered a swift clothesline blow to her throat.

Wu's heart began to race at what she witnessed. Her forehead skin furrowed, and her eyes widened a bit. As her uncomfortableness grew, she tapped the one-way mirror.

"This isn't aerosolized is it?" Joyce asked.

"No," a thunderous voice responded over the black speaker.

"Shouldn't we abort and call in medical?"

"Not yet, give it some time. Just let the process go."

A few more excruciating minutes passed. Joyce's attention was drawn to the sonorous beeping from her smartwatch. A flood of data streamed across the screen of the rectangular-faced device. "Their vitals are crashing. We have to do something."

"I said no. Hold steady." The speakered-voice responded again, this time more forcefully.

More and more the students' bodies were transformed into what could best be described as mechanical monstrosities. Their limbs were worn off and replaced with deformed robotic-looking appendages. Hands were replaced with what appeared to be tri-digit claw-like tentacles. Perspiration beaded upon Joyce's forehead as she observed all of this.

"I'm calling it." Immediately Joyce tapped the side of her smartwatch. Instantaneously, a group of paramedics clad in blue hazmat suits with stretchers and crash carts came into the room. The paramedics made a valiant effort to save the dying students, but it was to no avail.

CHAPTER SEVEN

REMEMBRANCE

A year and a half ago
Delohar, Lemalia

*B*lankenchip looked in Conrad's direction with a resoluteness to his face. "Alicia..."

She looked on at the destruction wrought by the Omega Prime Units and responded somberly, "I know."

Conrad paused for a moment and knew very well what she was about to do had repercussions. Repercussions that she would have to deal with for the rest of her life. She looked down briefly, and slowly raised her eyes up to the sky.

"Please, God, forgive me."

She pulled out a small rectangular control panel from one of the side slips in her modular tactical vest. Conrad pressed the center button on the device.

Thousands of miles above them, the Vigil Satellite Defense System's laser cannon came to life. The cannon calibrated its coordinates to Conrad's signal. Within seconds, a high-powered laser beam ripped through the cloudless sky. The beam lanced through the behemoth Omega Prime robots, completely incinerating them. Along with the metal wrenching, melting, and collapsing under the high-powered laser human flesh was seared away. Conrad could see the skin of the United People's Front soldiers' melt away like candles. Hundreds of screams echoed in her ear. Too many for her to shut out.

* * *

Now
Conrad Residence
Silver Spring, Maryland

Conrad shot up out of her bed at the sound of her cellphone ringing. Instinctively grabbing her Glock 17 from under her pillow, she brandished it. Her eyes quickly scanned the room for threats. There were none, just piled up boxes within a room in disarray. Lowering her weapon, she turned to her nightstand. Her cell phone screen displayed a name that she had not been expecting.

"Hi grandma," Conrad said as she answered her phone.

"Good morning, my dear Afua," Conrad's maternal grandmother, Dr. Phyllis Mensah said with her sweet Ghanaian accent.

Shaking her head, she put her weapon back under her pillow. "Grandma, why do you always insist on calling me by my middle name?"

"Because it is your name," Mensah responded firmly. "It's your heritage. I would be doing a disservice to you if I didn't remind you of where you come from."

"You mean Montgomery County?"

"Is that supposed to be funny?" Mensah said with a hint of ire. Her erudite tone had begun to show through.

"Relax. I'm just messing with you, Grandma," Conrad responded as she angled herself over the edge of her bed. She pulled the cellphone from her face and looked at the screen. "Grandma, you said good morning but it's past 3:00 AM here. It's still dark out."

"Afua, it's 7:00 AM here in Ghana so it's well into the morning hours. In fact, I've already gone for my walk with your grandfather and have planned out my lectures for today. What is your excuse?"

"Grandma, do you always have to make me feel like a slacker?" Conrad said as she made her way downstairs. As she made her way down the wooden staircase, toward the kitchen, she passed the empty rooms of her siblings.

"It is all in love, my dear," Mensah said with a smile.

"Obviously." Conrad said as she opened the fridge to get a bottle of *Perrier* water.

"So how are you holding up, my dear? I haven't heard from you in a while."

Conrad rested her hand against the counter table and gazed upon boxes of packed appliances and dishware. "I'm… I'm hanging in there."

"I understand." Mensah paused, "Have you heard from the twins?"

"No," Conrad said as she placed the Perrier firmly on the counter in front of her. "They've been keeping me from them."

"Oh Afua, I wish I was there with you. If I didn't have classes to teach this semester I would be there."

"It's ok grandma. You've done more than enough---taking care of the twins when I was going through my…phase."

Mensah's voice softened. "Stop that! I am your grandmother, and you are my responsibility, you understand, eh?"

"Yes, Grandma," Conrad said nodding.

"I just want you to remember you three are very important to me and your grandfather."

"I understand."

"And no matter what, don't let them keep you away from each other. The relationship between the three of you is too important, so don't ever let these temporary things keep you three apart."

Conrad's hand tightened around her phone. "Yes, Grandma," her voice cracking.

"Where are they now?"

"Camille is with some fosters up in Columbus, Ohio and Cameron is in Arlington with a family down there."

"Are they safe?" Mensah asked as her voice sharpened.

Conrad smiled. "Yeah, they are, I made sure of that."

"You have a security detail on them?"

"One of the perks of being the leader of America's homegrown super team. They just can't tell me specifics of their day-to-day activities."

"But I am sure you have figured a way around that," Mensah said as a grin creeped up on her face.

"I also have a surveillance drone suite tasked to them twenty-four seven."

"That's my granddaughter. You remind me so much of your mother." Mensah's voice started to lower slightly. "I miss her, Afua."

"I know, Grandma, I miss her too."

"Have you heard any more from your father's old friend? What's his name," she snapped her fingers, as if to conjure up his name, "the disgraced Defense Secretary?"

"Hanahan? I'm going to see him tomorrow."

"And from our last discussion you said he may have something to say about your parents—how they died?"

"He does. And I plan on getting answers."

CHAPTER EIGHT

PARALLAX VIEWS

September 25th
Federal Correctional Institute
Cumberland, Maryland

The clang of metal barred doors shutting behind her reverberated in Conrad's ear. She was led by two prison guards to Charles Hanahan's prison cell. Looking sharp in her skirted service uniform, she received lewd comments and leering stares as they made their way down a long hall lined with the cells of various male inmates. She resisted the urge to respond in kind. Instead, she provided her agitators with a stare that could burn a hole into a man's skull. Once they felt the heat of her stare, many of the inmates piped down.

The Cumberland FCI was a medium-security prison with a notable history. It previously housed several notorious inmates such as the Ponzi Schemer, Jack Abramoff, and Gambino crime associate Joseph Watts. It was now home to the disgraced former Secretary of Defense. After what seemed like ages, they finally came upon a 6 x 8 feet cell. Hanahan sat quietly on his bed reading a copy of the *Washington Post*. One of the escorting guards tapped on the bars of his prison cell.

"You got a guest, Hanahan," the lead guard said. As he reached for the cell door, his sleeve slid back to reveal a skull and arrow tattoo on his wrist.

Hanahan peered up and smiled as he saw Conrad standing there, reminiscent of when he first asked her to lead the Vigil team. "What a nice surprise, Alicia. Come to check on your old godfather?"

Her jaw tightened. "No, I need some answers."

Hanahan carefully folded his newspaper and placed it beside himself. "Guard, how much visit time do I have today?"

He glanced down at his watch and then to his other colleague. The lead prison guard then responded, "You have an hour left."

"That's more than enough time," Hanahan said as he raised his hands up.

The lead prison guard entered Hanahan's cell and placed cuffs on him. The guards ushered Hanahan and Conrad into a monitored visitor's room. After they entered, Hanahan's wrists were unshackled, and he took a seat in a hard-plastic chair. Conrad took a seat across from Hanahan.

"What's on your mind, Alicia?" Hanahan asked.

"Believe me, you don't want to know."

Hanahan looked down and snickered. "Are you still pissed about Lemalia?"

Conrad leaned in closer, her eyes laser focused. "You committed a political assassination of a foreign head of state, sir. Pissed is an understatement."

"You know why it had to be done, don't you?" Hanahan said as he leaned back in his chair. "The old political charades and games wouldn't work. Decisive action had to be taken."

"Stop being disingenuous. You created a global catastrophe by killing off a duly elected president."

"An election that was rigged. You know that firsthand," Hanahan said as he pointed in Conrad's direction. "It was your team that discovered the Network's endgame."

"It still doesn't make it right."

Hanahan straightened up in his chair. "It's not like elections haven't been meddled with before, Alicia."

She looked off to the side, her eyebrows furrowed as she let off a sigh. "You have got to be kidding me. We are not Putin's Russia, Charles!"

"But I know you're not so naïve that you think we haven't meddled in other peoples' politics. Just be real with yourself for a minute. America has always acted in its self-interest."

Conrad cocked her head to the side, with her eyes fixed on Hanahan. "So, how are you any better than Ramsey or Duvalier or any of the other members of the Network?"

"Simple. I do for country. They do for self." Hanahan leaned forward on the table with his fingers clasped. "Think about it, if they monopolized Duritium, one of the most unique versatile substances on earth, we would be subject to the economic whims of a cadre of elite, erudite pricks who think the world revolves around them."

"How are they any different from some of the politicians we have here?"

"That's the problem, they're not." Hanahan pointed to the window with his right hand, "I helped free the Lemalians from a puppet dictator—"

"And in turn you replaced it with civil war and chaos," Conrad interrupted.

"Well, that's why you were there to clean up, right?"

"No. We're there to do the right thing. As a matter of fact, I have Morrison in Lemalia now, to help them rebuild their security apparatus, no thanks to you. Even the ICC is looking to prosecute you for war crimes."

"Sucks for them. They can't have me because we're not a Rome Statue signatory. And if I remember correctly, they are also seeking war-crimes charges against you guys as well."

"The UN's ICJ is trying but they know they can't reach us. And if they look at the evidence, they can see we aren't the real war criminals," she said as she nodded her head in Hanahan's direction. "You are."

"What was it you said during the Joint National Security Committee hearing, 'you have to break a few eggs to make an omelet,' or something like that," Hanahan said with a slight laugh. "That's why I love you, Alicia, your delivery is always on time. Like I said before, you were my ace in the hole in taking down the Network."

"I thought nepotism had nothing to do with my appointment, sir?"

"Well, as I've said before, nepotism has been around long before the Conrads ever showed up in Washington."

She eased in her chair and crossed her legs. "Well, there's only one Conrad in Washington now."

Hanahan stared down at the table sullenly. "Look, I'm sorry about the twins. I know Ramsey planted that doctored waterboarding photo with DCWS. Have they reversed their decision since they found out the truth?"

"No. The Department of Child Welfare Services said my actions in Lemalia were proof enough I was an unfit guardian."

"I'm sorry," Hanahan responded dourly.

Conrad unfolded her arms and placed her hands flat on the table. "Camille and Cameron are safe. But I want to know about my parents."

"I'm not sure if this is the time, Alicia."

She slammed her hands on the table so forcefully it caught the attention of the prison guards. The second guard moved to separate the two, but the lead guard reached out his right hand to hold him back.

"Dammit, when's the time?!" Conrad demanded.

Hanahan looked down at the deep hand indentations in the table left behind by Conrad. "That's got to be a couple hundred pounds of force there, Alicia. You're getting stronger by the day. Getting you into the SHARP program was a great investment."

"Stop deflecting," Conrad said as her nostrils flared.

"I'm not. I'm just making an observation. Having enhanced strength and healing sure beats taking prednisone to calm down your flares."

"Shut up," Conrad said as she leaned into Hanahan.

Seeing the anger in her face, Hanahan relented. "The night your parents died; the police filings claimed their accident was caused by an exploding tire in your dad's car."

"I know, I've read the police report hundreds of times," Conrad said, flicking her wrist back dismissively. "Tell me something I don't know."

"At the scene they found the brake wires were cut, and the tires had micro-punctures. They were so small you couldn't tell by looking and was undetectable to the on-board tire gauge system." Hanahan glanced back at the guards then leaned in close to Conrad's ear, "It had all the features of foul play."

"Then why the hell didn't anyone look into it?

Hanahan looked away briefly before answering. "Because they couldn't find the perp, or suspected perps who set it up. But I know who it was." Hanahan rubbed his finger in the indentations in the metal table contemplatively. "You know your dad and me were best friends. We go back to our time on Delta Force. We were brothers, closer than brothers even." He wrenched his mouth to one corner. "But your dad didn't always have the best judgement when it came to partners."

"What do you mean?"

"After I retired from active duty your dad went on to serve as Assistant Joint Chiefs of Staff. When he left that post, he went into a private military contracting business with Harold Baltimore. They formed CoBALT."

"I know. They had a falling out a couple years after. What are you getting at?"

"Well, Harold and I didn't necessarily see eye-to-eye. I tried to convince your dad not to do business with him."

"But I thought Baltimore was also a part of your Delta Force unit?"

"Hmmph," Hanahan chuckled. "You remember that hungh? Well, Baltimore also invited me to join CoBALT, but I declined."

"Why?"

"Because I knew what kind of guy Harold is. Cutthroat—even more than me. His only concern was profit and everything else be damned." Hanahan folded his hands as his jaws clenched. "Your dad didn't see that soon enough. He was always too damn trusting, always trying to see the good in people. I think some of that's rubbed off on you, too."

"I never was a fan of Harold either," Conrad replied.

"Yet he didn't contest the stake in the company your dad willed to you."

"What does that matter?"

"Have you been paying attention to the financial statements they have been sending you? 'Cause if you did, you'd realize Harold hasn't been dealing with the most upstanding of characters."

"What do you mean?"

Hanahan pointed in Conrad's direction. "He used CoBALT to run guns for corrupt governments, warlords, and criminals. He even provided security for the United People's Front shadow cabinet."

"Are you kidding me? His people were in Lemalia during the war?"

"Yes," Hanahan pressed his right forefinger against his palm-side of his left pinkie finger. He stretched it as if he was counting off numbers, "Ramsey hired them to protect Erosin Analaise's handpicked cabinet officers. Throughout all the chaos there is no way you would've been aware. He's even sold weapons to General Dankwah and funneled cash into one of the dummy corporations that was funding Aldessa's campaign. Harold's been in your business this whole time and you haven't noticed."

"So, you're telling me one of his people killed my parents?"

"I have no doubt."

CHAPTER NINE

THE REBUILD

September 26th
Kalaran, Lemalia

Morrison's thoughts ventured back to the events of least year as he rode in the back of an armored Hummer. He gazed upon the continued poverty that many of the townspeople suffered as the vehicle rumbled along the rough terrain. They eventually reached the outskirts of the war-ravaged town that once served as the home of the country's largest Duritium mine. Making sure he had his cellphone; he tapped the inside pocket of his sports coat. The Hummer made an abrupt stop at the steps of an elaborate building which stood in contrast to the devastation that surrounded it.

As he stepped out of the vehicle, he caught sight of Intelligence Minister Lirwa Prashad as she walked down the stairs toward him. Morrison could not take his eyes off her as she walked toward him—her neat, bright blue tunic collard dress with red trimming set off nicely against her rich caramel skin. Morrison saw flashes of his ex-wife, Danielle, in her.

"Agent Morrison, I presume?" Prashad said as she extended her hand to greet him.

"Yes, Minister Prashad," Morrison responded as he shook her hand.

"I am glad you could make it," Prashad responded solemnly. "We have a lot to discuss in terms of shoring up our security apparatus in preparation for new elections."

"How many people live here?" Morrison asked.

"The town is about 10,000," she responded. "If you count seasonal contractors that number goes up to 12,000."

Morrison took note of the numerous children who were playing around bombed out houses. "But these kids live in squalor and their families are mining one of the most precious metals in the world."

Prashad nodded her head. "That's why we are trying to change things." She pointed into the direction of the elaborate building as they walked up its steps. "This new school was built to educate all of the children in this community. It's our first steps in making things right."

"How's this being funded?"

"We took the profits that would have gone to Network businesses, and instead re-routed them to expanding public works and aid targeted at the people of Kalaran."

"That makes sense. Extremism grows out of poverty and lack of access."

"Exactly, Agent Morrison," Prashad said as she pointed in his direction. "In order to avoid creating future recruits for the United People's Front, we've begun providing the resources to the community so they do not have to go down that path."

"How have things gone in that area?"

She turned to look up at him. "What do you mean?"

"I mean the investigations into the continued UPF insurgencies. What have your agents found?"

Prashad pulled a slim cellphone from her side pocket and tapped on the screen. A holographic image of UPF assets popped up.

"Remnants of the UPF mostly went underground after their defeat last year," she paused before continuing, "thanks to you and your team."

Morrison smiled. "Thanks, but we were just doing our duty ma'am."

"Please, you can dispel with the humility, Agent Morrison. All I'm saying is true. Thanks to your team's investments in rebuilding our nation, we've been able to narrow down the location of many of the UPF cells scattered throughout the country."

Prashad enlarged the holographic image.

"With the help of your team's surveillance drones we've been able to get granular detail on the comings and goings of top UPF leaders—including their assets and liabilities. It's allowed me to insert many of my clandestine agents into key UPF strongholds."

"I'm…glad the drones have been helpful. I'm just not so sure about its excessive use."

Prashad cocked her left eyebrow. "How so?"

"I do care about security, but there have to be boundaries on how much we invade into peoples' lives."

"Well, your leader, Captain Conrad, has other ideas. And I agree with her. The security and safety of a nation sometimes has to take precedence over the privacy of a few."

"Really?"

"Oh yes, we Lemalians don't have your American sensibilities when it comes to personal privacy. We care about our people's lives and sometimes that means encroaching on some of their privacy."

Morrison's eyebrows furrowed briefly.

"Come now, Agent Morrison—" Prashad said as she lightly tapped the back of Morrison's left arm.

"You can call me Terrell," Morrison responded.

She looked back with a warm smile. "Okay, Terrell, please follow me, President Legaud is waiting for us."

They walked into an ornate administrative office that housed the principal's office. Legaud leaned against a woodgrain finished desk, surrounded by his security detail. He wore a bright smile as well as a traditional multi-colored suit which had patterns similar to those found in Ankara cloth.

"Agent Morrison, it is great to see you again," Legaud said as he extended his right hand.

"Same here, sir," Morrison answered as he grasped Legaud's hand.

"I see you have met Minister Prashad."

Morrison turned to look in her direction. "Yes, she's brought me up to speed on the situation with the UPF insurgency."

Legaud nodded. "This is becoming more and more disconcerting Agent Morrison. I had hoped forming a unity government would have served as an olive branch to the other side---- but I was wrong."

"I understand, but sometimes you can't rationalize with radicals," Morrison said dejectedly.

"True, but although they are radicals, they are still my people."

"Sometimes even your own people can be your worst enemy."

"I see, but that was the reason I took on the presidency," Legaud replied. His statement was somewhat misleading due to the fact that he usurped the role after the newly elected president, Mohan Aldessa, was assassinated. This fact was not lost on Morrison.

"Speaking of the presidency, I've been coordinating with UN election monitoring officials to make sure the upcoming elections are safe and free."

"Thank you, Agent Morrison. I look forward to running a free and fair election."

Morrison nodded in agreement. "I pray for the same, Mr. President. I pray for the same."

CHAPTER TEN

TECHNO FUTURAE

September 27th
AlphA.I. Con
Palo Alto, California

The sprawling convention hall overflowed with a diverse crowd. They were wide-eyed and excited to see the latest tech innovations from AlphA.I. Stroud had helmed the company since its infancy and showed no signs of slowing down. He made his mark on this convention with the latest techwares. There had been rumblings that Stroud would be debuting a new device. As the crowds waited to see what the tech genius was planning, he sat in the waiting room with his Chief Operating Officer, Bridgette Huntley. With furrowed eyebrows and flared nostrils, Stroud looked in Huntley's direction. Without saying a word, she knew what this look meant.

"I apologize, sir."

"What are you apologizing for?" Stroud asked as he smoothed out his thinning, sandy brown hair.

Huntley looked down at the floor briefly with her clipboard braced under her forearms. "Let's not be coy, sir. We both know you're furious about what happened to the Beta group."

"Can you imagine the fall-out from this Bridgette?"

Huntley put up her hand, "There won't be any. Stiles and her team cleaned up the bodies, and we filed missing persons report with the LAPD. Most of them were loners without any family. They won't be missed."

"That's not the point, Bridgette. This was supposed to change the world, not get some college kids killed."

"Well, we've had something like this with some Variants we've recruited in the past."

"It's not the same," Stroud replied. He put his head in his hands. Huntley hesitantly walked over to him to stroke his back. He patted the top of her hand.

"This was the start," Stroud said. "The first real synthesis of man and machine. Something I've dreamed of since I was a child."

"The delivery system was off," Huntley responded. "Once we get the Adept, they'll be able to bypass this problem."

Stroud lifted his head up to look at Huntley. "Where are we on acquisition?"

Huntley lifted her left wrist, which was adorned with a sleek, dark black, metallic band with digital numbering on the top. She touched the top of the band. Instantly, a blue solid-state holographic display of a map of the United States emanated from the device. Huntley manipulated the image by sliding her thumb across the top of the band. The image zeroed in on the state of Illinois. "Stiles has a grab team set up for two weeks from now."

"Why so long?"

"The team has to do scenario run throughs before they approach."

"Are they using the predictive algorithm protocols?"

"Yes. It won't be the same as Japan."

"That was a freaking nightmare," Stroud said as he gestured with his left hand to Huntley. "How is the Asset by the way?"

"Doing well," Huntley said with a slight cough, "a little resistant but we are able to get what we need from her."

"Good, and how are the negotiations with Saisentan going? Are we close to getting this deal done?"

"Yes. Venturepointe's finalizing the details of the acquisition."

Stroud smoothed out his khaki vest as he got up from his chair. "Excellent, soon we'll expand our market share exponentially."

Huntley nodded in agreement.

"How are things going on Capitol Hill?"

Huntley's mouth twisted. "Our lobbyist are doing their best to get the privacy legislation blocked."

"And what about the subpoena?"

"I'm set to testify before the senate subcommittee in a few weeks. Don't worry I can handle this."

"That I have no doubt," Stroud said smiling. "That damn Malveux has been a freaking thorn in our side. We have got to do something about her."

"I agree," Huntley said.

A faint knock was heard on the door.

Huntley cocked her head in its direction. "Who is it?"

"You're up in three minutes," the producer responded.

"Thank you," Huntley replied.

Stroud looked in the mirror once more with a slightly crooked smile. "Bridgette, soon the world will see humanity's future doesn't lie with superhuman saviors but in embracing the man-machine singularity."

* * *

Convention Floor of AlphA.I. Con

Blankenchip and Bledsoe perused the various exhibits on the convention floor. He was drawn away by floating platforms powered by mini polarity engines. His eye also caught people with neuro enhancer devices attached to their temples. Blankenchip's brain started churning with ideas about how he could upgrade his own exoskeletal suit. As he peeked in on a demonstration on matter digitization, he felt a tap on his left shoulder.

"Anything interesting, babe?" Bledsoe asked as Blankenchip turned in her direction.

He kissed her on the cheek.

"Nah, just getting some ideas that's all. What about you?"

Bledsoe traced her eyes along the convention hall. She saw a demonstration on localized temperature control and smiled. "This is kind of a homecoming to me."

"I know, it's been a while since you've been in the Bay area, huh?"

"Yup, it has. This is where I grew up. Born and raised in San Fran. I do miss the weather sometimes."

"You mean the half-ass warm and half-ass cold climate in this area," Blankenchip said playfully.

Bledsoe grinned. "Yeah, right." She looked at her hands and paused before continuing. "You know, Dennis Stroud helped design the SHARP protocols that helped activate my powers?"

"Activate your powers?" Blankenchip asked quizzically. "I thought you were a complete norm before SHARP?"

"I thought the same, too. The DARPA research team did some genetic tests on me prior to the project, and they determined I was a latent Variant. In fact, Dennis Stroud was a part of the team that developed the subdermal tech that helps me utilize my powers."

"Really?" Blankenchip replied. "You know I didn't mean anything with that stuff I was saying with John."

Bledsoe waved him off. "I know. You tend to say a lot of stuff out of your ass so I let it slide."

Blankenchip shrunk back slightly.

"Yeah," Bledsoe continued, "I had no idea. They said I should have manifested in my early teens, but nothing happened."

"So, all of the genetic engineering and surgeries?"

"Weren't for nothing. They helped amplify and augment what was already there."

"And I thought I read your complete file. Even though we've been dating for over six months there are still things I'm learning about you, Karen Bledsoe.

You never cease to surprise me," Blankenchip said with a grin.

"Is that so?" she replied.

Blankenchip leaned into her space in anticipation of a kiss, but before their lips could connect, they heard a voice over the public announcement system.

"Please make your way to the center stage for the keynote address from AlphA.I. CEO Dennis Stroud."

Blankenchip nodded his head to Bledsoe, and they headed over to center stage. A congested mass of people huddled close. The tight space elicited a sense of claustrophobia. The convention lights dimmed, and a spotlight zeroed in on the black curtains aligned above the center stage. Stroud emerged from behind the curtain and trotted confidently upon the stage.

"Good afternoon, AlphA.I. Con! How are you all doing out there?" Stroud said—his lapel microphone boomed his voice throughout the auditorium.

Someone yelled out, "We love you, Dennis!"

"I love you all, too."

The crowd laughed. Stroud smiled back as he sauntered across the stage.

"I'm not good at this at all, you know, public speaking. My COO, Bridgette told me I had no choice. Or else the board members would push me out---I don't mean onto the stage but out of a job!" Stroud replied in a light tone.

The crowd reaction was a mix of glee and laughter.

"What does real change look like? Can anyone tell me?" Stroud posited to the crowd.

A few mumblings occurred in the midst of the audience. Stroud propped his right ear in the direction of the audience as if to sus out what was being said. A brave soul from the audience screamed out, "Real change looks like us!"

Stroud pointed back nonspecifically. "Exactly, real change looks like us." He paused and looked down with his right thumb pressed against his bottom lip as he paced across the stage. "Over the centuries we as a species, us, humans, have constantly looked to advance."

Suddenly, a digital screen dropped down from the ceiling. An image of a horse drawn buggy contrasted next to a new AlphA.I. designed automated car was clearly displayed.

"We evolve daily, there is no way we are going to stay the same. That's why we make advances in technology medicine and other areas. That's where we at AlphA.I. come in; we seek to evolve humanity to its rightful place."

The image on screen changed to the image of a sleek cell phone.

"Ladies and gentlemen, I would like to introduce you to the *Turing Two* cell phone. It can fully integrate with the national CYBRA AI operating system. As you may well know, the CYBRA program can integrate into any technological app, service, or program you have."

Stroud then drew his eyes into the throng of reporters that were a few steps from the stage down on the ground. He pointed to a reporter who raised her hand.

"What about privacy and proprietary rights in regard to CYBRA overriding other apps and programs on your new phone?"

"We have a shared agreement with a majority of tech companies regarding fees," Stroud responded. "Each company will receive a percentage of downloaded programs that CYBRA may have over-ridden."

"But does that really matter since your company has been acquiring tech companies left and right? You've basically monopolized every technological space," the reporter asked.

Stroud ignored that follow up question and looked to another reporter in the crowd vying for his attention. He pointed in their direction. "Yes, you in the brown blazer."

"Mr. Stroud, your company, AlphA.I. has multiple projects in almost all industries from defense contracting, to consumer electronics, highway management, and medical devices. Your products affect almost every facet of our lives. In fact, with CYBRA you're running the country's technological grid. Some may accuse AlphA.I. of pretty much running our lives. What do you say to those people who feel AlphA.I. is over-reaching, and essentially trying to rule over us?"

Stroud looked down briefly with a slight smile, and mischievous look. His Minnesota accent started to creep through as he began to speak, "Well, that's good question, uh…what's your name?"

"Raquel, sir," the reporter responded.

"Well, Raquel, there is no question we as a company aim to impact the world, but in no way are we trying to take over peoples' lives. AlphA.I.'s motto is: 'Humankind. Evolved,' and we believe that's best accomplished through technology. Thank you very much," Stroud said as he exited the stage.

He waved to the crowd as he walked off into the backstage area. As he got behind the curtain, the producer removed his microphone. Stroud was visibly shaken by the concluding line of questioning. He eyed Huntley in the corner of the hallway. She let off a cautionary glance in his direction. Before Stroud could head in her direction, he heard a familiar voice.

"Nice job Dennis."

Stroud turned to see Lawson wearing a smart grin on his face.

"Doug, are you here to congratulate or hate?" Stroud asked bluntly. Huntley quickly made her way in Stroud's direction as the men began their conversation.

"Look, Dennis you asked if I would be there for your debut, and here I am."

"Ok, so what do you think?" Stroud asked with some slight hesitance.

"I think it's brilliant, effective, and at the same time deplorable," Lawson said flatly. "What you're proposing with your phone and CYBRA, is horrifying."

Stroud raised his hands in protest. "You don't get what we're trying to do Doug. CYBRA will unify this country and the world."

"You're insane, Dennis!" Lawson said as he pointed his finger in Stroud's direction. Huntley saw this and gave a scowl in Lawson's direction as she came to Stroud's side. Lawson ignored the look.

"Do people understand how you're precious CYBRA A.I. system actually works?"

"What are you talking about, Doug? You sound like the mad man now."

"I've seen the schematics and the code behind CYBRA. Do people know what your system's algorithm actually does?"

"Ok, that's enough. I am going to have to ask you to leave," Huntley said, shoving her body in between Lawson and Stroud. She waved over for the security personnel in the back corner of the room.

Lawson put his hands up as he backed away. He looked beyond Huntley to lock eyes with Stroud. "Ok, I'm out of here but Dennis I am not going to let this go. I will make sure people know the truth."

Huntley glared at Lawson as he walked off with security behind him. She looked back at Stroud, who was slightly shaken. Huntley lightly touched his shoulder.

"Are you OK, sir?"

Stroud touched her hand. "I'm alright, Bridgette. Just give me a second. Just surprised Doug would come at me like that."

Huntley firmly grabbed Stroud's shoulder. "Dennis don't worry. I'll take care of everything."

CHAPTER ELEVEN

PIERCING THE VEIL

October 6th
Lawson Residence
Palo Alto, California

Evening set on the suburban cul de sac that Doug Lawson called home. He sat at the dinner table with his wife and confidant, Pauletta.

"Babe, when I talked to Dennis it seemed like he had no clue what the ramifications were of his new A.I. system," Lawson said after taking a sip of his White Zinfandel.

"But you saw the schematics and the code behind the program?"

"Yes."

Pauletta pointed her fork in Lawson's direction. "By a legit route?"

The curve of Lawson's lips rounded up in a smile. "Well, as legit as they can come." He drove his fork into his medium-rare steak. "Someone inside leaked the information to me." He pulled up his phone and slid his right thumb across the screen and squinted intently at it. "I believe she goes by the name Echo."

"Clearly a pseudonym," Pauletta responded as she impaled her salad. "How do you know it's even a she?"

Lawson put down his phone and looked at his wife with bright eyes, "Because a guy wouldn't have as much concern as a girl. I'm just saying…"

Pauletta smacked the side of her husband's right arm playfully as he let off a slight chuckle.

"Besides, I did a background trace on her IP address and cross referenced it with the employee listing in the operations division. All the employees that are in that division are female."

"OK, Mr. detective, so what is so catastrophic about CYBRA?"

Lawson placed his phone at the center of the table and tapped the screen once again. Immediately a green-hued holographic image of a network of cellphone towers beamed upward from the screen.

"From what I could ascertain, the CYBRA system is an integrated A.I. network that emits a constant radio signal throughout cellphones, upgraded vehicles, basically anything electronic. It not only emits signals but also receives signals."

"What other kind of signals?"

"Brain Waves."

"What?!" Pauletta exclaims. "How? You'd need a direct touchpoint, like an EEG electrode or an actual brain implant to make that happen."

"That's what I am not sure of. But I'm going to find out," Lawson said as he drove the side of his right fist lightly into the table.

Pauletta put her utensils down and clasped her fingers into a sling to rest her chin on. "Wow Doug. So essentially they've created a way to read people's minds?"

"It's a little more complicated than that, but yes. And if they could read minds, they could also theoretically control them."

"So, what do you plan to do about this?" Pauletta said as she pushed her plate away.

"I have to call this out," he said contemplatively. He folded his hands together and looked his wife in the eye. "I am going to reach out to anyone who'll listen—congress, the FCC, the California governor's office, press. Anybody who will hear me out."

Lawson was interrupted by a rumbling noise upstairs.

"What is that?" Pauletta asked as she quickly rose from her chair. "Was that Cademon's room?

"I don't know," Lawson quickly replied as he rose from his chair. "Let me check it out."

Lawson's heart thumped fast in his chest as he raced up the wooden staircase. He lightly grabbed on to the railing to keep himself on balance as he tried to get up to his oldest child's bedroom. He nearly tripped over the scattered assortment of toy trucks, action figures, and electronics that led to Cademon's room.

He finally reached his son's door. Lawson nearly wrenched the door's handle off as he thrusted it open. Horror filled his heart as he saw furniture toppled over as well as blood splatters on the carpet and wall. "Oh my God!" Lawson screamed as he hurried to his son's bed but saw nothing but streaks of blood on the bedsheets along with torn pillows, and a comforter.

"Pauletta! Get up here!" He immediately ran to the bathroom that adjoined Cademon's room.

Despair washed over him as he saw his son's body in the tub with three bullet wounds in his chest. Lawson let out a blood curdling scream as he cradled his son's dead body. He rocked his son inconsolably back and forth. "Pauletta!" he screamed once more but was met with no response. Lawson gently placed his son's body down into the blood-drenched tub.

Hurrying down the opposite end of the hallway, he rushed to his daughter Amaris's bedroom. Lawson slipped on the blood seeping out from underneath Amaris's bedroom door. He reached up from the ground with tears flooding his eyes to grab the door handle to his precious five-year old's bedroom. As the door creaked open, he saw Amaris's body, laid out on the ground with blood streaming from the back of her head from a pointblank bullet wound.

Lawson continued to weep as his blood-stained shirt pressed against his daughter's head as he held her. The loss overwhelmed him. His body crumpled to the ground. Somehow, he gathered the strength to lift his body off the ground and slowly made his way to the stairwell. He violently called out his wife's name as his body, limp with grief, trudged down the wooden staircase.

"Pauletta! Pauletta!" Tears clouded his eyes so much he couldn't even see a few feet in front of him. He used the back of his hand to wipe away the tears. When he arrived at the base of the stairs, he saw his wife slumped over on the dinner table. Blood oozed out of her chest and drenched the tablecloth.

"No, no, no!" Lawson screamed as he rushed to his deceased wife's side. He collapsed over her. He sobbed to the point of almost choking on his own mucus. The click of cocked pistol was heard. Lawson looked up through tear-filled eyes to see a ski-masked figure. They pointed a silencer-tipped Glock pistol in his direction. Lawson's eyes widened. Before he could utter a breath, a bullet pierced his skull.

PART TWO

THE ADEPT

(NKINKYIM: ADINKRA SYMBOL OF VERSABILITY)

CHAPTER TWELVE

I'M RATHER UNIQUE

October 8th
Jones Household
Hyde Park
Chicago, Illinois

"Itrish come on now, you're gon' be late now!" Clarice Jones shouted up to her seventeen-year-old daughter. When Mrs. Jones's Jamaican accent got thicker, her daughter knew she was serious.

"Alright, Mommy, I'll be down in a sec, now!" Itrish Jones replied as she leaned her head back to put in her contact lens. The lens fit well on the first try, which was a first for her. She brushed her dark braids off her shoulder as she rushed to get her bookbag and roller bag together to head to school. As she walked from her adjoined bathroom to her main room, one could see her walls adorned with posters of an array of hip-hop legends such as: Nas, A.Z., Notorious B.I.G., KRS-One, Rakim, A Tribe Called Quest, and Public Enemy. She filled her bags to the brim with books, overnight clothes, and other supplies. Just as if on cue, her younger brother, Anthony, came to her doorway.

"Hey, 'Trish my phone's acting up again, can you fix it right quick for me?" he said as he thrusted the sleek gun-metal, gray phone in his older sister's direction.

"Right now, really? Did you restart it?"

"Yes! Three times," he said vociferously. "I even went back to read the instructions and it's still not working."

"I'm about to go. Can't this wait?" Itrish said as she straightened out her school uniform.

"Please?" Anthony said with sad eyes. He moved in to hug his big sister softly. "Pretty please?"

"Aaaaagh!" Itrish screamed as she raised her hands. "Don't give me that look! You know I can't say no to that."

Itrish eyed the phone. "Isn't this the *Turing Two*?"

"Yeah."

"And it's already breaking?"

"Yeah."

Itrish shook her head. "Hmmm, Janky. Give me this."

She grabbed the phone. As soon as she touched it, the pupils of her eyes emanated a white glow. Her fingertips let off a slight static charge and a glowing circuit-like pattern radiated from her fingertips to the back of Anthony's phone. After five seconds, she handed the phone back to her brother. "Here you go, I even upgraded it with a holographic interface. Happy now?"

Anthony jumped all over his sister. His twelve-year-old arms almost squeezed the life out of Itrish. "Thank you, thank you, thank you! Did I tell you you're my favorite sibling?"

Itrish smacked her lips slightly. "Really? I'm sure Laurel and Magnus would love to hear that."

"Just don't tell them," Anthony said with a mischievous smile before he ran out of his sister's room.

"Itrish!" Mrs. Jones shouted again.

"Coming, Mommy!"

Itrish hurriedly ran down the wooden staircase of her parents' venerable rowhouse. The click clack of her roller bag's wheels rumbled through the house as she came down the stairs. Itrish kissed her mom on the cheek as she got to the base of the stairs. "I'm sorry, Mommy, Anthony was slowing me down."

"Don't go blaming your brother, Itrish Jones. You know you're the only one to blame for your tardiness, young lady," Mrs. Jones said, lovingly chiding her.

"Yes, Mommy." Itrish said as she ran through the door to place her luggage into the family's Honda minivan. After her mother made her way into the driver's seat, Itrish commented, "Mommy, you know you don't have to talk to me like I'm one of your students."

"I know, my dear, but it always gets the response I want out of you, sweetheart." A smile traced across Mrs. Jones's face as she started the vehicle. Itrish smiled back as she shook her head. She pulled the front lever of the passenger chair to slide back to a more comfortable position.

"You're a junior now, how are you feeling?" Mrs. Jones asked as she pulled into the side street and into the main arteries of Chicago rush hour traffic.

Itrish looked out of the passenger side window before she turned to look at her mother. "I don't know, kind of blah, I guess."

"'Blah?'"

"I don't know how to explain it," Itrish said with a half-smile. "I've already got the SATs and ACTs out of the way. The Variant Aptitude Tests are almost done. I'll be happy once those things are over with."

"What are your thoughts on that?"

"I feel like I'm being paraded around like a Westminster dog, just for them to tell me I'm 'worthy.'"

"You do sometimes shed like a Border Collie..." Mrs. Jones said, laughing with a broad smile.

"Mommy!" Itrish screamed.

"Calm down, calm down, girl, you know I'm just playin', chile." She turned the minivan down the exit to the right. "Seriously, you've been blessed with a gift, Itrish."

"I know, Mom but being at VERGE for the past few years has been tough," Itrish said stroking the right side of her cheek.

"I understand sweetheart. But once you manifested after middle school, we knew we couldn't keep you in a regular school."

Itrish fiddled with the Pandora bracelet given to her by her mother—a sweet sixteen gift. "Was it tough for you and dad to come to the decision?"

Mrs. Jones firmly gripped her steering wheel and sighed. "Itrish, sweetheart, you have no idea. Especially with it being an overnight charter school. Your father and I struggled to decide what to do. It wasn't easy but it was the right thing to do."

Itrish gave a slight nod at her mother's words. As their minivan pulled up to the curb, she eyed her friends as they entered the school. Her attention completely shifted from their conversation to catching her friends' attention.

"Don't forget, your father will pick you up at the end of the week."

"Yes, Mommy."

Before she opened her side door, Mrs. Jones gently patted her forearm.

"Hey, don't forget Itrish, you are my blessing, and you are here for a reason, sweetheart," Mrs. Jones said with a smile. Itrish smiled and hugged her mother before she left.

CHAPTER THIRTEEN

THE GIFTED UNLIMITED

Two Hours Later
VERGE Academy
Chicago, Illinois

Gail Gowan's green eyes carefully scanned the student aptitude tests. She capped off her twenty-five- year secondary education career by serving as the VERGE Academy's principal. The years had been kind to her, she barely looked her fifty years of age. The only signs were the slight streaks of grey interspersed with the black hair she inherited from her Japanese mother.

A heavy knock on her office door's frosted glass was heard.

"Come in," Gowan said with some mild bass in her voice.

The door creaked open.

"Good morning, Principal Gowan, were you planning on moping about all day or meeting with the potential candidates?" Mary Ellen Raymond, Gowan's assistant principle, said with a broad smile.

Gowan waved Raymond in. "Well, you know moping is my superpower."

"Is there something you haven't been telling me?" Raymond said with a wry smile. She walked up to the right of Gowan's wooden desk, which was laden with multiple student photos, files, and papers. "I only thought you were a telepath."

"An out of practice one at that," she replied. Gowan lifted her right wrist to display a gleaming, dark blue, metallic bracelet with a rectangular LCD screen in Raymond's direction. She jingled her wrist around. "With this thing, I'm as normal as anyone else."

Raymond touched the bracelet. "So, you volunteered to try the SHAN prototype? I thought Saisentan was still a ways from perfecting it."

"They are, from what I understand." She glanced at the bracelet, "I just thought I would try it to see if it really worked."

"Does it?"

Gowan shook her head. "Not all the way, I can still pick up flashes of thoughts even with this thing on. Plus…" she tapped the bracelet's LCD screen and the device unlatched from her wrist, "it gives me a freaking headache."

"At least it can come in handy if some of our kids become unruly," Raymond said. She lifted the bracelet from Gowan's desk for a closer look.

"I hope our kids will never need it."

"I hope so too," Raymond said. "Maybe Saisentan will be able to speed it past the developmental phase once they merge with AlphA.I.?"

"Speaking of AlphA.I., isn't one of their reps coming in today for the Variant Aptitude Tests?"

"Yes, but it's funny they usually bring in a low-level HR person for the evaluations but this time they're bringing in Bridgette Huntley."

Gowan paused. "Wow, they're bringing the big guns."

"Well, we do have an impressive incoming senior class," Raymond said as she peered over Gowan's shoulder to see Itrish Jones's picture.

* * *

Three Hours Later
Basement level Training Simulator
VERGE academy

"Duck!" Itrish shouted to her classmate, John Gallagher. Gallagher was in the sights of a mechanized energy cannon. Luckily for John, he was a Variant blessed with an advanced metabolism and superhuman speed. He could reach speeds of up to two-hundred miles per hour on a bad day. He was only seventeen, but nowhere near his peak. Even though he had amazingly fast reflexes and speed, he was known to get easily distracted. Thankfully, he heeded Itrish's warning and sped out of the way of the oncoming plasma cannon blast, as his blond hair whooshed back as he ran.

"Thanks I.T.," Gallagher shouted back to her with a smile.

Itrish's skin warmed from the intensity of the blast even though she was well out of the line of fire.

"Hey, 'Trish," Malik Anderson, another classmate, said over their wireless earpieces. "Can you shut this thing down?"

"Is Nas the greatest MC of all time," she responded matter-of-factly.

"I can't with you sometimes," Anderson chuckled. "I swear you were born in the wrong decade with those old-school hip-hop references."

Itrish smiled as her eyes illuminated with a bright white glow. The barrel of the mounted plasma canon started to turn rapidly from right to left and electrical sparks flew from the back of the cannon. The cannon barrel lowered, and immediately the device shut down.

As the three teenagers engaged in their conflict, their every move was scrutinized by the trio of Gowan, Raymond, and AlphA.I. COO, Bridgette Huntley. Data from their form-fitted uniforms were relayed on-screen to the three women. They watched intently through a large, one-way, glass mirror from a perched position, inside the observation deck. Gowan sat in a small tri-sectioned office chair in front of an elaborate computer panel. She pulled the microphone on its malleable stand closer to her mouth.

"Great work," Gowan said. "But Malik, you probably could have used a telekinetic maneuver to free up Itrish to take that cannon out."

Huntley crossed her arms as she glanced over Gowan's shoulder down at the action below. Her initial facial expression was flat, then her eyes widened, almost in a mix of surprise and glee as she witnessed the demonstration of Itrish's abilities.

"Tell me more about that student." Huntley asked as she hovered over Gowan's shoulder.

Gowan's back stiffened. "You mean Itrish?"

"Yes, her."

Gowan typed on the touchscreen computer panel in front of her. The holographic projector base to the left of the panel lit up and displayed Itrish's headshot.

"She is a level 4 technopath, with the ability to control all electronic and technical devices. She can virtually take over any piece of tech from a nanite to a quantum computer."

"Including large digital and wireless networks?"

Gowan raised her eyebrow. "Yes, and that's child's play for her."

"What about techno-assimilation?"

"To a small scale she has the ability to assimilate small objects like cellphones, small tablet computers, smart watches," Raymond said, butting in on the conversation. "We project she could reach omni-level status by her twenty-first birthday."

"Really? Fascinating," Huntley said as she cupped her right hand under her chin. "There's only one other multi-level technopath that I'm aware of. I thought omni-levels were purely theoretical. She sounds like an amazing young woman."

With a smile of pride on her face, Gowan swiveled around in her chair to face Huntley. "You have no idea."

Down below, the trio relished their seeming victory during the training exercise.

"I think we won," Itrish said as she looked on at the metallic wreckage of what was once a plasma cannon.

"Good work guys," Raymond's booming voice said over the PA system. Immediately, the debris and environment around the trio of youngsters started to fade to reveal a large, almost warehouse-like space with sterile, gray walls lined with rectangular light panels. The trio of Anderson, Itrish and Gallagher dusted themselves off as the solid-state holographics of the training scenario receded.

The main entrance door slid wide open and the trio of the three women that previously observed them walked through. Gowan led as the two other women flanked her. Gowan clapped her hands as she walked to her students.

"Great work, guys!" She gave each one of her student's congratulatory hugs. Anderson received Gowan's embrace but looked over her shoulder and saw Huntley.

"Is she here for the VAT?"

Gowan looked back at Huntley. "Yes, she is." She extended her hand out in Huntley's direction. "Guys I would like to introduce you to Ms. Bridgette Huntley from AlphA.I."

"Wow! How did you manage that, Principal G?!" Gallagher asked enthusiastically. "You got the head of the number one tech company in the world. I am impressed."

"Well John, I'm just doing my job," Gowan said as the students greeted Huntley.

Huntley's eyes pierced Itrish's own as she stared intently at the young technopath. "Hi, Itrish, right?"

"Yeah, that's me."

"I was impressed with your level of control during the exercise. Was it hard to do?"

"Let me ask you a question before I answer yours."

Huntley paused. "Uh, sure, ok."

"Why is AlphA.I.'s board lily white? I mean absolutely no black people. Why is that?"

Huntley tightened her mouth. "We at AlphA.I. have a commitment to diversity and are actively recruiting a person of color to join our board."

"Just *a* person of color?"

Gowan nudged Itrish in the back. Itrish in turn peeked back at her before she answered. "I guess I'll get my answer another time. To answer your original question, it was a walk in the park."

"Amazing."

"No, I'm just kidding. It took me a while to get this good." Itrish glanced in Gowan's direction. "With Principal G's help, I've been able to get better with my abilities."

"I bet it was tough getting this adept with your powers?"

Itrish looked in Gowan's direction with lifted eyebrows. Gowan nodded for her to answer. "Well, at first it was but the more I practiced, the better I got." she said. "And I couldn't have gotten this good without these guys here." She pointed with both her thumbs to Anderson and Gallagher behind her.

"Interesting. We could use someone like you once you graduate," Huntley said. She pulled out a business card from her right blazer pocket and pushed it in Itrish's direction.

Reluctantly, she received the rectangular piece of hard-stock paper, and replied, "Ok, thanks."

CHAPTER FOURTEEN

MIDNIGHT MARAUDERS

Student Quarters
VERGE Academy

"Didn't that lady creep you out?" Anderson asked Itrish as he handed her a bottle of water from his minifridge.

"I don't know," Itrish said as she scanned her tablet computer. She was seated on the top bunk bed. The tablet's screen images flashed across rapidly. Her eyes glowed as she utilized her technopathic abilities to easily control the device.

"That cold-eyed stare was enough to give me goosebumps, Trish," Anderson said, seated at his desk, which had a Trinidadian flag tacked to the corkboard right above it. He glanced at his laptop screen displaying an article on the recent rise of missing Variants across the country.

"It felt like she saw you as an Extra Value Meal," Anderson said as he turned in Itrish's direction.

Itrish smiled. "I always thought of myself as the main entrée at a five-star restaurant."

Anderson flashed a smile back. "You're my entrée, baby."

"That was corny as hell," Itrish replied as she shook her head.

Suddenly, Itrish's body was levitated off the top bunk. She was startled briefly but soon came to the realization it was Anderson's doing. As she floated closer to Anderson, their eyes locked and their lips eventually touched.

"Let's keep it PG people!" a familiar voice shouted. Anderson and Irish turned to see Gallagher in the doorway.

"Really, John?" Anderson huffed.

"Yes, really Malik." Gallagher threw up his right hand in protestation. "Don't forget that we share a room during the school week."

"Yes, and I always tell you that around this time is our," Anderson said as he motioned between himself and Itrish, "time."

"Whatever, dude, we've all known each other for too long for there to be this secret stuff. We're the three amigos," Gallagher said as he flopped himself on to the lower bunkbed. He almost bumped his head against the underside of the top bunk. Being 6'1 in height actually had its disadvantages at times. Recovering quickly, Gallagher immediately pulled his cellphone from his pocket.

Anderson shook his head. He noticed his friend's attention being pulled into his phone. "What are you looking at?" he said as he reached over to grab his friend's phone. Gallagher used his super speed to quickly move it out of reach.

"Manners, Malik?" Gallagher retorted, wagging his finger in Anderson's direction. "I know your mom taught you about grabbing stuff that isn't yours, right?"

Just as quickly as he swiped up his phone, Gallagher could feel it wrench from his hand. The phone jutted up from his hand and flew directly into Anderson's.

"I loaned you the money to get this phone remember; So technically, it's mine as well," Anderson said with a smirk. "Now let me see what's got you so into your phone." Anderson scanned the article. "Why are you reading about Vigil?"

"The article is a puff piece on their surveillance drones, and how they're invading peoples' privacy."

"You mean those fascists are getting even more Big Brothery?" Itrish said disdainfully.

"'Big Brothery?' Is that even a word?" Gallagher asked with cocked eyebrow.

"Would you like some fries with that Haterade?" Anderson said as he playfully nudged Itrish's right elbow. "Now what did they ever do to you?"

"For starters, they slaughtered hundreds of people in a foreign country with their Deathstar laser. And now they've deployed a whole drone army on the world!"

"But come on, baby," Anderson pleaded. He spread his arms wide. "You have to look at the big picture. They were in a war. I'm sure they had a reason for it."

Itrish leered at him. "Come on, Malik. You know they had other options. They have that one guy, Arrowhawk right? He could've done something without all the collateral damage. Think about how many people died. It's crazy!"

"You know I.T. that's not a hundred percent true, "Gallagher rebutted. "They said he was injured during the time. He couldn't have helped."

Itrish gently took the phone out of Anderson's right hand and pointed to the screen. "That was just the beginning, this is even worse. Now, they can put a drone hit out on anybody. It's scary."

Anderson folded his arms. "Naw, I don't believe that. You're being a little out of pocket 'Trish! C'mon now, they still have to abide by the rules."

She motioned her right hand in Anderson's direction. "Now how many times have we seen that not to be true? Politicians act like they're above the law, police officers in this very city get away with murdering innocent black people all the time. How much more a bunch of super-powered people with no accountability?"

"I got an idea," Gallagher said as he folded his arms. "We can make our own super team. Keep them in check, like you said I.T."

"What kind of nonsense…" Anderson began to say in protest.

"No, I'm serious." Gallagher said, as he leaned forward. "We can do our own thing. Look, my cousin is an engineer, but she also is a Variant like us. She's brought up the idea of making her own super-team…"

Itrish threw up both hands shoulder-height. "Hold up. What business does an engineer have trying to be a superhero? First of all, they have no training. Second, how are they going to pay for it? Third, the government would never allow it. Should I go on?"

"Well, she was in the Army reserves for three years and also part of the first class of VERGE Academy students. And as for the other stuff…" Gallagher looked away somewhat confused. "We haven't figured it out yet."

"My point exactly."

"Well, I know one thing." Gallagher fired back.

"What's that?" Itrish asked.

"Out of the three of us here," Gallagher began to say with a mischievous smile, "you're the only one who can actually do something about those drones up there."

"John, you're crazy." Anderson said. "Trish's abilities are great but there's no way in hell she can tap into their system. They got way too many firewalls to keep any hacker out." Anderson nodded his head in Itrish's direction. "Even the world's greatest hacker."

Gallagher motioned in Itrish's direction. "So, you said that Vigil's unleashed a drone army on the planet, and you didn't agree with it. Then, what are you going to do about it?" His deep blue eyes focused in on Itrish. She looked back at him with equal intensity. Itrish then looked in Anderson's direction where she was welcomed with a slightly worried and disapproving look. She clenched her jaw and looked down to the floor with an intense stare.

"I'm gonna do it," she said confidently.

Gallagher's arms shot up into the air. "Yes!"

Anderson tapped Itrish on her forearm. "You know I don't like this at all babe. Who's to say you don't get caught?"

"Don't worry I won't," Itrish said boldly.

* * *

Four hours later
WGN TV Headquarters
2501 West Bradley Place
Chicago, Illinois

The cover of night made it easy for the three teens to sneak atop the WGN TV building. As one of Chicago's oldest independent television stations, it was a city treasure. They stood a good distance away as not to be seen by any bystanders. Anderson looked in Gallagher's direction.

"John, can you take a quick peek around, so we don't run into anybody?"

"Sure." The friction from Gallagher's feet left a blazing trail in concrete ground as he jetted off to do a quick reconnaissance tour of the building. And in what seemed like less than five seconds he returned.

"We're good. Nobody around that could spot us."

Anderson nodded. He looked at Itrish. "One last time Trish. You sure you want to do this?"

"Yeah, I am," she said, as she looked up at the rooftop satellite.

"Ok. God help us," Anderson said under his breath as he closed his eyes and placed his right hand on his forehead. Slowly, the trio felt the ground disappear beneath them as they ascended to the top of the building. They landed gently on the rooftop. After they landed, Anderson leaned over and clenched his knees.

"You ok, baby?" Itrish asked as she patted him on the back.

He waved her away. "Yeah, I'm fine. It's just that John," he motioned in Gallagher's direction, "gained like fifty pounds—could barely lift his behind."

"Get the hell out of here, Malik," Gallagher protested with a slight chuckle, "You know I weigh about a buck fifty soaking weight. It's your fat ass who has the weight problem."

Itrish shook her head and laughed. "I don't know what I'm going to do with you guys." Her gaze went up to the large satellite transmitter perched upon a metallic base with prominent wiring with computer paneling attached. Just a few feet away from the dish was a newly installed guyed cellphone tower. Itrish walked over to the structure and noticed the insignia of AlphA.I. emblazoned on one of the metallic stanchions holding the tower in place. She traced her eyes up to the tower and noticed an array of antennae with a concave shape that was unlike anything she had seen before. Nestled at the mid-section of the tower were three cameras. Itrish motioned her hand up to these devices. The pupils of her eyes released a warm, white glow. Immediately sparks spat out from the back of the cameras' housing units.

"That's better." Itrish said contentedly.

"I didn't even notice those cameras up there babe," Malik said. "Good call shutting them down."

Itrish nodded her head.

Gallagher folded his arms behind his back pacing around the base of the satellite dish.

"So, you think you can pull this off I.T?"

Without looking in Gallagher's direction she responded, "Watch me work."

Itrish calmly walked over the base of the satellite dish and removed a panel off the fiber optic relay unit. Her hands erupted with a slight glow as she grabbed the exposed wiring. As Gallagher and Anderson looked on, Itrish tapped into the satellite dish's radio emitter and countermanded its original signal. Strands of glowing energy steadily crisscrossed up her hands, torso, and head like circuitry.

The transmitter's radio signal was re-routed from the television station's satellites to the Vigil Satellite Defense System array. With thousands of satellites hurriedly orbiting earth, pinpointing the exact location of the Vigil SDS was like trying to find a needle in a haystack. Using the various telecommunications relay satellites, she bounced a radio signal that grew concentrically. She could feel her head pounding as she reached out further to expand the signal. A scarlet ribbon of blood trickled down her right nostril as she strained to expand the radio signal's radius.

"Trish, that's enough!" Anderson shouted.

Anderson's words fell on deaf ears. Itrish's focus was on reaching the Vigil Satellite Defense System's Command and Control unit. Once their protocols were breached, she essentially had the world's deadliest space-based weaponry in the palm of her hand.

A few minutes passed and she finally got the signal to the Command-and-Control unit's radio receiver. The unit's onboard computer system was one of the most advanced, if not the most advanced system in the world. It governed all the SDS's surveillance, intelligence, and offensive capabilities. Itrish began to tap into the computer's mainframe and programming.

"Dammit," Itrish whispered.

"What is it?" Gallagher asked.

"They're program firewall is legit. I haven't seen anything like it."

"You could read their programming code?"

"Yes. It's bananas," Itrish responded.

"Do you think you can get around it?"

Anderson nudged Gallagher's shoulder. "Don't encourage her. She's damn near killing herself because you dared her to!"

"I didn't put a gun to her head!" Gallagher retorted.

"Both of you shut up," Itrish said as she cringed.

She employed a brute-force hyper-sequencing technique to overcome the Command-and-Control unit's firewall. Finally, success had been achieved. She saw the various 0's and 1's composing the program's binary code.

"Got 'em!" Itrish said triumphantly.

"What?!" Gallagher asked.

"I'm in. Let's see what we can do about these killer drones."

CHAPTER FIFTEEN

SOUND BOMBING

Vigil Satellite Control Center
Fort Meade, Maryland

The piercing sound of ringing alarms tore through the darkened confines of the Vigil Satellite Control Center's main hub. Its interior resembled NASA's mission control center in Houston with banks of computers in neat rows facing an array of large LCD screens. Multiple technicians in blue uniforms manned the computers.

Satellite Control Director, Kellita Davis's countenance changed as she heard the clanging alarms. She burst out of her office, which overlooked the hub below.

"Austin, status report!" Davis shouted down to Lead Control Specialist, David Austin.

Austin pulled up a schematic on his large recumbent computer screen. He tapped on the screen's tactile interface. A larger version of the schematic appeared on the center LCD screen.

"There's been a breach of the Command-and-Control module. No active NRO repair activities have been logged and radar has not picked up any space debris that may have physically caused this," Austin responded.

"So, it's a remote breach," Davis said as she observed the schematic. "Possibility of foreign actors?"

"Not likely, ma'am," Austin said as he tapped his screen. "We've repelled dozens of attacks from the Chinese, Russians and Iranians. This hack is next level."

Davis peered down contemplatively. "Do we have any video of what's going on?"

"No, whoever is doing this has knocked out visual spatial capabilities."

"What's been compromised so far?"

Austin swiftly typed on his keyboard.

"Navigational systems, eighty percent of offensive capabilities, and sixty-five percent and counting of drone deployment systems."

"Well, damn," Davis said as she scratched her head. She observed the percentages that Austin just spouted out displayed clearly on the LCD screen. In front of her the description of the breached capabilities blinked in bright red lettering. Davis' blood pressure started to rise as she dwelt on the possibility of an outside attack. Her twenty years of experience with NASA and the NRO then began to kick in.

"What capabilities are online?"

"We still have radar, lidar, radio frequency and about thirty percent of drone deployment capabilities intact."

"Ok, run a piggy-back on the source."

"Already on it." Austin furiously typed away on his keyboard. Sweat beaded up on his top lip as he saw the percentages of their control capabilities slipping by the moment. His eyes lit up as a geo-location popped up on his screen. "I have it ma'am; it's within a five-mile radius of downtown Chicago."

"Brilliant," Davis said as she reached into her right pants pocket. She pulled out a 5 x 7 inch pristine silver cellphone. Davis carefully pressed her right thumb against the phone's surface. Immediately, a soothing voice oozed from the phone.

"Hello, director, how may I assist you today?"

"Patch me through to Captain Conrad," Davis said with a hint of trepidation.

Almost instantaneously, Conrad's face appeared onscreen.

"Director Davis what's going on?" Conrad asked curtly.

"Sorry to disturb you at this time of night, ma'am," Davis said as she saw the time reading 1: 25 AM.

"It's alright Kellita, I was up anyway," she said as she looked over the holographic designs of the Mirador.

"The SDS has been compromised. It seems to be an outside non-state actor. We're waiting for final analysis to confirm, but we are confident it's an independent hacker."

"OK, how much have we been compromised?"

"We've tried to put up more firewalls but whoever they are, they've been able to work around it. Almost like a living computer virus."

"Offensive capabilities still intact?"

Davis looked up in frustration at the onscreen image of the SDS and its various points of compromise. "We're hanging on by a thread. We've shut down the SBL's solar array charging unit, thank God. Drone capabilities are down to fifteen percent."

"Are the tactical drones on-line?" Conrad asked.

"About five percent---primarily non-lethal ordinance. The other ten percent are surveillance drones."

"Any location data on the source of the breach?"

"Yes Ma'am. We've narrowed it down to a five-mile radius of downtown Chicago."

"Whoever pulled this off would need a massive amplifying signal to get into our system," Conrad said knowingly. In the year since the team reworked the satellite system, she made sure to know the ins and outs of the SDS. "Have you cross-checked any of the local TV and Cable stations to see if any of them are emitting a high frequency radio bandwidth?"

Davis looked in Austin's direction, who happened to be listening in on the conversation as well. He slid his rolling ergonomic chair over to another screen to his left and typed a few digits on screen.

"Director Davis, I got it," Austin shouted. "There's a massive spike in radio frequency output at the WGN television station."

"Did you catch that, Captain?" Davis said over the phone.

"Yes, he was loud enough, I could hear halfway across DC," Conrad replied dryly.

Davis smiled at the remark.

"Ok, dispatch Chicago PD and local FBI to the location," Conrad said. "And send the tactical drones to the location."

Davis paused for a second. "Are you sure Captain? Don't you think sending out local PD and the feds is enough?"

"No. Whoever hacked our system has shown they're pretty formidable. I don't want to take any chances on compromising the safety of the police and federal officers dispatched to investigate. You said the drones had non-lethal ordnance, right?"

"Yes, sonic canon package."

"Then let's send them out," Conrad said abruptly.

"What about civilians?"

"You know better than anyone those drones are tailored to be pinpoint accurate---even with just radar guidance. Collateral damage will be zero."

Davis looked down away from the cellphone screen. She then looked back at it and began, "Offensive strikes require—" and before Davis could complete the sentence, Conrad interjected.

"I've already entered in the remote authorization code. Initiate the strike." Conrad's image blinked off the phone's screen.

Davis's hands shook as she put the phone away. She nodded in Austin's direction, "Send out a message to Chicago PD and local FBI on level one emergency channels to respond to the breach. Patch me through to the drone deployment matrix."

"Yes, Director," Austin said compliantly. He slid his chair over to an adjacent computer screen, which was much different from his other two screens. This screen was horizontally elongated with a yellowish shimmer from the overhead fluorescent light reflection. Austin tapped the screen and the words: *Director Tactical Protocols* appeared.

Davis slowly walked up the short spiral stairs into the Director's office. It was designed with two-way glass, which allowed her to observe everything that was going on in the hub. At the far end of the office was a half-mooned shaped control panel with keyboard lettering. Above it was a high-definition LCD screen that measured about five feet across and three feet in height.

She placed her right hand on a biometric scanner embedded in the panel. Immediately, the screen came to life and the same words that were on Austin's screen appeared on the large LCD as well. Mechanical whirring sounds emanated from the floor panels as they retracted back. Slowly, a reclining metallic chair rose from the floor. The chair was adorned with cushioned arm rests with tactile control sticks; along with a headpiece that looked similar to a soldier's helmet that was affixed to the chair's headrest. Davis sat in the chair and immediately she was enveloped by multiple harness belts. She put on the helmet and took hold of the joysticks. The large LCD screen's text immediately converted to a highly detailed radar image of the targets. From what Davis could gather, there were three humanoid shapes atop the building.

Davis carefully moved the joysticks forward and over 20,000 miles up in space, the hatch of the SDS's number three drone housing module opened. Immediately, a swarm of over one- hundred micro-drones, like the Perdix drone design, were deployed. The drones propelled through geostationary space using mini assist-controlled boosters. They moved like a collective of ravenous locusts through the cold expanse of space to eliminate their targets.

* * *

WGN TV Headquarters Rooftop
2501 West Bradley Place

"What the hell?" Itrish blurted out.

"What happened?" Anderson asked emphatically.

Itrish backed away from the satellite dish. "They shut down power to their laser. I couldn't touch it."

"But you shut down their other stuff?"

"You know it," Itrish said as she dusted her hands. "That thing won't be operational for a while."

"I know one thing for sure," Gallagher said. "You just violated about a thousand federal statutes."

Itrish shrugged her shoulders. "It was worth it."

"We'll see," Anderson said with a slight hint of unease. "Let's get out of here."

Itrish and Gallagher gathered close to Anderson. He closed his eyes and they lifted off the ground. They hovered over the expanse of the rooftop and gently landed three floors down, behind the television station in its fenced-in parking lot.

As soon as they landed, they heard a buzzing sound.

"Do you guys hear that?"

"What?" Itrish asked.

"Look," Anderson said as he pointed up to what appeared to be a group of bats descending on them. It was too late before they could make out that it was not a horde of shrieking bats but a swarm of drones. They screamed in anguish as the impact of the directed sonic pulse devastated their ear drums. The drones swept above them and out of their line of vision.

"Oh my God, what was that?" Gallagher shouted as his ears still rung.

"I don't know," Itrish interjected. "But I've never seen anything like that come from a bunch of drones."

The micro-drones hovered high above the trio as they readied for another pass. The drones' sonic cannons started to charge up and their propellers started to spin relentlessly as they headed toward the teenagers caught dead in their sights.

CHAPTER SIXTEEN

UNCOVERED

WGN TV Parking Lot
2501 West Bradley Place
Chicago, Illinois

Itrish's eyes were transfixed. The incoming drones doubled back to make a second pass. One could mistake her intent stare as one of fear, but in fact she was reading the schematics of the drones as they barreled toward the three of them. Her head filled with numerous data points and program prompts. Just before the unending swarm of micro-drones discharged their weapons, their propeller blades slowed down to a hovering stand still.

"What did you do, I.T.?" Gallagher asked, looking confused.

"Simple. I told them to stop."

"Nice work, baby," Anderson said assuredly.

* * *

Vigil Satellite Control Center
Fort Meade, Maryland

"What the hell?! They locked me out!" Davis said as she observed the end result of Itrish's actions.

Davis removed the helmet and leaped out of the control chair. She hurriedly made her way out of her office and down to the main control hub. Austin turned in Davis's direction.

"I see things didn't go so well with the drones."

"The hell they didn't," Davis retorted. She walked up behind Austin's chair and leaned over his shoulder. "Did our mystery hacker take out the surveillance cams in the vicinity?"

"I don't think so," Austin said as he typed away on his keyboard. "Let me check something." He clicked on a video file. A grainy image of the exterior of the WGN building popped up.

"Switch camera views."

Austin complied and clicked on another key. The image changed from the exterior to the back-parking lot's camera---three fuzzy images appeared near the poorly lit parking lot.

"Enhance that image," Davis said as she pointed at the screen.

Immediately, Austin slid his finger across his mouse's rollerball. With each swipe of his finger the image enhanced to make out three young people. Davis drew her head closer to the screen. "Damn, they're kids."

"Let me run a quick facial recognition on them," Austin said. He clicked on *Control R* on his keyboard and immediately small boxes encapsulated the faces of the trio onscreen. Next to each box was a cycling image of multiple people, running almost like a slot machine. The images eventually matched the ones on screen. Davis's eyes widened.

"Wow, they're just kids." Davis said as she backed away from behind Austin's chair. "Go ahead, package that info into send it to the Vigil Prime Server. We'll let Captain Conrad and the team decide what they want to do."

* * *

October 9th
Bridgette Huntley's Office
AlphA.I. Headquarters
Palo Alto, California

The bright California sun shined through Huntley's floor to ceiling office windows. She enjoyed the panoramic sunsets of the Valley when she worked late nights. Huntley read over her tablet computer as she reclined in her comfortable, brown, leather chair. Her relaxed moment was cut short by an intra-office alert on her tablet. She tapped on the screen. A holographic image of her assistant, Morris Peterson, illuminated from the tablet's holographic projector.

"Tell me what's going on, Morris," Huntley asked tersely.

"We had a breach in one of our new network nodes. Specifically, the Chicago region."

"Chicago?" Huntley leaned forward, "Who was it?"

Peterson's holographic image receded to video footage atop the WGN tower. The image was grainy with a top-down angle.

"Hold it. Why is the quality so poor? This thing looks like found footage from World War Two. I thought we're supposed to be the leader in high-definition video."

"I apologize, Ms. Huntley," Morris's holographic image popped up again. "Whoever breached the node interfered with the video system, too. But we were able to salvage a good portion of it."

The original video image superseded Morris's image as it enlarged. As the video enhanced, Huntley could make out the tops of three heads, but not their faces. "Can you rotate the angle on it?" she asked.

"Sure."

The video angle shifted around and enlarged to reveal the faces of Gallagher, Itrish and Anderson. The corners of Huntley's mouth curled up in glee.

"We identified them as three Variants native to our database: Malik

Anderson, John Gallagher, and Itrish Jones," Peterson said. "Ms. Huntley, we determined it wasn't just our system that was breached but also a federal satellite system---specifically, the Vigil Satellite Defense System."

"Really?" Huntley said, eyebrows raised. "Even our best technicians couldn't touch their security firewalls. I'm glad to see our sponsorship of the school is going to good training."

"Exactly. Based on the data we have so far, we believe it was the technopath, Jones, who was the main culprit in the breach," Peterson said. "She even staved off what appeared to be a flock of weaponized drones."

"Drones?! How and from where?"

"We believe the drones were deployed in response to the Vigil SDS breach. Likely a counter-measure."

Images of the drone attack flooded the holographic image. Huntley stroked the angle of her jaw with her right forefinger. "This is more impressive than what I saw at the VERGE school."

Huntley abruptly cut off Morris's transmission. She reached into her designer, leather, crocodile skinned Brahmin purse to pull out her cell phone. As she drew it closer to her, the device instinctively scanned her face and unlocked. She delivered a simple order over the phone.

"Adept extraction is a go."

CHAPTER SEVENTEEN

YOUTH MOVEMENT

October 10th
Vigil Headquarters
Sublevel Two
Pentagon
Arlington, Virginia

"Can you run us through what happened, Alicia?" Pendleton asked, sitting next to her. Blankenchip and Bledsoe filled out the rest of the table. Across from them were large screens projecting the images of: Morrison, Fighting Bull, and Arrowhawk.

She shifted forward in her chair and tapped the table's embedded control panel. A holographic image of the SDS, along with pictures of Itrish alongside her profile details popped up.

"Yesterday around 1: 30 AM eastern, we had a breach of the SDS. We had some of the best minds redesign our firewalls. This young lady, Itrish Jones, tore through them like a wet paper towel."

Itrish's image enlarged as Conrad continued to speak. "I was alerted to the breach by Director Davis. At the time we were aware of the breach, our primary visual capabilities were knocked out. We were basically blind with exception of radar. Jones single-handedly disabled eighty-five percent of our offensive capabilities."

"Was she able to breach the SBL protocols?" Blankenchip asked.

"No," Conrad said as she leaned back in her chair. "Thankfully, we were able to shut off its power."

"What about countermeasures?" Bledsoe asked.

"That gets me to the next point. I authorized non-lethal drone countermeasures."

"Are you crazy?!" Blankenchip blurted out. "With a whole bunch of civilians around?"

Conrad quickly swiveled her head in Blankenchip's direction. "Aaron, I knew the risks. That's why I deployed the non-lethal complement of drones—if you bothered to listen."

"Captain, Aaron has point," Bledsoe responded gruffly. "I don't think it was smart to deploy those drones on a bunch of kids?"

Conrad stood up from her chair and glanced in both Blankenchip and Bledsoe's direction. "This girl breached our satellite defense system. Can you imagine what would've happened if she took control of the SBL?

Pendleton gently patted the back of Conrad's left arm. "I think what Alicia is saying has merit. There was no way to know if it was a foreign actor or something worse trying to take over the SDS. We all know from the last year and a half the risk sabotaging the SDS." He turned to look directly in Bledsoe and Blankenchip's direction. "Plus, those kids aren't just run of the mill teens. They're Variants."

"With all due respect, sir, that's not fair," Bledsoe retorted. "You don't know how it is when you first manifest. You don't have all your abilities under control in the beginning. They may have just lost control…"

"To be clear," Conrad interjected, "Jones was the one who breached our system. Not the other two. With respect to their abilities, these kids are at a VERGE academy, whose sole focus is to help Variants control their abilities."

"I know, Captain!" Bledsoe shot back. "My son attends the VERGE Academy in San Diego, so I know their purpose. But they're just kids, and we need to cut them some slack."

"We've already reached out to the administration at the Chicago VERGE Academy about the incident," Pendleton interrupted. "I've arranged a meeting between us and their principal today at one this afternoon, their time."

"So, I am assuming we're not going in guns blazing," Arrowhawk said over the screen.

"No, this is more of a soft outreach," Pendleton answered. "As a matter of fact, no combat uniforms. I don't want to spook them."

"Smart move," Arrowhawk said. "I doubt DOJ would want to press charges against minors on domestic terrorism charges."

"Good point, John. By the way, how are things going in Japan?" Pendleton asked.

Arrowhawk leaned forward in his ergonomic chair, bringing his image closer to the camera. "We've been briefed by my PSIA liaison about the Harada situation. They've already interrogated Harada's inside man, Takayasu. Unfortunately, we weren't able to sit in on it. From the report it seemed that Takayasu arranged through contacts within Saisentan to enhance Harada's Gijo Hei. Their chief technologist was originally involved in the PERSD program and was the one running the covert enhancement operation that gave those Gijo Hei their cybernetics."

"So, I'm assuming they've cleaned house of that chief technologist?"

"Exactly," Fighting Bull chimed in. "They have another guy, Sora Fujihara, who's taken over. We have a meeting with him in a few days to discuss exactly how much of Saisentan's tech was used by Harada."

"Sounds good," Pendleton said before looking in Conrad's direction. "Alicia, is there anything else?"

Conrad shifted her gaze from Arrowhawk and Fighting Bull's images to turn to Morrison's onscreen. "Terrell how is the security detail going on in Lemalia?"

Morrison shook his head. "Not good. The UPF is launching attacks daily."

"How is President Legaud doing?"

"As best he can. Loyalists to the PNDP and remnants of the UPF are still launching terrorist attacks on the capital, even as they're prepping for new election. We're looking into who's backing them."

Conrad tapped on the table's embedded touchscreen panel. Immediately, a holographic image with numbers and military icons that detailed the UPF's recent attacks. "Yeah, based on these reports there have been about twenty attempts on his life just within this past month alone."

Pendleton motioned to one of the uniformed support officers in the room. They walked over and handed him a manila folder. He lifted it up. Written on the cover in stenciled block text were the words, *ICC Confidential.*

"Not to mention there's a war crimes investigation in the International Criminal Court against him."

"Which is totally baseless," Morrison interjected. "The mere fact the case has gotten this far is ridiculous."

"Well, the ICC thinks they have legitimate grounds." Pendleton said as he clasped his hands together.

"It wouldn't be the first time the ICC had beef with America," Fighting Bull pointed out. "Past administrations' sanctions against ICC judges; I'm sure haven't endeared us to them."

Morrison waved his hand. "We all know the charges against Legaud aren't true. To be honest, it should be us on trial."

"You really think so. Terrell?" Conrad snapped back.

"Alicia, I know. President Legaud was stuck in a hard place. He had no other choice but to come to us. Look, all I'm saying is this man wants to protect his people and he's being persecuted for it."

"But he's far from a saint, Terrell," Pendleton said. "He took over the presidency by default."

"Not to mention he dissolved parliament when he first took office," Arrowhawk chimed in.

"I get it, Mark," Morrison retorted. "But in the end, we have to look at the big picture. He's trying to stabilize his country after a huge civil war. And he's also willing to give up power, just for the stability of his country."

Pendleton tilted his head slightly to the side as he nodded. "True, Terrell, but we still have to deal with the nuances of what's happened. We can't gloss over what he's done and how he got to power, no matter how benevolent he seems."

"I'm not ignoring that, Mark. That's why I'm here, to make sure he does things the right way."

"Fair enough," Conrad said. "We'll see you back stateside in a few weeks."

"Copy that, Alicia," Morrison replied.

Conrad motioned in Pendleton's direction.

"We'll be waiting to hear about what you two find in Japan," Pendleton said looking at Arrowhawk and Fighting Bull onscreen. He looked down to the rest of the table. "Alicia, the rest of you are heading over to the VERGE Academy. Its time these kids realized who they're messing with."

CHAPTER EIGHTEEN

NOW YOU'RE MINE

Three Hours Later
Rooftop Helipad
VERGE Academy
Chicago, Illinois

The Avian landed atop the helipad in silence. The newly installed sound dampeners made the team's entrance a lot less jarring than previous times. As the main hatch opened, the walk-ladder from the ship's undercarriage extended onto the brick-red colored helipad. Principal Gowan and Assistant Principal Raymond waited patiently for the team to deplane.

"Good morning, Principal Gowan," Conrad said. She extended her right hand as she removed her Garrison cap.

"Good morning, Captain Conrad," Gowan reciprocated as she grasped Conrad's hand. Conrad raised her eyebrows at the sight of the bracelet on Gowan's right wrist.

"That's the coolest piece of wearable tech I have ever seen. What is that?"

Gowan looked down at the bracelet. "Oh, this thing's just a prototype. It's called Superhuman Abilities Nullifier, or SHAN for short."

"Interesting," Conrad said. "I thought they were completely theoretical at this point."

Gowan gave a nervous smile. "No, it's gone past theory. I'm just testing it."

"Don't want to accidentally peek into somebody's mind I'd guess, right? Never know what you might see," Conrad said with a knowing smile.

"I see you've done your research, captain," Gowan replied firmly.

"Always."

Gowan felt the incessant poking of Raymond's right forefinger into the small of her back. Raymond tried to subtly—but failed miserably—to get Gowan to introduce her to Vigil's team leader. Gowan relented and in turn motioned to Raymond. "This is my assistant principal, Mary Ellen Raymond."

"It is such an honor to meet you captain. I'm a huge fan of yours," Raymond said with her ebullient smile. Her dimples became more pronounced as she giddily shook Conrad's hand.

Conrad in turn extended her right hand to introduce the rest of her team members. After they exchanged pleasantries, Gowan led the team down a long, red-colored walkway lined with tracking lights to the elevator. The group of them fit within the cavernous elevator compartment. The interior of the elevator was lined with bright metallic panels with an alternating wood-framed finish.

The elevator arrived at the ground floor and opened to expose the school's administrative hub. It was an open office space with dozens of staff members milling around. The team drew stares as Gowan escorted them to her office. Upon entering Gowan's office, there was a long, rectangular, black leather chair that comfortably accommodated Bledsoe and Blankenchip. Conrad sat in a rolling leather armchair, right next to the couch. Gowan made her way to her desk. Raymond opted to leaned against the front of Gowan's desk. The VERGE Academy principal tapped a few strokes on her keyboard and turned to look in the direction of the Vigil team.

"When I received a call from the Defense Secretary about you coming, I have to admit I was shocked but also excited. But when I later found out why, I began to worry."

Conrad leaned forward and looked directly at Gowan. "There is nothing to worry about as long as you can help us. Early yesterday morning, our satellite defense system was hacked by one of your students." Conrad pulled out her cell phone from her jacket's right breast pocket and tapped on the screen. A holographic image of Itrish Jones accompanied by Gallagher and Anderson popped up. "We believe it was these three students."

Gowan shook her head at the images. "I see, I can say that I am a little bit disappointed to hear this because they are some of my best students." She leaned back in her functional leather office chair. "Not that I don't trust you captain, but do you have any proof to substantiate these claims?"

The static holographic images immediately transitioned to a grainy video of the students escaping the rooftop of the WGN TV station.

"We pulled this from the closed-circuit security camera from one of the television stations downtown. We believe that Jones, she's the technopath, right?" Conrad said, looking to Gowan.

"Yes."

"She used the TV station's satellite set up to jam our signal and override our defense system's protocols." Conrad closed the image and put the cellphone back into her jacket pocket. "Because of this serious breach, we wanted to talk to them."

"Do you have some sort of warrant?" Gowan asked.

"No," Conrad said succinctly. "As you know, the Superhuman Terrorist Act doesn't require a warrant in order to detain a suspected superhuman terrorist."

Gowan rose swiftly from her chair. "Are you calling my students terrorists?!"

Bledsoe calmly intervened. "Look, Principal Gowan, we are not calling your kids terrorists. We just want to know what your kids may have been doing out late on a school night."

Raymond looked back at Gowan with a concerned look. Gowan flashed one back. "We have backup security footage of the students leaving campus."

Blankenchip's ears perked up. "Backup? What happened to the primary video?"

Gowan tapped her desktop keyboard again and rotated her computer screen in full view of the team. "The primary video was scrambled."

"Any idea who it was?"

"We believe it was Itrish that scrambled it," Gowan said.

"Hot damn!" Blankenchip blurted out. "The girl is good. What can't she do with tech?"

"Was that a rhetorical statement, Lieutenant Blankenchip?" Gowan asked sternly.

Blankenchip smiled, leaned back in the couch, and shrugged. "However, you want to take it."

Raymond reached over Gowan's desk and typed in a few keystrokes and immediately the screen changed to illuminate the letters of the school in bright red on the screen. "I think I can explain that, but I'll need to go a little in depth with who we are and what this school is about."

She tapped the keyboard once more. "The Variant Encompassed Research and Group Education academies focus on teaching Variants how to use their powers and encourage them to integrate into the larger society. The school comprises grades eight through twelve."

"Why isn't it K through 12?" Blankenchip interrupted.

"Because most Variants manifest during puberty," Raymond responded. "We have a very structured curriculum that strengthens both the minds and bodies of our students. Since about the mid-nineteen sixties we've seen the emergence of superhumans, specifically Variants---individuals born with special abilities. The first documented Variant was Gregor Kirilenko in Saint Petersburg, Russia. The first documented American Variant was Duane Newman, who was born in Odessa, Texas in 1953." Raymond paused for a moment. "These early Variants had nowhere to learn how to control their abilities, how to relate to their non-powered peers, or what to do with themselves. Previously, our government only had a patchwork system to train and integrate Variants into mainstream society. We want to assure they won't be a harm to themselves or others. That's where we come in as the mainstay of Variant education and training."

"We've also had corporate sponsors to supplement the federal monies we get to run the schools," Gowan added.

"Nice picture show," Blankenchip responded. "You still haven't answered my question. How much tech can this girl control?

Annoyed, Raymond tried to maintain a professional tone. "To answer your question, Lieutenant Blankenchip, Itrish is a multi-level technopath, on her way to becoming an omni-level technopath."

Bledsoe raised her hand. "Omni-levels are theoretical. There's no human body that could achieve that type of technological mastery."

"Oh, you would be surprised," Raymond said assuredly. "Itrish is beyond what we've seen in other technopaths."

"Wow, this is something else," Blankenchip said as he leaned forward in his chair. "At least we know where our federal dollars are going to."

Raymond continued, almost dismissive of Blankenchip's comment. "The VERGE Academy has been a true benefit to the public. Multiple Variants have been recruited in all areas of industry, civil and military service—"

"As a matter of fact," Gowan said as she interrupted Raymond midsentence, "Itrish is actually being evaluated for recruitment by most of the major tech companies."

"Do you happen to have a list of the companies looking at her?" Conrad asked.

"Yes," Gowan said. She took a manila folder with the printed text, *Recruitment Class Evaluations*, from her top right desk drawer. She pulled out a sheet of paper from it and handed it to Conrad. She quickly scanned it and peered up in Gowan's direction.

"We need to see her."

Gowan tapped her phone's intercom button. After a quick beep, the voice of Gowan's assistant came on the line. "Yes, Principal Gowan?"

"Please send an administrative escort to pick up Itrish Jones to my office."

There was a brief pause before her assistant responded. "May I ask why?"

"Because she has some very special guests here."

* * *

Intro to Political Science Class
Second Floor

"So, Dominic, you believe the effects of redlining had no undue burden on African American communities in Chicago?" Calvin Porter asked his student.

Dominic Tristan loosened his uniform collar before answering. "Yes, Mr. Porter, I believe so. I think even though this country has had a terrible history of segregation, with modern civil rights we, uhm for the most part, have overcome most of the barriers that keep different ethnic groups from living together." Tristan pulled up pictures of famous African Americans on his holotab. "Now, we see there have been many prominent African Americans who live in extremely affluent areas even in Chicago, amongst white people." His voice cracked slightly. "I'm not saying discrimination doesn't exist, but I don't think redlining played a part in the living conditions of many African Americans."

"So, do you think African Americans intentionally moved to low income, high crime areas?" Mr. Porter asked his student.

"No! That's not what I am saying at all," Tristan protested emphatically. "I'm saying I believe there is no evidence that redlining played a role in their current condition. I believe other things like low paying jobs and some racial prejudice played a part."

Itrish's hand shot up.

"Go ahead, Itrish," Porter said pointing in her direction.

"I disagree 100%." She also pulled out her school-issued holotab and brought up an image of the Federal Housing Administration neighborhood maps from the early 1930's. "You can see on this map from the 1934 FHA map the red outlines were the areas where primarily African Americans lived. It was these same areas that the FHA explicitly denied loans to. It's no coincidence that these where African American neighborhoods. And the whole purpose of the FHA was to increase home ownership among U.S. citizens---well, certain citizens."

"But why is that relevant now?" Porter questioned. "Like Dominic pointed out, there are plenty of African Americans living in affluent neighborhoods here in Chicago. They seemed to be doing all right."

"Because they are the exception and not the rule, Mr. Porter," Itrish said as she reached into the holographic image and manipulated it to shift into a pie-chart displaying homeownership rates broken down by ethnic group. "Homeownership is the main way people build wealth in America; when you block peoples' ability to own homes by denying them loans, you keep them from building wealth. That leads to a cycle where those who don't have access to capital aren't able to climb the economic ladder." Itrish turned to Dominic Tristan. "Then you create a permanent underclass, and that's a problem for everyone."

Porter smiled and nodded, clearly encouraged by the spirited discussion. Just then, a knock was heard at the classroom door.

"Oh, hello can I help you?" Porter asked.

"Hi, I'm David Nix, the administrative escort," the main replied. He looked to be in his mid-twenties, with a buzzcut.

"I've never seen you before. Are you a new hire?"

"Yeah, they just brought me on a few weeks ago."

"Ok, who are you looking for?"

"I am here to escort Ms. Itrish Jones to Principal Gowan's office."

The students in the class let out an ominous "OOOOOO." She waved them off as she got up from her chair.

"Really?! You guys need to stop," Itrish said as she gathered her things. She slid her cellphone into the side compartment of her bookbag.

"Right this way, Ms. Jones," the escort said as he ushered her out of the classroom. He had a muscular build and wore a well-fitted vest and trousers. Itrish noticed an earpiece in his left ear—different from the ones most escorts used.

"So, how long have you been working with Principal Gowan?" Itrish said as she pulled down the straps of her bookbag—tightening them around her shoulders.

"For a few weeks now," he answered with a stilted half-smile.

"Oh, ok." She tapped the side compartment of her bookbag. The brief spark of light that arose from her hand upon contact with the compartment went unnoticed by the man.

The pair walked down the main hall to the stairwell that led to the ground floor. The halls had students milling about, trying to hustle to the next class. As they ascended the stairs, the escort stayed about one foot behind her. On the ground floor, Itrish noticed the population of students had thinned out. The escort tapped her on her shoulder and directed her to the adjacent corridor instead of the one that lead to Principal Gowan's office.

"Hey, I think Principal Gowan's office…"

Before Itrish could complete her sentence, the escort grabbed her by the shoulders and slammed her against a locker. He placed his hand over her mouth with his left hand. With his other hand he pulled up his vest and retrieved the holstered SFP9 Heckler & Koch pistol from his waistband. The man placed the barrel against Itrish's cheek.

"Don't even think about screaming," the man said. He tapped his earpiece. "The Adept has been contained."

"Good. Get to the rendezvous point. Extraction protocols are in place," a non-descript muffled voice said over the line.

"Copy that," Itrish's captor said. He quickly holstered his weapon and turned her around to bind her wrists with handcuffs he pulled from inside his vest. Before he could corral her, she threw a right hook that connected with his left cheek. The man shook off the blow. He instead twisted her right arm and swiveled her around pinning her against the wall. The man abruptly latched the bare, metal handcuffs around her wrists. He lifted her up by her right arm and pushed her forward down the long hallway. Roughly twenty feet away, Itrish could see the service elevator down the hall.

Just feet away from the service elevator; Itrish's captor was suddenly slammed against the front of the service elevator's large metallic door. The captor landed gracelessly on to his right flank region. He shook his head as he tried to recover from the blow. The captor looked around to see who hit him as he readied his weapon but saw nothing. He could see Itrish bound and screaming as she ran toward the elevator. The captor reached into his right vest pocket and retrieved six small metal balls. He hurled them in Itrish's direction. She lost her balance and tumbled to the ground as she slipped on the metal spheres.

Itrish's captor trotted toward her. As he advanced, he was thrust to the ground by an unseen force. The impact of his fall caused his weapon to jut out of his hand.

"Stay down this time," a voice said behind the captor. He looked up to see Malik Anderson's face looking down on him. The captor struggled to reach for his weapon just inches away from his right hand, but Anderson telekinetically moved it out of reach and it into his own hands. Anderson waved his right index finger in the captor's face.

"No, no, no. I can't have you doing that, bruh." Anderson then telekinetically lifted the captor and slammed him forcefully headfirst into the row of lockers just to his right. The blunt head trauma left the captor unconscious. Anderson calmly walked over to Itrish. She felt a slight tug at the center of her handcuffs. After three seconds the shackles were torn from her wrists.

"I'm sorry I couldn't get to you sooner, "Anderson said as he lifted her up off the ground. "I'm glad you sent that 9-1-1 message to my phone."

Itrish hugged him. "Thank you!" Her embrace was so tight it almost squeezed the air out of Anderson.

Anderson smiled. "Come on let's—" his comment was cut short as he convulsed and was brought down to the ground. Itrish was mortified by the sight. As Anderson's body slumped to the ground, she saw another man dressed in a short-sleeved polo shirt, cargo pants and tactical boots wielding the taser that downed her boyfriend. She turned to the right and saw the red fire alarm lever. Without hesitation she lunged for it. As the sonorous alarm permeated the school hallways, the man in the polo shirt pulled another weapon from his right cargo pant pocket. He fired on Itrish. As the sharp edge of the projectile pierced the skin of her neck, she reached for it, but it was too late. Her vision blurred, and she barely heard the man radio the rest of his team.

* * *

Principal Gowan's Office

The fire alarm's thunderous sound sent a rush down Gowan's spine. She quickly pulled up the school's closed-circuit video feeds on her desktop computer.

"What is it?" Conrad asked as she got up from her chair.

Gowan lifted her left forefinger to indicate to Conrad to give her a second. The principal's eyes scanned the multiple boxed images onscreen. She noticed her students left in an orderly fashion, but in the video feed from the ground floor service corridor displayed a quick flash of a man in the polo shirt coat leaving through one of the exits. "Who is that?" Gowan whispered under her breath. Mary Ellen Raymond heard her colleague's whisper and came around to see what was on Gowan's screen.

"I've never seen him before," Gowan told Raymond as she pointed to the screen. She tapped her keyboard to enhance the man's face, but his image was blurred.

"Dammit," Gowan muttered in frustration.

"I need to know what's going on," Conrad said commandingly.

Gowan looked in Raymond's direction. Raymond in turn tapped a key on Gowan's keyboard and lifted her holotab to project Gowan's screen holographically in full display of the rest of the team.

"Is he one of your administrators?" Conrad asked.

"No, he's not one of ours." Gowan said ominously. "I just tried to run facial recognition on him, but I couldn't get a match.

"You guys have facial recog abilities?" Blankenchip said. "A high school?"

"You'd be surprised, Mr. Blankenchip," Gowan responded. "Some of our former students have come up missing in the past. We want to make sure this doesn't happen under our watch."

"Like we said earlier, some of top tech companies in the world sponsor our school," Raymond interjected. "They provide us with a variety of technological tools—facial recognition being one of them."

"Considering we educate Variants; you can imagine there are people out there who seek to harm them. We've experienced some of our former students going missing so one can never be too cautious." She pressed the side clasp of her SHAN bracelet—the device immediately popped off her wrist. Gowan rubbed her right wrist from where the bracelet once adorned. She looked in Raymond's direction. "I'm going to run a quick psi-scan."

The VERGE Academy principal gripped her temples. She was a level two telepath---able to read minds but unable to control them. The arduous task of reaching into the minds of the almost six-hundred students, staff and administrators was burdensome. Blood trickled from Gowan's nose as she continued her psionic search for the man in the image. Raymond tried to hand her a tissue, but Gowan waved it away.

Conrad looked in Raymond's direction. "Hand me your holotab."

Raymond complied. Conrad touched the holotab screen to her wristwatch. The originally displayed holographic image disappeared, and instead was replaced by a scrolling array of faces, moving at an imperceptible speed. Raymond looked on in amazement.

"What did you do?"

"I've interfaced your holotab with our server. I'm seeing if I can get a hit on this guy from our database." The images continued to scroll holographically as Gowan eventually broke her silence.

"Itrish."

"What about her?" Bledsoe asked.

"She's been taken," Gowan said as she wiped the blood from her nose. "I can't tell by whom exactly but I'm not picking up her psionic signature."

"Why can't you track her? Shouldn't you be able to still track her down beyond the school?" Blankenchip asked.

She shook her head. "I can't. Whoever took her, set up something that's blocking my abilities. I can reach out to those students and staff in the area, but something is holding me back from expanding my search."

Conrad looked in Blankenchip's direction. "I need you down there to assist with evacuation."

"What about Mr. Mystery date?" Blankenchip growled back.

The scrolling facial images eventually settled on that of a young thirty-something male with closed cropped hair. A holographic schematic of his vital statistic popped up.

"Garrison Cane," Conrad said as he read through his information. "Age thirty-two, former Navy Seal, honorable discharge, went into private military contracting about five years ago." Conrad looked in Blankenchip's direction. "That's our mark."

Blankenchip begrudgingly complied. He reached with his right hand to tap the dorsal side of his metallic left wristband. Immediately metallic tendrils flowed out of the wristband and up his arm, shoulder, and eventually encased him in his exoskeletal armor. He rushed out of Principal Gowan's ground floor office to help the school security guards usher out the students from the school. Blankenchip sprinted up the stairs to the second floor to clear out the classrooms. He continued down the ground floor corridor.

Thermally scanning the row of lockers closest to the service elevator, Blankenchip was able to make out a humanoid form within locker U8. He pulled on the handle, but it was locked. Blankenchip decided not to use his weapon for fear of injuring whoever was behind the door. He instead opted to use his armor's augmented strength to rip off the locker door. As soon as it was off its hinges, Anderson's unconscious body slumped down. Before Anderson fell fully to the ground, Blankenchip caught him.

Blankenchip ran a quick vitals scan on Anderson to confirm he was in fact alive. Anderson's beating heart and faint but present pulse assured Blankenchip he was still alive. Blankenchip lightly tapped the side of Anderson's cheek but was unable to revive him. Growing impatient, he violently shook Anderson. The shock of being forcefully revived instantly caused Anderson to react reflexively. He pushed Blankenchip back with a telekinetic thrust. The telekinetic blast threw Blankenchip back against the wall, temporarily dazing him. Blankenchip then quickly recovered and pointed his SPLATT gun at Anderson.

"Who are you?" Anderson demanded.

"Freaking Santa Clause. Does Vigil ring a bell?"

Anderson began to calm down after Blankenchip intoned Vigil. "You-you're the armored guy, aren't you?"

"Yes. Blankenchip," he said as he lowered his weapon. "You're that Malik kid, aren't you?" His helmet retracted back to reveal his face as he extended his hand to Anderson.

"Yeah," he said as he shook Blankenchip's hand.

"What happened to you? Who stuffed you in that locker?"

Anderson rubbed his low back. "I don't know. They attacked me from behind, I didn't get a good look at the one who tazed me."

"They?" Blankenchip asked. "How many of them were there?"

"I saw the one that was trying to take Itrish but the second one, like I said, I didn't get a look at them."

Blankenchip radioed Conrad. "Alicia be advised, we got multiple assailants. Look sharp."

"Copy that," Conrad said over the radio link. She and Bledsoe were still in Gowan's office trying to zero in on the multiple assailants through surveillance footage. Detailed holographic images of the school and the surrounding ten-mile radius were displayed.

"Is that live surveillance footage of the school?" Raymond asked.

"Yes," Conrad said as she carefully scrutinized the images.

"But how?"

"She's using our satellite convergence protocols to key in on the school and the surrounding areas," Bledsoe said. "We're basically creating a visual dragnet to identify Itrish's kidnapers."

"Oh," Raymond replied. "I'm guessing from the many drones you have in service?"

Conrad gave Raymond a slight glare. "Actually, *your* student took out most of our drones, so this is directly from our satellite feed."

Raymond slinked back.

"There they are." Conrad pointed to an image of a non-descript dark grey Chevy Tahoe.

Conrad nodded in Bledsoe's direction and the pair rushed out of Gowan's office and headed toward the school roof. As they made their way to the helipad, Conrad radioed Regent Chiu.

"Regent I need the Avian ready to move in a few seconds. We have a situation."

"I figured as much judging from the sirens and emergency personnel flooding the streets," Chiu responded over his headphones.

"I need you to initiate cordoning protocols, I don't want any bystanders getting hurt in the commotion."

"Already done. Chicago PD has already set up a perimeter around the school and those guys only have a few options to make their exit."

"Good work, we're heading up to you," Conrad said.

Chiu smiled at the remark. "I guess we are going to be in pursuit from above."

"You got it."

Conrad and Bledsoe made their way to the helipad where the Avian awaited them. The ship's vertical thrusters came alive, and a plume of exhaust fumes were left behind as they blasted off toward the escaping captors. Conrad threw off her service uniform jacket into the jump seat and undid her collar tab. She walked over to a silver-colored vertical panel next to the cockpit entrance and pressed her hand against the biometric scanner. The panel suddenly slid open to reveal a rack of vertically aligned weapons. Conrad pulled out a modified Sig SG 553 assault rifle with a carrying strap.

The Avian's clear glass windscreen distilled real-time digital readouts of the truck's speed, occupants and even tire pressure. It didn't take long for the ship to come right above the fleeing SUV as it careened down North Lincoln Avenue. Conrad gave them a warning over the Avian's exterior loudspeaker.

Despite the warning, the vehicle continued to speed along. It soon began to turn on to North Western street, in the direction of Welles Park.

Conrad shook her head and looked in Bledsoe's direction. "They always take the hard way, don't they?"

"Yes, indeed Captain," Bledsoe replied with a smile. The pair walked over to the center of the ship on top of a circular platform with an elevated control panel at the edge. Conrad tapped on a red button on the control panel and immediately rappelling harnesses projected from the roof of the ship. Bledsoe and Conrad strapped themselves in.

"Karen, when we deploy, I need you to generate a localized fog cluster."

"Copy that, Captain."

Conrad then called out to Chiu, "Regent, we're ready."

Chiu looked back at the two women from the pilot's cockpit. "STARS deployment in… three, two… one…" suddenly the platform beneath them opened, dropping the pair down right on top of the fleeing vehicle.

Conrad almost slipped off of the SUV's roof as she landed and her harness detached. Her clunky formal shoes were of no help. She mentally chided herself for not packing her combat gear, even if it went against Pendleton's direction.

The SUV's driver heard the thump of Conrad's landing right above him. As soon as he heard her, he swerved to shake her off the SUV. The swerving motion almost threw Conrad off balance as she tightly gripped the edges of the rear passenger doorframes.

Bledsoe hovered about twenty feet above the SUV; with a buoyant localized wind cluster. Her eyes lit up as she generated a small mist in the vicinity of the vehicle. The fog covered a distance of about one city block. The driver's road vision was essentially gone. He turned to the occupants in the back cabin.

"Cane, they have they're weather witch flooding the area with fog."

"I'm on it," Cane answered back. He grabbed a grayish colored rifle and positioned himself through the back-passenger door window. Using the telescopic site on the weapon, he zeroed in on Bledsoe. He steadied the buttstock of his rifle firmly against his left, inner shoulder and fired a small, metallic disc. The disc landed on her chest, sending a jolt through her body. She quickly lost her concentration. The cloud of fog that blinded the escaping men suddenly dropped. Consequently, Bledsoe lost control of the wind gust that kept her aloft. Seeing this, Chiu immediately released a STARS retrieval harness from the Avian to grab Bledsoe before she crashed into the pavement below.

Meanwhile, Conrad struggled to avoid being thrown off the SUV. The driver continued to run roughshod through the streets. Now that his vision was cleared, he could focus on the road. Cane switched to a conventional pistol and aimed it at the roof. With the aid of her enhanced mental perception, she deftly moved to avoid the weapons fire, coming through the car roof.

Conrad rolled over the edge of the SUV's roof to the driver's side window. The driver, after he saw Conrad's face, immediately reached for his Glock-17 in the middle console. He pointed the weapon in her direction and squeezed the trigger. She moved out of the way of the gunfire as the driver's side window shattered. She could hear the pistol click as it ran out of bullets. Conrad immediately rolled back around and reached over the edge of the roof of the SUV into driver's side window frame to grab the steering wheel. The driver yanked the steering wheel right, to wrest it from her control. As they struggled with the steering wheel, they ran over a baseball mound, sideswiping the fencing around the dugout. Conrad bounced up off the car roof like a rag doll as she struggled to maintain her grip.

The driver's attention was so fixated on Conrad that he failed to see the rod-iron gazebo quickly coming into view. Just seconds before impact, she leapt off the SUV's roof and landed into the thicket of rose bushes next to the structure. The SUV's grill crumbled around the gazebo's main staging frame. The driver's head slammed violently against the deployed airbag as the vehicle made impact.

The two men who held Itrish in the back of the Tahoe were shaken up.

Cane grabbed the unconscious Itrish from the back seat. His associate, who was still recovering from Anderson's telekinetic lashing, stumbled out of the back seat with blood dripping from his right hand. He called out to Cane while he grasped his wounded appendage.

"Where is she?"

"I don't know, Russell," Cane said as he trained his weapon with one hand in the direction of the rose bushes.

"Did you call this in?" Russell asked as he tried to staunch the blood coming from his wound.

Cane continued around the rose bushes and gazebo. "No need." He then lifted up Itrish's body and threw her over his right shoulder. "Let's go."

The pair quickly retreated from their damaged SUV to head for the Queen of Angels Catholic Church. Cane took the lead while Russell maintained the rear. Not getting but a few feet away from their vehicle, Russell suddenly dropped to the ground.

Cane turned to look back to see his partner writhing in pain. Right next to his partner's legs were several shells. He looked up to see Conrad aimed her rifle in their direction. Cane tried his best to fire on Conrad with his left hand, but his shot was off as he struggled to balance Itrish over his right shoulder. He fired three more rounds which forced Conrad to take cover. He gripped Itrish's legs tight against his chest and began sprinting. Before he could get beyond just a few feet, he was hit behind his kneecaps with SPLATT rounds. Cane collapsed to the ground with Itrish's body falling in front of him.

Conrad slowly walked toward Cane with her rifle still trained on him. Cane reached into his right pants pocket to retrieve a metallic disc. Just as Conrad got within ten feet from Cane, he flung the disc in her direction. She shot it out of the air before it could even land on her. Conrad pointed her rifle in Cane's direction firing a round into his left shoulder. He fell flat on his back.

"Who do you work for?" Conrad asked him as she continued to aim her weapon.

Cane laughed. "You don't want to know, Captain."

She shot him in the right shoulder as he fell completely on his back. Conrad walked over his body. The barrel of her rifle was squarely over his forehead.

"At this close distance, even non-lethal rounds would split your skull. Now, again, tell me who you work for."

As she spoke, he reached for an object in his right pants pocket.

"I'll be damned if I talk to you." He quickly slammed the side of his right thigh with a small pen-like device. Almost instantaneously Cane's body turned limp, and he began to gasp for air. Conrad quickly threw her weapon aside and grabbed Cane by the collar. She saw Cane continue to struggle for air. Within a few seconds he stopped breathing. Conrad used her right index and middle fingers to palpate for a carotid pulse, but none is found. She then tapped her right wristwatch to assess Cane's vitals, but there were none. Conrad turned to walk over to Itrish. She checked Itrish's carotid pulse which was intact and bounding.

"I've recovered Jones," Conrad said as she radioed Chiu over her earpiece. "We need to send out a clean-up team."

"Copy that, Captain, I'm en route."

"Have we secured her parents yet?" Conrad asked.

"Chicago PD has already sent a team out there."

CHAPTER NINETEEN

INSURANCE POLICIES

Jones Household
Hyde Park
Chicago, Illinois

John Jones heard three gentle knocks on his door. He walked over to the front door and peeked through the peephole to see a throng of uniformed Chicago police officers. As the father of four children, he was constantly in a state of worry. His heart fell into the pit of his stomach as he opened the door.

"Can I help you, officers?" he asked in his Kingston accent.

The lead officer flashed her ID and badge. A flash of dark blonde hair peaked out from underneath her officer's cap. "Officer Delany. Are you Mr. John Jones?"

"Yes."

"Is your daughter Itrish Jones?" She lifted up Itrish's photo.

Jones nodded his head. "Yes. What's wrong?"

The officer came closer. "Sir, your daughter was the subject of an attempted abduction."

"My God," Jones blurted out. "While at the school?"

"Yes."

"Where is she?"

The police officer raised her hands to calm him. "She is fine, sir; she is in a secure place. We believe whoever was behind this may come after your family as well. "

"Why didn't you call first?!"

"Sir, in situations like this, we feel it best to see the family in person."

"Take me to my daughter," Jones said sternly. "I want to see her."

"I understand your concern, sir. We will get you to her as soon as possible but we need to know if the rest of your family is here with you."

"It's me, my wife, and my youngest."

"Good, we'll need you all to come with us now so we can get you to your daughter."

Jones nodded and called up the stairs to his wife. Clarice Jones walked downstairs.

"John, what's going on?" Mrs. Jones asked with a sense of confusion.

"These officers say Itrish was almost kidnapped at school."

"My God."

"She's fine, though," Mr. Jones said reassuringly. "They're going to take us to see her."

Officer Delany again stepped in. "Yes ma'am, if you can get your son and gather your things, we can take you to her."

Mrs. Jones nodded and headed upstairs to get Anthony as well as her belongings. After a few brief minutes, Mrs. Jones and Anthony came downstairs, and Joseph Jones reached into the coat closet to gather their things. After putting on their coats, they walked out the door to the three cruisers outside their house. They were ushered into the last of the three cruisers. Delany made her way to the lead cruiser and sat down in the passenger seat. She lifted off her cap to remove a blonde wig and began picking the false skin off her face.

Her partner looked over to her. "Those facial prosthetics are a bitch to get off, aren't they?"

"Yeah. "

He started the car as his partner pulled out a cellphone from her right pants pocket. She dialed pound eight on the touch screen and lifted the receiver to her right ear.

"This is Stiles. We've secured the family."

CHAPTER TWENTY

NEW STATE OF AFFAIRS

October 12th
Office of the COO-Cybernetics Division
Saisentan Corporation
Tokyo, Japan

"Welcome to Saisentan, Mr. Arrowhawk," Sora Fujihara, Saisentan's chief operating officer of the cybernetics division, said as he extended his right hand. He stood about 5'8 inch in height. It was a notable contrast to Arrowhawk's 6'4 inch frame.

"Thank you, sir, it's a pleasure," Arrowhawk said as he grasped Fujihara's hand. Fujihara then turned to greet Fighting Bull.

"How have you all enjoyed your time so far?" Fujihara asked as he firmly grasped Fighting Bull's hand. She noted his dark hair peppered with gray.

"Agent Hamato," Fighting Bull turned to point to PSIA agent Yuriko Hamato, "was kind enough to provided us with an extensive tour of the facility."

Hamato extended her hand and gave a slight bow to greet Fujihara. "It is good to see you again Mr. Fujihara." She stood about 5'3 inches in height with shoulder length hair. Fujihara motioned for the three of them to take a seat in the office chairs across from his desk.

"How can I help you?"

"Firstly, we want to thank you, Mr. Fujihara, for seeing us," Hamato started to say. "Your help in rooting out corruption within the company was much appreciated. But we have to ask, what do you know about Codai Harada's use of Saisentan technology?"

Fujihara folded his arms and leaned back in his leather chair. "I believe we have provided you with all of our files regarding our former technologist's misdeeds. He was the main person attached to cybernetically enhancing Ms. Harada's honor guard." He tapped on his desktop computer's keyboard. Immediately, the screen popped up with multiple documents and diagrams. "From the files I sent over to the PSIA, you can see Takayasu had been receiving payments through a shell company that was managed by Credite Suisse. I believe the account was managed by a…" Fujihara stopped to read his computer screen, "a Florian Birchler."

"Yeah, he was the Network's old banker," Arrowhawk said.

"Yes. Apparently, she had been funneling money to him for the past year and a half. The first prototype enhancements were developed around ten months ago."

"Do you know anything about that?" Fighting Bull asked.

Fujihara shook his head. "No, I don't. We don't have any biological enhancement projects run through this division."

Fighting Bull leaned in. "Mr. Fujihara, do you know anyone else involved outside of Takayasu?"

"I'm sure there are many lower-level researchers on the ground who were involved. We've been doing a review and are weeding out the culprits." Fujihara turned in Hamato's direction. "We will gladly share whatever information we find out."

"Thank you, sir," Hamato replied.

"It is the least I could do after all of your hard work in tracking down my Kaori."

Arrowhawk raised his eyebrow. "Kaori? Excuse me, am I missing something?"

Hamato turned in Arrowhawk and Fighting Bull's direction. "Mr. Fujihara's daughter, Kaori, was abducted several months ago by unknown assailants. We believe they may have been foreign agents. There have been many leads, but nothing substantial.

"But I do appreciate your trying," Fujihara said appreciatively. He turned to Kaori's photo on his desk. "I miss her very much."

"We believe her kidnapping may have been linked to her being a Variant," Hamato said.

"Why?" Fighting Bull asked.

"Because of her unique powerset. She is a technopath, the only one in our country."

"What kind of leads do you have so far?" Arrowhawk asked.

"We have some, but as I mentioned earlier, nothing definitive."

"Let me know how we can help," Arrowhawk said, looking in Fujihara's direction.

Fujihara leaned forward in his chair and laid his forearms flatly on his desk. He stared at Arrowhawk and Fighting Bull intently. "I need you to find my daughter no matter what."

Arrowhawk nodded. "Tell us more; do you know anyone who would want to harm you or your family?"

"No."

"We have already looked extensively at Mr. Fujihara's personal and professional associates," Hamato said. "And they all have been cleared."

"I see," Fighting Bull said. "How about corporate rivals? Any competitors looking to get a professional advantage on you or the company?"

"Maybe some of Takayasu's old friends would want to come after me, but I would not think any of them would come after my family."

"Yes," Hamato interjected again. "As a matter of fact, she was taken months prior to us uncovering Watanabe's dealings with Harada."

"Ok, has anyone looked into Harada pulling some strings behind the jail cell?" Arrowhawk said as he glanced in Hamato's direction.

"Highly unlikely. She has been under strict surveillance since your team captured her."

"Hmmph, I see." Arrowhawk looked down at Fujihara's desk which was covered in a neat array of documents. Most of the text were written in Japanese, but one in particular was written in English and read: *Final Merger Proposal Proposition.* He pushed the other documents aside and lifted the multi-page document to Fujihara's eye line. "What's this?"

Fujihara leaned forward, squinting. He turned to his top right drawer and pulled out his reading glasses.

"That's the final draft of our merger proposal with AlphA.I." Fujihara said as he took the document from Arrowhawk. "They send out the final proposals to all of the department heads to see if there were any last-minute changes that needed to be made."

"I also see on there, "Arrowhawk pointed to the bottom corner of the page, "Venturepointe Consulting?"

"Yes, they have been taking the reins on making sure this is a smooth transition."

Fighting Bull motioned toward Fujihara. "May I take a look, please?"

"Yes, of course," Fujihara said as he passed the document over to her.

She flipped through the first few pages. "The merger will be finalized in a few weeks."

"Yes, the joining together of these two companies would provide a powerhouse in the tech space. With our specialty in cybernetics and human integrative tech and AlphA.I.'s knowhow with software and communications, it is a match made in heaven," Fujihara said.

"Ok, and I see that so far, both countries' Federal Trade Commissions have greenlit this process. Interesting," Fighting Bull said as she continued to flip through the document. "May we take this?"

Fujihara straightened up in his ergonomic chair. "I cannot provide you with the original version, due to trade secrecy."

"We understand but it could help us find your daughter," Fighting Bull said as she leaned forward.

Fujihara crossed his arms and looked up to the ceiling ponderously then back to Fighting Bull.

"I can provide you with a redacted version for your viewing."

"Thank you, sir," Fighting Bull replied with a smile.

Fujihara tapped on his keyboard. A few seconds later, Fujihara's assistant walked in with a freshly bound copy of the redacted merger report and handed Fighting Bull the bound document.

"Thank you so much, Mr. Fujihara. We appreciate your help," Fighting Bull said as she rose from her chair. Arrowhawk and Hamato both gathered their things and began leaving as well.

"You are more than welcome," Fujihara said as he stood from his seat to shake everyone's hand. Before he let go of Arrowhawk's hand he said, "Just don't forget to bring back my daughter."

* * *

Nine Hours Later
Ritz Carlton
Tokyo, Japan

Fighting Bull leaned forward in her high-back chair. In front of her was a circular desk with a laptop computer and neatly stacked pages. Her eyelids started to lag after spending hours poring over the Saisentan documents.

Her phone buzzed. She looked on the screen. Fighting Bull tapped two letters on her keyboard and pressed her right forefinger into a biometric sensor before her screen dimmed. Within seconds the dim screen receded, and Conrad's image appeared.

"Good morning, Alicia," Fighting Bull said.

"Hey, Cynthia," Conrad responded. "You look exhausted," Conrad noted. "What time is it over there?"

Fighting Bull's eyes tracked down to the timestamp on the screen. "About midnight."

"You still good to go?" Conrad asked.

"Yeah," she said, rubbing her eyes. "I've been trying to sift through all the intel we got from our meeting with Saro Fujihara."

"What have you found?"

"On the Harada side, not much new. But we did find out interesting information about Fujihara himself."

"What was that?"

"His daughter was kidnapped over ten months ago."

"What leads do they have so far?"

"From what we see, the PSIA has pretty much turned over every stone and come up empty. They attributed it to foreign agents, but I don't see why they'd target Fujihara. The only viable reason is that she's a Variant."

"Interesting. What's her story?"

Fighting Bull grabbed a sheet from her stack of neatly arranged documents. "Her name is Kaori. She's twenty-three, a graduate student at Tokyo University of Technology's School of Bionics, Computer and Media Sciences. An avid soccer player. She lived at home with her parents and her thirteen-year-old brother Yuuto, who also is a Variant."

"What's her powerset?" Conrad asked calmly as she wrote down notes on a sheet of paper.

"She's a technopath—able to manipulate all forms of tech within a roughly 100-yard vicinity. Apparently, she can also techno-assimilate; graft any piece of tech to her body and repurpose it."

"That's interesting. Same thing happened when we went to the Chicago VERGE Academy. A bunch of ex-spec ops guys tried to kidnap the Variant who breached the SDS."

"It's funny they didn't have these VERGE schools when I was coming up." She folded her hands before continuing, "Danforth told me that after the CIA recruited me, the bigwigs in Washington thought it would be best to formalize the Variant educational system. You know," Fighting Bull said with the corner of her mouth turned up, "you don't want those genetic freaks running around with the regular folk."

Conrad shook her head. "I never saw the wisdom in that, you know? How can people be any more afraid of people born with powers than those who get theirs in a lab?" she asked, pointing to herself.

"I couldn't agree with you more, but back during that briefing, for just an instant, you sounded like those DC bureaucrats."

"C'mon, Cynthia, you know me; it had everything to do with them breaching our security. Those kids are way out of their league."

Fighting Bull's eyes pierced into the screen as she viewed Conrad. "You know I was like that when I was their age, just getting used to my abilities."

"But you're different..."

"And I bet your best friends are all Variants..."

Conrad put her head down then looked up. "Well, they are..."

Fighting Bull looked at her with a cocked eyebrow and mouth twisted to the side.

"Really, Cynthia, please don't play me like that."

"I'm not," Fighting Bull said, cutting her off. "Back to what I was saying—am I really that different though, Alicia? I can turn into virtually anyone in the world. That makes me dangerous. And it makes a lot of people uncomfortable."

Conrad leaned back in her chair. "That's why I'm glad you're on our side." Fighting Bull shook her head with a smile before Conrad continued again. "But you see what I'm saying, though, Cynthia..."

Fighting Bull bowed her head slightly and motioned in Conrad's direction. "Yes, but you know what you did was wrong, right? I didn't want to say anything in front of everybody, but Karen and Aaron were right. Even a non-lethal drone strike was reckless."

Conrad glanced down briefly. "It pisses me off to admit it, but you're right."

"I know," Fighting Bull said with a wide smile.

Conrad's eyes looked back down to her notes. "So, with these dual kidnappings," she began to say, "you think it's just a coincidence?"

"Hell no," Fighting Bull said with some bass in her voice.

"Yeah, I didn't think so either."

"I'll send you what we have on Fujihara," Fighting Bull mentioned as she placed her pages back on their neatly arranged stacks. "Maybe we can piece together what is going on with our two technopaths."

"Copy that," Conrad said as she laid her notes to the side. "Anything else you've found?"

"Well, there is an impending merger between Saisentan and AlphA.I."

"Yeah, I heard a little bit about it, but nothing too in depth."

"Well, they have been working together for a while, even before the merger. They've done joint ventures in the area of remote neuro-links for control of cybernetic limbs in children with birth defects. As a matter of fact, the CEO of AlphA.I. had cybernetic limbs designed by Saisentan."

"I see, and who's handling the specifics of the merger?"

Fighting Bull looked around on her desk and reached over to one of her paper stacks to pull the cover sheet of the final merger proposal. "Venturepointe Consulting. Aaron's son works for them, right?"

"Yeah. He's interning there. I'll have Aaron see what info he can get from him." She paused then said, "without violating any federal trade laws."

"Sounds like a plan Alicia," Fighting Bull responded.

"Where's John by the way?" Conrad asked.

"He's in his hotel room sleeping, I figured I'd be nice and let him sleep while I took the check-in with you."

"I see," Conrad said with a mischievous smile. "Were there some strenuous extracurricular activities that got him tired?"

"Alicia, please. He wishes."

"So, you guys haven't had any time to explore things, on a… more personal level huh?"

"Is that why you paired us on this assignment?"

"Not the main reason, but it's a bonus."

"A bonus?"

"Yep. Just make sure I get a wedding invite."

"I am not going there with you. Bye, Captain!"

As the two women completed their conversation, Arrowhawk slept deeply just a room over. His cell phone suddenly blared a rhythmic jingle. Arrowhawk wiped the crust out of his eyes and reached gingerly for the phone. As he brought the screen closer a broad smile came upon his face

"Hello, gorgeous, to what do I owe this call?" Arrowhawk said groggily.

"John don't even go there," Agent Cristina De La Vega replied. "I'm married with a kid and what we had was a long time ago."

"And did I ever tell you how lucky Kevin is to have you as his wife?"

"Many times. And aren't you and Agent Fighting Bull an item now?"

Arrowhawk paused before answering. "It's complicated."

De La Vega sighed. "When is it *not* complicated with you, John?"

"Well, you know me, Tina," Arrowhawk said with a quick chuckle.

"I know you didn't just call to talk to me about my complicated love life. What's up?"

"Were going through the ringer on oddball cases here. The San Fran Bureau even tapped us to assist on the murder of a Silicon Valley exec and his family. But there was one in particular that I wanted to give you a heads up on. A few weeks ago, a group of hikers found a shallow grave with the bodies of over a dozen college students."

"My God," Arrowhawk responded with shock. "Any ideas as to the cause?"

"The running theory is that the cause of death was organ failure due to rapid cell decay."

"What?" Arrowhawk said as he scratched his head. "How? Especially with a bunch of college students."

"The Hazardous Evidence Response Team found their bodies covered in a metallic coating; unlike anything they'd seen before," De La Vega replied.

Arrowhawk pressed the phone close to his ear. "You think it may be a possible superhuman terrorist event?"

"I'm not sure but it's highly unlikely. Another thing that was interesting was that DNA analysis of the bodies showed some evidence of a virus.

Nothing in the scope of conventional biowarfare agents."

Arrowhawk typed in some notes on his phone as she spoke. "Virus, huh? Terrell's wife, or ex-wife is an infectious disease specialist at NIH. Let me see if he can get her to take a closer look."

"Thanks, John. Also, there was one other thing," De La Vega said as her voice softened.

"Yeah, what's that?"

"We did get a positive I.D. on one of the bodies, "she paused briefly, "and it was Coryn."

Arrowhawk's heart almost stopped. Coryn Baisden was his cousin. She constantly hung around John and his brother Alan when they were kids. He remembered she was a sophomore studying finance at UCLA. Coryn would often text message him about how she would participate in on-campus studies to make a little cash.

"I'm sorry, John."

Arrowhawk steeled himself and responded, "Have her parents been notified?"

"Not yet. We were going to wait until we identify all of the victims and contact each family at the same time."

"Ok," Arrowhawk said as his voice cracked. "Give me everything you have on this case."

CHAPTER TWENTY-ONE

TAKE A LOOK AT YOURSELF

October 14th
Vigil Headquarters
The Mirador
Washington, DC

The refreshing cool breeze off the Potomac kissed Conrad's face as she stood out on the observation platform. She had overseen every detail of the design and building of the Vigil team's new headquarters, the Mirador.

The structure was a sweeping spiraling architectural wonder—rivaling the Washington Monument in stature but besting it in aesthetic. The Mirador's façade was outfitted with Duritium reinforced glass that was impervious to both bullets and directed energy weapons. Built on an artificial island structure, it was specially designed to accommodate the team's nautical equipment. As a matter of fact, Conrad moved her things into the Mirador. This seemed more like home to her than the empty house she once shared with her siblings.

Captain?" Officer Grace Norris said as her holographic image appeared before Conrad.

"Yes?"

"I wanted to let you know Ms. Jones is awake now."

"Thanks, I'll be down."

She exited the observation platform through the sliding doors that led to the main elevator. The elevator opened and she made her way down to the living quarters. As the doors opened, she was greeted by agent Norris, who handed her a holotab.

"Thanks, Grace." Conrad said, taking the device from Norris.

She walked into Itrish's quarters. The room was arranged elegantly, with a queen-sized bed with an ornate, wood frame along with desk and leather chair. The walk-in closet had glass façade sliding doors. What little pieces of personal effects that Itrish had, were neatly laid atop an ottoman next to the bed.

Conrad could see the young woman with her legs draped over the edge of the bed as she walked in. She stared up at Conrad with her big, brown eyes.

"Where are my parents?" Itrish asked.

"And good morning to you, too, Ms. Jones," Conrad said sarcastically as she pulled the leather chair from the desk to the front of the bed.

"I've been holed up in this place for days," Itrish said with arms spread wide, as if to emphasize her point. "I don't know anyone here. I'm away from my friends and family." Itrish leaned forward in her bed. "If you were me, would you think it was a good morning?"

"I can't disagree with that, Ms. Jones—"

"Just call me Itrish," she said abruptly. "You make me sound old, like I'm thirty or something, calling me 'Ms. Jones,'" Itrish said as she clutched the locket given to her by her grandmother.

Conrad recoiled internally about the thirty-year-old remark. "Ok, thirty's not ancient Itrish," she said, given she was in her mid-thirties.

"According to who? Definitely not me."

Itrish looked around at her sumptuous room, filled with all the comforts that any teenager would want. "With all of your drones and satellites you can't tell where my parents are?"

"We know your family was captured," Conrad replied. "Where they are, we don't know but their captors have reached out to us and want to exchange you for them."

"Then let them!" Itrish exclaimed.

Conrad shook her head slowly. "I'm sorry, Itrish, I can't do that."

"So, am I in protective custody or just in custody?" Itrish asked, as she thrust her forefinger in Conrad's direction.

Conrad's eyes tracked downward as she let off a short sigh. "You are not in custody, but I do have to say that what you did, breaching our firewalls and over-riding or satellite defense systems were technically criminal offenses."

"Not the way I see it," Itrish said as she tightly folded her arms across her chest. "It was an act of civil disobedience."

"You think so? What you did was punishable with jailtime."

"So, is this what this is? A pretty cell to keep the little, black, Variant girl in her place?"

"No," Conrad said as she rose from her chair. She walked away toward the far corner of the room and leaned against the wall. She calmly crossed her arms. "What is your deal, Itrish? You obviously are extremely talented and bright, and that's even before we factor in your powers. What's your problem with us?"

Itrish folded her legs crosswise on top of the bed mattress. She interlocked her fingers and began circling her thumbs clockwise. "You failed us."

"We protect this country, this world, day in and day out. How have we failed you?"

Itrish's voice broke slightly as she began, "When I first saw you on TV, over a year ago, I said 'Ok, this could be me.' A black woman with superpowers." She looked up and raised her hands in Conrad's direction. "I was hyped! But when I saw what you did in Lemalia—all those people dead."

Conrad gently cupped her cheek with her right palm. "We... I didn't have a choice."

"You always have a choice," Itrish said as she looked at her with piercing, brown eyes.

Conrad got up from against the wall and took a seat back in the leather chair. "Itrish you'll learn things are not that simple." She looked at her hands. "You said you were excited to see a black woman with superpowers." She lifted up her gaze to match Itrish's. "I had to go through a lot of pain to get these powers."

Itrish leaned back against the pillows on her bed and folded her arms. "How?"

"You probably know a little bit about my story. I was one of the first women on an elite special force's unit. What a lot of people don't know is that I had lupus before I volunteered for the program that gave me powers."

"My God," Itrish whispered under her breath.

"Yeah. That was painful enough—lot of meds I had to take to keep my flares at bay."

"But how did they let you in the army?"

"I knew people. Got medical exceptions, and I wouldn't take no for an answer."

"Wow."

"The process of becoming who I am was probably just as bad. But I knew in order to fulfill my duty I had to make a tough choice." Conrad clenched her fist and pressed it against her bottom lip before continuing. "That's what I did in Lemalia. I made a tough choice."

"I see. But what you did though. How can you live with your conscious? Isn't it hard to sleep these days with all those deaths weighing on you?" Itrish asked, looking dead on at Conrad. Her gaze reminded Conrad so much of her sister's.

"Y-You're right, it's not easy," Conrad said as her eyebrows furrowed. "But it's not because of what happened in Lemalia," she said, as she desperately struggled to break eye contact.

Luckily, Conrad was saved by another holographic alert. "Captain, it's Officer Norris, you're needed down in the Briefing Room."

"Copy that, I'll be down." Conrad stood up from the leather chair. Before she left, she turned back to look at Itrish.

* * *

Five minutes later
Vigil Briefing Room
Fifteen Floor
The Mirador

"What's with the old-school folders, Mark?" Blankenchip asked. He pointed to the stack under Pendleton's arm, as he entered the briefing room.

"These," he said waving a folder. "are the files I had to pull up on some of our perps from the battle of Chicago."

"'Battle of Chicago'?" Bledsoe said with a cocked right eyebrow. "Are we really calling it that now?

Pendleton smiled at the remark. "Whatever you want to call it, but I had to pull up the DoD hard files on Itrish Jones' kidnappers." He placed the folders on top of a rectangular platform device on the briefing table.

"Have any of the survivors talked?" Conrad asked.

"Not one of them. They've all pleaded the fifth," Pendleton responded.

Bledsoe leaned forward in her chair. "And we still can't track down where those prisoner swap demands are coming from?"

Pendleton shook his head. "They're using burner accounts and cutting off any communication before our tracking system can get a lock on them."

He clicked the right-sided button of the small wireless mouse that was paired to the rectangular platform. Immediately, the contents of the folder appeared in holographic form. Headshots of the attempted kidnappers appeared in full view of the team. "Those were the two who infiltrated the school. The files on the driver didn't come up on our database. It seemed like all electronic records—federal, local and state—were all scrubbed."

Blankenchip pointed at the kidnappers' holographic images. "The only way I could see that happening is if someone introduced a logic virus." He referenced the type of computer virus with malicious code that triggers an event when certain conditions are met.

"Who do you see having that capability?" Conrad asked as she pointed in

Blankenchip's direction.

Blankenchip's chair creaked slightly as he leaned back in his chair, scratching his head. "It could be anybody. Feds-wise, I would say someone in NSA or even IARPA. Civilian side could be a number of tech companies; any of the divisions of Alphabet, Facebook, and whatever's left of Binary Technologies."

"Binary was Duvalier's old company, right?" Bledsoe asked.

"Yeah," Conrad answered. "I know they cleaned house after Lorraine Duvalier got thrown in jail, but I'm sure there are still some bad apples in that company."

"I doubt it's Duvalier's company," Blankenchip replied. "They developed software primarily. These guys had tech that could cancel out superhuman abilities. This is way beyond their scope. We need to focus in on those possible suspects."

"I'm glad you brought that up, Aaron," Pendleton said. He pulled out a plastic bag with one of the damaged discs from his vest pocket. The device had a small, red, evidence tag tied to it. "Tech forensics looked into these things and it seems like these little guys are keyed to negate the abilities of Variant superhumans. As far as they can tell, it has no effect on Augments or Contingents."

"Do we know who designed them?" Bledsoe asked as she reached over to take a closer look at the disc.

"They traced it to a small firm in Japan called CyberSense. These were commissioned years ago by the Japanese government to deal with Variant prisoners. These little guys apparently emit an electromagnetic pulse that blocks the neurotransmitters in Variants' brains, to keep them from mentally accessing their powers."

"You said were," Blankenchip said. "What's CyberSense up to now?"

"Nothing," Pendleton answered. "They were acquired by Saisentan."

Conrad's eyes keyed in on the holographic faces of the men. "You mentioned you had to go back to old DoD files. These guys were ex-special ops?"

Pendleton nodded. "All of them were in some special operations division of all of our military branches." He clicked on each picture, and microfiche-like images of dossier pages popped up. "Cane was a former SEAL team six and Russell was ex-Delta Force. Both honorably discharged with the highest commendations. After they left the service their whereabouts were unknown."

"Makes sense," Bledsoe said in agreement. "What do we know about their personal lives?"

"Most of these guys kept a low profile and had no family. I'm having the research division piece together more solid profiles on these guys." Pendleton clicked the mouse again and the images of the men vanished. "Along with running more recon on the Jones family's whereabouts."

"Mark, what did their captors say?" Conrad asked.

"What they've always said. They want the Jones girl." Pendleton continued with his arms folded, "But this time they say they'll execute one family member for each day we delay."

"And Chicago PD never located the impersonators who showed up at the Jones's home?" Bledsoe asked with her hands tightly folded.

"Nope," Pendleton said as he shook his head. "The remains of the stolen police cruisers were found at Navy Pier. There were only charred police uniform remnants. No identifiable DNA traces were found."

"How do we know they're not dead already?" Blankenchip asked.

"They sent both verifiable video images as well as voice recordings."

"Dammit, what kind of tech are they using to block our tracking protocols?"

"I'm not sure, Aaron, but it's pretty damn sophisticated."

Bledsoe raised her hand. "Have they given you exchange parameters?"

Pendleton pressed the touchscreen panel in front of him to activate the briefing table's holographic system. "Yeah. The Field Museum in two days, at 10 pm. No other support staff outside of the core members of the team."

"Pull up the schematic of the museum for me, Mark," Conrad asked as she crept forward in her chair.

Suddenly a side-by-side image of the museum's schematics popped up. Conrad pointed up at them.

"We have multiple exits and entrances. This could work out to our tactical advantage."

"You aren't seriously debating giving up Itrish, are you?" Bledsoe asked as her maternal instincts kicked in.

Conrad shook her head. "No. Typically we'd use Cynthia for a bait and switch, but since she's not here, we have to look at other options."

She turned to look at Pendleton. "How tall is officer Morial?"

"About 5'4," Pendleton responded quickly.

"Same height as Itrish," Conrad said as she rolled the tips of her finger atop the meeting table.

"What are you thinking Alicia?" Pendleton asked pensively.

CHAPTER TWENTY-TWO

RECKONING

Office of the President and CEO
AlphA.I. Headquarters
Palo Alto, California

"Bridgette, what in the hell did you do?" Dennis Stroud said as he got up. Huntley's back arched slightly in the leather chair across from Stroud's smart desk. She lightly gripped the chair's brown leather-bound armrests as Stroud's melodious voice sharpened.

"Dennis, bring your voice down, let me explain—"

"Don't condescend to me," Stroud said as struck his desk with his right fist. His synthetic skin tore, exposing metallic plating and wiring underneath.

"Now, see what you did, Dennis?" Huntley said matter-of-factly as she looked at the cracked desk surface. "You've ruined the desk's A.I. interface. It's basically useless."

He peered down at the damaged desk, then he quickly turned his focus back on Huntley. "I don't give a damn."

She got up from her chair with hands raised in a calming fashion. "Listen to me Dennis, everything's under control."

"The hell it is!" Stroud said as he eased back into his chair. "First, you screwed up the beta testing for CYBRA and then you lost the Adept. Things are not under control."

"Dennis, I get it—"

"Not to mention, now the Adept is in the custody of Vigil!"Stroud said before Huntley could defend herself.

"Those were just minor setbacks," Huntley said as she slinked back into her chair. "Stiles and her team have secured the Adept's family. We've negotiated an even exchange. And we have contingencies in place."

Stroud shook his head and leaned back in his chair. He placed his head in the palms of his hands. "This wasn't supposed to happen this way, Bridgette." He looked gravely in Huntley's direction. "Those were kids who were killed in the beta testing—they could have been my own." Stroud's voice broke as he said this.

"But they aren't your kids," Huntley replied coldly. "They're Variants. It was a necessary sacrifice to see the ultimate vision come to pass."

Stroud lowered his head as he nodded.

"The conversion process didn't go as planned," Huntley said. "The viral matrix didn't fuse properly with their DNA, even with the Asset's cellular signature added to the vector's genetic sequence. I'll have Dr. Breckenridge look at it again."

"No, I'm going to pay him a visit in person. No more screw ups."

Huntley nodded and cocked her head slightly to the side. "Don't worry, Dennis, we can still do this, your dream can still become a reality."

"Yes," Stroud said somberly.

Huntley walked over to him and gently squeezed his right shoulder. "You're a visionary, Dennis. You've mapped out man's next evolutionary step."

"That's true," Stroud agreed. "Variants are a tool, but they're not man's ultimate evolutionary endpoint. They're a means to a greater end."

"Exactly! When everyone else thought it was impossible to create a nationally integrated A.I.-based infrastructure system, you saw that it wasn't." She moved to his right. "Look at you now. What do those naysayers have to say, now? We've pretty much acquired Saisentan. We'll soon have Asia and the Americas on lock. Dennis, think about it, we're on the verge of something monumental."

Stroud gently patted Huntley's hand on his shoulder. "I appreciate the sentiment, Bridgette." He relaxed back into his chair.

"Anytime, Dennis, you know I'm always there for you." Huntley replied with a smile.

Stroud looked at the damage he wrought on his smart desk. "I never expected my upgrades to be so strong." He pushed back slightly from the desk, "You know, there was a time when I used to work at DARPA, in the SHARP division as a matter of fact. Doug and I imagined how best to perfect the human body. He was all about genetic augmentation and I was all about machine enhancement." Stroud paused to look at the exposed metal underneath the torn synthetic skin on his hand. "There is something about cold steel, just the purity of it. Something our dirty human DNA, with all its mismatches and nonsense genes, could never compare to. Doug and I had some good times, even though we did grow apart. No matter what, we always respected each other."

Stroud turned to look up in Huntley's direction. "Do you know what happened to Doug?" He pulled out a holotab from his top desk drawer. Immediately an image of the cover of the Palo Alto Weekly illuminated into a holographic image before their eyes. The headline read: "Tech Ethicist and family murdered in execution style mass murder."

"God," Huntley whispered under her breath. She put her head down and pinched the bridge of her nose.

"Was this your doing?"

"I suggested, and I mean *suggested*, to Stiles that it would be best if Doug Lawson weren't around to mess things up."

Stroud raised his eyebrows. "I didn't know you were that cold-blooded. I like that, though."

Huntley moved back a bit. "You're not upset?"

"No, it's regretful. But Lawson stood in the way of what we're trying to do. Although we were friends, that's not important. Sacrifices have to be made for man's evolutionary promise."

"Okay," Huntley said as she tried to reorient herself.

"At least Stiles is putting the cybernetic enhancements we gave her to good use. What about blowback, though?"

"Stiles covered her tracks pretty well."

"I'm not talking only about that. What about the congressional blowback, I mean? They've been getting on our tails about this privacy crap."

Huntley put her hand up. "Don't worry, I'm all set for the senate hearing tomorrow."

"Good." He then tapped the screen of his holotab. Immediately Itrish's profile picture came up. "So, tell me how we plan on getting the Adept back?"

* * *

October 15th
Communications, Technology, Innovation and the Internet Subcommittee hearing
Senate Chambers
Capitol Hill
Washington, DC

Huntley was welcomed by a mass of photographers. A cacophony of flashbulbs erupted in her face as she entered. She was ushered into the chambers by security as her attorney trailed behind her. Huntley doesn't bother to shield her eyes from the bright light; it seemed like she was born for this. As the COO of AlphA.I., she was as much the face of the company as Stroud was. Whereas Stroud loved being among adoring crowds, she relished being in the arena facing off against any real and perceived enemies of the AlphA.I. agenda.

As Huntley made her way to seat, she saw the gallery filled with supporters. Some of her advocates wore, "We Love Bridgette" and "AlphA.I. 4 Ever" t-shirts. Many of these people took pictures of her with their Turing Two phones. A few of them had AlphA.I. designed neuro-enhancer devices attached to their temples.

Huntley was sworn in by subcommittee chairman, Senator Bryan Bence from New York. Bence looked to be about 5'10 inches in height, with a slightly muscular build. His years as a former football player turned senator were evident in his physique. As Huntley sat down, she lightly tapped her hand under her table. Bence opened for questioning.

"We are here to discuss the issue of national data privacy. The tech revolution has made many improvements in our lives. Many of these have been beneficial and many others deleterious. Within this revolution has been the commoditization of data—which in many ways has become more important than financial assets. Since the beginning of the New Road initiative, AlphA.I. has been privy to majority of American citizens' data. That amount of power under one entity can be extremely dangerous. We have asked AlphA.I. Chief Operating Officer, Bridgette Huntley to testify on her company's alleged privacy violations." Bence paused and looked in Huntley's direction. "Are you ready?"

"Yes, Chairman Bence," Huntley responded.

"Good, let's get down to brass tacks," he said as he arranged his papers. "This committee has been investigating alleged privacy violations committed by AlphA.I. over the past several months. As you know, probably better than anyone on this subcommittee, that the New Road Initiative has provided unfettered access to the data of nearly all Americans—"

"Excuse me, Chairman Bence," Huntley interrupted, "it's actually ninety percent of the U.S. population."

Bence cocked his eyebrow. "Yes, but either way, AlphA.I. has amassed huge amounts of data on all of us. That kind of data monopoly is dangerous."

"But to be fair Chairman Bence, the legislation that put the New Road Initiative in place was supported by many individuals on this very subcommittee," Huntley replied as she nodded in Senator Sylvia Royce's direction. Senator Royce slid a lock of her dark brown hair behind her right ear as she nodded back.

"Very true but it doesn't diminish the reason why we are here. I'll let my colleagues on the subcommittee state their concerns." Bence eased back in his chair and turned to look at ranking member, Senator Nicolette Daniels.

"I yield the floor to ranking member, Senator Daniels."

Daniels arranged the glasses atop the bridge of her nose before beginning. "Thank you, Mr. Chairman. Ms. Huntley, we've received numerous reports concerning AlphA.I.'s involvement in unauthorized data-mining targeting potential customers. Is this true?"

Huntley shook her head. "Absolutely not. Whenever people sign their privacy agreement, they acknowledge we have the right to use their data."

"But Ms. Huntley," Daniels said as she pointed her pen in Huntley's direction, "people who even opt out cannot use your products. And since your products permeate virtually every aspect of our lives, they're virtually shut out of the tools to engage in modern society."

"Well, there are consequences for not complying."

"That's just part of what I am getting at. Many of my own constituents who've opted out of these agreements still have their data utilized by AlphA.I."

Daniels motioned to one of her staff members to hand a spiral bound document over to Huntley.

"As you can see in this report," Daniels began to say, "multiple complaints have been made to the FTC concerning data privacy violations committed by AlphA.I."

Huntley flipped through the documents and looked up at the row of senators. "I am aware of these complaints and our lawyers are addressing this."

"Well, that still doesn't mitigate the reality of these complaints. What do you have to say about this?"

Huntley's attorney leaned into her ear.

"Due to the sensitive nature of these allegations, I've been instructed by my legal counsel not to answer."

"Hmmph," Daniels grunted. "Fair enough, since I don't think I'll be getting anywhere with this. I yield back the balance of my time."

"Thank you, Senator Daniels," Bence replied. "I would like to recognize Senator Royce for her opening questions."

"Thank you, Chairman Bence," Royce smiled brightly as she replied. She tapped her holo-tab to pull up her notes. "How are you doing today, Ms. Huntley?"

"Very well, Senator Royce, thanks for asking," Huntley replied as she nodded.

"Good," Royce responded. "As we all know, The New Road Initiative has been a game-changer in terms of streamlining our nation's communications, transportation and financial infrastructure. We've seen improved efficiencies in global communication and logistics. Not to mention, we have been less vulnerable to cyberattacks since bringing our national tech infrastructure under the AlphA.I. umbrella. While there have been steep declines in nationwide traffic accidents thanks to AlphA.I.'s smart grid infrastructure, and improvements in medical data transfer, which has been vital in dealing with pandemics and communication between public health jurisdictions. I say all this to say that many of these advances could not have been achieved without giving up something. In this instance, it's our data. I personally believe it's a worthwhile trade-off…"

"Excuse me, Senator Royce," Bence interrupted, "but is there a question somewhere in your statement?"

Royce glared back. "Yes, Mr. Chairman, I was getting there." She cleared her throat and continued. "Ms. Huntley, what initiative does AlphA.I. have on the horizon to protect our national data?

Huntley leaned toward her microphone. "Thank you for that question, Senator Royce. We at AlphA.I. have created the CYBRA artificial intelligence operating system which has a self-scrubbing function purposed to shield data compromise—especially by foreign adversaries. Since CYBRA's A.I. system runs the New Road infrastructure, we have made sure to keep out any potential hacking from countries such as North Korea, Russia, and China. It's a program the likes of which no one has seen before."

"Thank you, Ms. Huntley," Royce responded. "I yield back the balance of my time."

Bence looked at Malveux to his left. "The chair recognizes Senator Malveux."

"Thank you, Chairman Bence," Malveux said as she arranged her papers. She turned her gaze to Huntley. "Ms. Huntley, thank you again for appearing before this subcommittee."

Huntley nodded in response.

"I agree with Senator Royce that the New Road Initiative has been an amazing development. Although, I am also concerned about the lack of privacy millions of Americans have encountered as a result. Your company's data reach is expansive, but you've also become the privatized chief surveillance apparatus of America. That's something in a free and fair society we cannot stomach. My question to you is, in a democratic society such as ours, how will AlphA.I. make sure our freedoms are maintained?"

"Mr. Chair?" Royce interjected. "May I say something?"

"Senator Malveux has not completed her questioning…"

Royce completely ignores Bence. "I find it ironic that Senator Malveux accuses AlphA.I. of creating a surveillance state when Vigil, led by a close associate of the senator, is engaging in those very same tactics."

Malveux's nostrils flared as Bence responded. "The senator from California will cease her questioning, as she is not currently recognized." Bence nodded in Malveux's direction. "Please continue, senator."

"Thank you, Mr. Chairman. As I was saying, how does AlphA.I. plan on being a good corporate citizen when it comes to respecting our personal liberties?"

Huntley took a sip of water before answering.

"Senator Malveux, I would like to respond by echoing a statement made by your goddaughter, Alicia Conrad. 'Sometimes you have to break a few eggs to make an omelet.'" Huntley thrust her forefinger into the table. "This country has the most efficient infrastructure the world has ever seen. America is running as smoothly as a well-designed machine. And some minor sacrifices had to be made in order to accomplish this grand goal."

Malveux shook her head. "But you're missing the point. We aren't machines, we're human beings."

"Well, Senator Malveux, maybe it's time we evolved."

* * *

National Institute of Allergy and Infectious Disease
National Institutes of Health
Bethesda, Maryland

"How are the titers looking?" Doctor Danielle 'Dani' Morrison asked her infectious disease fellow, Doctor Darnell Randall.

He tapped his tablet's screen and pulled up the recent antibody titers on their vaccine study patient that they were rounding on. His eyes widened.

"This is amazing Doctor Morrison; his antibody titers are at a protective level."

Dani nodded. "And to think we were able to do this without an injection." She walked over to Randall to look at his computer screen. "This epidermal powder immunization modality is looking to be more effective than the old way of doing things."

"And who knows, it can probably be used for other types of infusion therapy."

"If this approach could be applied to convalescent serum therapy, then it's game over," Dani replied with a smile. Suddenly her phone buzzed. She grabbed her phone and looked at the screen.

"Excuse me, I have to take this."

"Sure, Doctor Morrison."

Dani nodded and stepped away to take the call at the nurse's station. "Hello, Terrell."

Terrell Morrison's voice crackled over the line. "Hey Dani, how are you doing?"

She cupped the phone receiver close to her mouth. "I'm fine, Terrell. I'm at work so I can't really talk much." Her voice quivered a bit as she spoke to her now ex-husband. It had barely been a year since the divorce was finalized.

"I understand. I won't keep you long," Morrison replied as the pitch of his voice dipped low.

"I'm sorry to sound like I'm rushing you off the phone. But I'm just a little crunched for time. What's going on?" Dani said, as she tried to recalibrate her tone.

"I'll make it quick then. I have a big favor to ask of you."

Dani looked down at her feet as she leaned against the curved nurse's station counter. "I'm listening?"

"About a month ago, a pair of hikers found the bodies of a bunch of UCLA college students in a shallow grave in L.A.," Morrison said. "As a matter of fact, one of the students killed was related to one of my teammates."

Dani covered her mouth with her right hand. "Oh my God, I am so sorry."

"Thank you. I'll send your regards to him. We think it was some sort of virus that killed them."

Dani tucked her phone between her shoulder and cheek as she folded her arms. "Any signs that it's a biological attack?"

"We don't know," Morrison responded. "It had such a limited scope, and no group has taken responsibility yet. So, at this point it's unlikely."

"Ok, what do you need me to do?" Dani asked as she adjusted the Pandora bracelet Morrison had given her.

"Can you analyze the data from the FBI forensics team? Maybe, pinpoint the origin of the virus to give us some clues?"

"Well, I can do my best," she said as she positioned the cellphone closer to her ear. "But typically, the CDC would be the ones to tackle something like this."

"I know, but since you're the expert on novel viruses I figured it would be best to reach out to you first," Morrison said with a smile that unfortunately Dani couldn't see.

"Ok, I'll see what I can do. Have them send over whatever they have. I'll take a look."

"Ten four, Dani."

Dani got up away from the nurse's station and switched the phone to her other ear. "So, I hear you're the point man for nation building in Lemalia."

Morrison brought his phone close up to his ear "No, I'm just trying to help out. Make sure the country's security infrastructure is in tip-top shape as it gets back on its feet."

"That's noble, Terrell."

"Thanks, Dani. There are just a lot of international antics going on. The International Criminal Court has brought, what I think are bogus charges against Lemalia's president."

Dani looked down at her bracelet. "I know. But I'm sure you'll be alright."

"Thank you." He paused briefly. "But had I known how tough this would be, I probably wouldn't have taken the assignment."

"I'll tell you this: you have more guts than me," Dani said as she smiled.

"Oh really? This coming from the woman who's traveled to disease ravaged countries to treat thousands of people. I beg to differ, Dani. I think you've got all the guts."

His compliment elicited the brightest of smiles on Dani's face. "Aww, flattery will get you everywhere, Mr. Morrison."

"Is that so, Mrs. Morri—" he paused to correct himself, "I mean Dr. Dani."

Dani quickly changed the subject. "Ok, so I have to go but I'll be looking forward to getting those data sets and samples."

"Will do," Morrison said solemnly as he gently pulled his phone from his ear.

CHAPTER TWENTY-THREE

COURTS OF JUSTICE

October 16th
Pre-Trial Chambers
International Criminal Court Headquarters
The Hague, Netherlands

Papers shuffled about in the hands of the seven judges in the ICC's Pre-Trial Chambers. Each of them rifled through the charges filed by Chief Prosecutor, Olesugun Olutanji against former U.S. Secretary of Defense, Charles Hanahan. As they were aligned on the long raised wooden bench, Olutanji stood patiently next to his desk.

The lead judge, Dembe Businge, from Uganda pressed her glasses over the bridge of her nose as she inspected the documents in front of her. She meticulously examined each page as Olutanji started to rock from side to side.

Businge looked down from the bench. "You have quite a list of charges, Olesugun."

"Yes, your honor," Olutanji said respectfully. "But there are many travesties that Secretary Hanahan has to account for."

"I see," Judge Louis De Silva, the ICC's Brazilian representative on the bench said. "Crimes of aggression, war crimes, and genocide are all listed in this filing."

"That is correct your honor. I believe there is ample evidence to support these charges against the secretary in regard to his assassination of a foreign president as well as his involvement in starting a foreign civil war," Olutanji replied.

"But that can't fall squarely on his shoulders," Bertram Balasingham, from the UK chimed in. "There was a wide-ranging confluence of events that led to these outcomes."

Olutanji nodded. "I agree your honor, but our focus is Secretary Hanahan. He was the one that utilized ex-American military to assassinate Lemalia's rightfully elected resident, Mohann Aldessa…"

"But hold on, Olesugun," Moroccan Judge, Amina Mohammed interjected. "We know Mr. Aldessa was aided to the presidency by an illegal, criminal, international organization. And many of their members are now in custody or are fugitives."

"I understand Judge Mohammed. The Network was the main power behind a potential illegitimate president being installed into office. But he still did not deserve to die. He should have been prosecuted in a court of law where he could face legitimate justice. Not justice at the end of a gun barrel."

French judge, Pierre Trudeau rapped his knuckles against the table. "Exactly! We live in a world of laws." He leaned over to look down the bench at his colleagues. "Secretary Hanahan violated multiple international laws with the assassination of president Aldessa."

"Not to mention, he ignited tensions that triggered a civil war in that country," South Korean Judge Minu Kim said.

"Ok, you have made an impassioned speech. You have given us some grounds to go forth with this," Businge said. "But I have to ask, don't you think it's concerning that the main driver for this case is the brother of Erosin Analaise; the same man who sought the violent overthrow of the current president?"

Olutanji looked away from the bench and stroked his forehead. "Yes, Judge Basinge, it is but because this referral was pushed by the brother of a former rebel, it does not make it any less valid."

Argentinian Judge, Juan Corleto, stepped in. "Olesugun, I agree with you, but with him being held in a country that is not a Rome Statute signatory, it, well, it makes this all moot, don't you think?"

"In fact, no," Olutanji said as he motioned in the judge's direction. "The provision in the Rome Statute allows for the ICC's jurisdiction in the case where a crime is committed in the territory of a State Party, of which Lemalia is."

Corleto leaned back in his chair and tapped his armrest with the tips of his fingers. "I see. Fair enough. But how do you plan on getting him back here for prosecution?"

Olutanji turned to the desk behind him and shuffled through his briefcase to locate a few documents. It took a few moments, but he pulled out seven bound documents and walked over to the bench of judges.

"Here are copies of the extradition petition I planned to send to the United States' Department of State once I received approval for you for an arrest warrant," Olutanji said as he handed a document to each member.

Each judge flipped through the petition. Kim looked up from the document and in Olutanji's direction. "This is a great effort you've put into this but let us be honest. Even if we did grant you that warrant, how likely is it that the Americans would extradite?"

"Judge Kim is right," Businge noted as she pointed her pen in Kim's direction. "You have laid out a compelling case, but we haven't any means to compel the Americans to hand him over."

Olutanji clenched his right fist. "Your honor, you know something must be done. We cannot let him get away with murder."

Trudeau raised his right hand and turned left to look at Judge Basinge. "But if there is a chance we could acquire Hanahan don't you think it's only right to grant the warrant?"

Businge mulled the possibility in her head. "Perhaps."

"Well then let's grant him the arrest warrant," Trudeau said emphatically with arms raised. "It may be an exercise in futility, but we may yet convince the Americans to send him to us. It does not hurt to try."

Businge looked reflectively at the petition in front of her. She turned in Trudeau's direction, her glasses sliding slightly below the bridge of her nose. Trudeau could see her leer over the frames like an old schoolteacher. She flashed the same look in Olutanji's direction. "All right, we will grant the warrant. But be warned Olesugun, I don't believe much will come out of this."

"Yes, I understand. Thank you, your honor," Olutanji replied with a broad smile.

"You're dismissed counselor." Basinge said as she got up from her chair. The rest of the judges slowly filed out of the chambers except one: Pierre Trudeau. He picked up the extradition paperwork and walked over to Olutanji as he packed away his documents.

"Do you have a minute Olesugun?" Trudeau said as he looked over his shoulder to see if there were any stray judges still in the room.

"Yes, sure, Judge Trudeau. How can I help you?"

"I have to say I am extremely proud that you are trying to bring this man to justice," Trudeau said as he scowled at Hanahan's photo in the extradition petition. "Not too many people are willing to take on this challenge. Especially, when it comes to Vigil possibly being entangled in this."

He nodded in acknowledgement. "Thank you, sir. I feel like a lone soldier. It doesn't matter if it's an American or not. We all must abide by the law."

Trudeau placed his hand on Olutanji's left shoulder. "I agree with you wholeheartedly, my friend." He leaned in to get closer to Olutanji's ear. "I just want to let you know I have a strong feeling we will be able to bring Secretary Hanahan to justice."

Olutanji swiftly looked back to Trudeau. "Really? You think the Americans will give him up that easily?"

Trudeau chuckled. "No, not easily but I believe we can get what we need to get Hanahan here to stand for his crimes." He looked away briefly and then turned back to look Olutanji in the eye. "Trust me."

CHAPTER TWENTY-FOUR

SACRIFICE PLAY

October 17th
The Field Museum
Chicago, Illinois

The moonlight through the Field Museum's skylight illuminated the bones of Maximo the Titanosaur. A group of four cloaked drones circled around the perimeter of the building. Real time data from their scans streamed across the computer screen of the team's nondescript van. The exterior of the van was a dull gray with dirty worn tires. The interior of the vehicle was different, outfitted with some of the most technologically advanced devices anyone had ever seen. This same data was streamed to Pendleton on the large LCD screens in the Mirador's briefing room.

"Perimeter scans show no bystanders around. No exterior boobytraps or dangerous ordnance as well," Conrad said over her radio link with the Mirador.

"Copy that, Alicia," Pendleton said. "You have tactical cameras on?"

Conrad placed her enhanced tactical glasses on. "Alright, Mark, we're heading in."

'Good luck, Alicia.'

The rear door of the team's van flung open. The three team members emerged with a fourth person in tow. As they entered the museum's west entrance, Bledsoe felt a sharp lancinating pain shoot from the top of her head down the side of her face. Conrad noticed as she grabbed her head.

"Karen, are you ok?"

"Yeah, I'm fine. It's just a headache."

They slowly made their way into the center of the main level. As they continued further, they saw a woman with her face covered with a skull mask, standing just below the Titanosaur exhibit with her arms folded behind her back.

"That's far enough," the masked woman said. Her voice had a mechanical tone to it.

Conrad raised her fist. The team immediately halted. "We're here for an even exchange. Itrish Jones for her family."

The masked woman motioned for the fourth member of Conrad's contingent to come forward. Conrad stretched out her arm to prohibit them from leaving. "No, we want to see her family first."

The masked woman nodded and tapped on her earpiece. "Bring them out."

Slowly, the Jones family was brought out into the main level .John Jones was last. He was ushered up from the Montgomery Ward lecture hall from the ground level with the barrel of a submachine gun pointed at the small of his back. He saw his wife and his young son lined up in front of the Titanosaur exhibit. Jones rushed toward them but was snatched back by his captor. The three members of Itrish's family were eventually aligned behind the masked woman.

"They're all here," the masked woman declared. She motioned for the young woman to come forth.

Conrad removed her blocking arm to allow her to walk forward. Itrish's brother walked forward first, her father came second, and her mother trailed behind. As they crossed paths, Itrish's mother rubbed her hand against the young woman's right arm. Mrs. Jones' eyes looked at the young woman carefully, then quickly averted her gaze.

As the young woman came over to the masked woman's side, she was grabbed by one of the armed captors and pulled off to the side. The masked woman and the rest of the visible captors then fled through the exhibit of the Ancient Americas. Conrad tapped her earpiece to contact Pendleton.

"The Jones family has been secured. We're headed toward our exit."

"Copy that."

Just as Pendleton cut out, Bledsoe grabbed her head.

"Karen, what's wrong?" Conrad asked.

"Dammit, my head is splitting."

Meanwhile, as the captors escaped through the exhibit, they passed a myriad of displays with variable lighting. The masked woman removed her disguise to reveal the face of Jane Stiles. She pulled out her cell phone to make a call as her team shackled the young woman's wrists. As Stiles put the phone to her ear, she took a closer look at the young Variant. She noticed that side of her face had an uncommon translucence to it.

"Hold on a second," she said as she tucked her phone away. Stiles grabbed the young woman's shoulder and turned her around. She could see that it was Itrish, but she looked at her hairline. There was an uneven alignment to it. Stiles reached for her hairline and pulled off a braided wig. The digital facial prostheses tore in the process, revealing the true identity of officer Morial.

"Shit!" Stiles said in a low voice. She pulled out her pistol and shot Morial in the chest—hitting her in her armor. Then in almost one smooth motion, Stiles immediately radioed one of her men.

"Faulk, they pulled a bait and switch. Engage now."

"Are the SHAN nodes in place?" Faulk asked as he peered through the scope of his rifle.

"Yes! If you have a shot, take it!"

Faulk nodded from his perch along one of the ornately designed pillars that overlooked the main level below. He radioed two of his other teammates.

"You heard the woman, gents. Contingency protocol is in effect."

Faulk peered through the sites of his M110 Semi-Automatic Sniper rifle and unleashed three rounds in the team's direction as they headed toward their exit. His bullets hit the glass displays surrounding Vigil. Conrad reflexively tried to protect herself with her forearm as glass shattered in her face. Instinctively, she reached around her back to grab her modified Colt Commando rifle and aimed her weapon back in the direction of the gunfire. She felt the kickback from her rifle against the inside of her right shoulder as she let off three rounds. Faulk quickly ducked to avoid Conrad's weapons fire.

"Karen!" Conrad shouted. "I need you to lay down some cover precipitation. We'll rain them out of their sniping position."

As Bledsoe tried to summon a localized storm, her head started to thump, and she could not conjure up anything. "I can't Alicia. Something's blocked my powers."

"Dammit," Conrad said as she tapped her wristwatch. "Don't worry about it."

"You called down the drones, didn't you?" Blankenchip asked Conrad as he fired back in the direction of Faulk and the other pair of snipers on either side of him.

"Of course, you sick old bastard."

Blankenchip shook his head in admiration.

"You just make sure you and Karen cover the Jones family," Conrad said as she motioned her head over in the direction of the family.

Blankenchip nodded. Conrad kept her rifle in low ready position as she quickly ran crouched down toward the Triceratops display. As she made her way to the display, she was hit in the mid-calf by a high caliber bullet.

"Aaaaagh!" Conrad yelled as she stumbled forward, right behind the bony triceratops display. She pulled up her pant leg and looked down at her calf to see there was mild damage but no penetrance through her BDU pants. Thankfully, she had this version of her BDU pants reinforced with a Duritium/biosteel microweave. She turned her head down to look at the small display on her wristwatch.

"It's about time those drones came in."

Bullets suddenly shattered The Field Museum's roof glass windows. They hit one of the heavy-set snipers perched on the second level. He fell backward as bullets pierced his chest and neck.

"Drake!" Faulk screamed as he saw the man taken down by the hail of bullets. His head swiveled around to see a trio of micro drones quickly descend through the destroyed glass windows. He quickly rolled forward and took cover behind a support pillar as the lead drone unleashed a salvo of bullets in his direction.

Meanwhile, Conrad saw the third remaining sniper aim his M39 Marksman rifle in her direction. He let off multiple rounds that tore into the triceratops display that she took cover behind. She quickly lifted her rifle and braced it against her shoulder. After three quick trigger pulls, bullets pierced the sniper's chest and skull. He fell to the ground without a sound. Faulk, who still took cover behind the pillar, took a glimpse to see his other partner fall to the ground from Conrad's bullets. He tapped his earpiece.

"Stiles! I'm getting killed up here. She's called a drone strike!"

"Don't worry, I got it." Stiles pulled out a small, sleek, black, rectangular device from her inner coat pocket. She depressed the device's center button.

Conrad could hear the drones' rotors slowing down. She peaked her head up from behind the triceratops display to see her drones spiraling down to the ground. Conrad violently tapped her wristwatch, trying her best to regain control of the drones.

"The hell is going on?" Conrad blurted out to herself.

A large crashing sound was heard as the drones smashed into each other and eventually hit the ground. As this happened, Faulk used flash bang grenades to cover his escape. Conrad lost her visual. She tapped her earpiece.

"Aaron, what's your twenty?"

Blankenchip fired off his rifle on one of the attackers. "Barely making it." He slapped the side of his helmet to activate his countermeasure analysis program. There were data points outlining how many people were in the path of their intended secondary extraction point. Behind him, the Jones family members hunkered down, trying their best to avoid getting in the line of fire.

Blankenchip motioned to Bledsoe to follow him.

"Alicia, we're making our way down to the lower level of the Ancient Egypt exhibit."

"Copy that."

Conrad sprinted through the long corridor in the direction of the aforementioned exhibit. As she rounded one of the corners, she was met by three attackers. Conrad slide-tackled the first. As the back of the man's hit the ground, she rammed the buttstock of her rifle into his face. Its impact collapsed the bridge of his nose and knocked him out.

The second attacker, clad in a grey flak jacket, fired in Conrad's direction. She swiftly did a front roll to avoid his weapons fire. She reached to her side holster to pull her Glock 17 pistol. She fired three bullets with uncanny accuracy in the man's leg and arm. The third attacker shot five rounds at Conrad—slamming her against the wall from the impact. She took a brief moment to collect herself before she raised up her Glock once more. It took all of three seconds before the third attacker was downed.

"Alicia, where the hell are you?" Blankenchip screamed in Conrad's earpiece.

"Stop whining, you old bastard! I'm on my way."

Blankenchip's armor was taking enormous amounts of gunfire while Bledsoe did her best to shield the Joneses while she returned fire with her Taurus pistols.

One of the attackers that shot at them pulled a red oblong disc from his thigh pocket. Quickly, he flung the disc in Blankenchip's direction. It bounced two times before it landed by Blankenchip's feet and emitted a bright flash.

"Aaaaagh! Fuck!" Blankenchip yelled as he tried to recover from the flashing light. As he tried to reposition himself, he noticed that he couldn't move.

"What the hell?" Blankenchip said as his heads up display streamed data concerning his armor's integrity. All his systems were off-line, including his basic mobility functions. He was frozen in place. His eyes widened as the attackers advanced.

Suddenly, two of the attackers were hit from behind with assault weapons fire. The third attacker turned to see Conrad firing on them. He raised his rifle in her direction, but he was met with a stiff boot to his chest along with an elbow strike to the head which snapped it back. As he fell to the ground, he began losing his grip on his rifle. Before the rifle hit the ground, Conrad swept it up by its carrying handle. In a sinuous motion, she gathered up that attacker's rifle. She aimed it at a fourth attacker and squeezed the trigger three quick times. Bullets pierced the man's head and chest. His lifeless body slumped to the ground instantly.

As Conrad dispatched the attackers, Bledsoe ushered the Jones family through the lower-level exit. Blankenchip's armor was still frozen with him inside. He struggled to reach for his wristbands to retract his armor. Mrs. Jones hid herself in front of Blankenchip, allowing his armor to protect her from the attackers' weapons fire even with him frozen in place.

After John and Anthony Jones made it safely through the exit, Bledsoe ran back to help gather up Clarice Jones. As Bledsoe ran back to grab her, she tapped the side of Blankenchip's wrist to deactivate his armor. She in turn grabbed Blankenchip's arm and also Jones.' At this point her uniform was the only protective armor they had.

The fifth attacker saw his opening. He turned his attention from Conrad and instead aimed his weapon at the trio of Jones, Blankenchip, and Bledsoe. As Bledsoe ushered Clarice Jones to the exit, the attacker began firing on them. Five bullets hit Bledsoe in her lumbar region. The impact of the bullets dragged both Bledsoe and Blankenchip to the ground and exposed Clarice Jones.

"No!" Conrad shouted, as she lunged toward the last attacker. He squeezed the trigger. She was helpless as Clarice Jones's body fell lifeless to the ground.

PART THREE

AWAKENING

(HW E MUDUA: ADINKRA SYMBOL FOR EXAMINATION)

CHAPTER TWENTY-FIVE

DISCOVERY

October 18th
Interrogation Room
FBI Field Office
Los Angeles, California

Joyce Wu tapped her right heel feverishly. She sat in an uncomfortable metal chair with leather cushioning. On the weathered, rectangular, metal table in front of her was a half-filled glass of water. Across from her, a pair of equally uncomfortable looking chairs—likely the ones intended for her interrogators, she thought. She shivered as the cold air from the vent above bored down on her as she turned to her right to see a smudgy one-way mirror in sore need of Windex.

Wu jumped up at the sound of the squeaking hinge as the door opened. Agents De La Vega and Johnson entered the room. A large manila folder was tucked under De La Vega's right shoulder. Johnson carried a nine by eleven-inch tablet computer in his right hand. As Wu watched them make their entrance, it was a study in contrasts—Johnson with his tall height, freckled skin, and bright red hair and De La Vega with her darker skin, shorter height, and natural curly hair. The female FBI agent placed the folder on the table in front of Wu. De La Vega removed her phone and placed it on the table as she took her seat.

"Please state your name for the record," De La Vega asked as he pressed 'record' on the phone.

She cleared her throat. "My name is Joyce Wu."

"And where do you work, Ms. Wu?"

Wu rubbed her hands together rapidly. "I'm sorry, but before we go on, can you turn down the air in here? It's freezing."

Johnson glanced over to De La Vega. She smiled and nodded back at him before she turned her gaze to Wu. "Sure."

A film of small icicles formed on the lower rim of De La Vega's eyelids. Her pupils emitted a bluish glow. Instantly the temperature warmed up. Wu's eyes widened at this sight. De La Vega blinked twice, and the film receded from her eyelids and the bluish glow receded from her pupils.

"Whoa, you're a…?"

De La Vega nodded her head. "Afro-Latina? Yes."

"No, that's not what I meant—"

"A Variant?" De La Vega said before Wu completed her sentence. "Yes, that too." She leaned forward closer to Wu. "Now, as I was asking, where do you work?"

"I'm the director of new technology outreach and an operations assistant for AlphA.I."

"And can you describe your relationship with Mr. Doug Lawson?" De La Vega said as she continued her line of questioning.

Wu's eyes veered down to her shaking hands. She clasped them together in a vain attempt to calm them. "I didn't know Mr. Lawson directly. I mean I knew of him, not personally though. His work with the Hexagon group is well-known."

Agent Johnson looked down to his tablet computer and tapped the screen two times. He turned the screen toward Wu. "Well, we have records of multiple emails between you and Lawson informing him of your concerns about AlphA.I. But I believe you were using a pseudonym." Johnson turned the tablet back to himself. "Echo was the name I believe."

"That's right," Wu responded confidently. "I knew I couldn't talk to anyone on my job."

"So, you leaked company information to Lawson, hoping he would what? Be your indirect whistleblower?"

Wu looked furtively at the glass of water on the table. "Yeah, something like that."

"And so, you reached out to the FBI once you found out about his murder." De La Vega stated.

Wu nodded her head slowly. Her hand shook slightly as she reached for the glass to take a sip.

"Ok, so in your original report you mentioned," De La Vega said as she read documents in the large manila folder, "AlphA.I. had been running field trials on a new program—an app I believe?"

"It was supposed to be an app that connected all of your electronics through proximity linking."

"So," De La Vega began asking, "what's the deal?"

Wu looked up fervently at both agents. "It's just a front. It was really a delivery system for a virus."

"What kind of virus?"

"I don't know," she shook her head. "But I was in charge of recruiting beta testers to see how they responded."

De La Vega quickly closed the manila folder. "You are going to have to give us a little more than that, Ms. Wu."

"I wasn't involved in the planning. I was just the one who recruited potential candidates." Wu cringed as she recalled what happened. "It was like something you would see in a horror film. Like their bodies were turned inside out. But instead of guts, it was metal and wiring."

Johnson pointed in Wu's direction. "So, that's what happened to those college kids buried in the Angeles National Forest?"

"Yes," Wu said as she collapsed her head into the palm of her right hand. "I just, I couldn't do anything, they-they wouldn't let me."

"Who wouldn't let you?" De La Vega inquired as she leaned forward.

Wu looked away. "One of the directors, I couldn't see who it was---they were in the adjacent room, behind the one-way mirror like the one you guys have."

De La Vega scribbled a note within a page in the manila folder. "Ok, so what exactly were they trying to do?"

"From what I can remember from the roll out meetings, they were working on creating a perfect symbiosis of man and machine."

De La Vega's eyes widened. "Essentially they want to create cyborgs or something?"

"No, not cyborgs, something more organic. A way to seamlessly integrate humans and technology. And it's not the first time they've conducted tests on people."

De La Vega looked in Johnson's direction then back at Wu. "What do you mean?"

"They've been conducting experiments on people—specifically Variants."

"What?"

Wu leaned forward in her chair.

"Not only was I in charge of recruiting the beta testers but I created the algorithm to identify the best candidates. My program works by predictive analytics. It's able to pinpoint perfect candidates based on age, geography, gender and superhuman ability—"

"Hold on," De La Vega interrupted. "Superhuman potential?"

"Yes, we wanted Variants specifically."

"Why?"

Wu put her hands in the air. "Because from what I've heard, our CEO, Mr. Stroud, figures they'd be the best candidates to conduct field tests on." She turned her head to the side. "I've heard rumors that he hates them."

"I don't get it."

"He's never forgiven them for what happed in Minneapolis."

"The Minneapolis event was the result of a known super-powered terrorist," De La Vega said. "Not an entire group of people!"

"From what I've heard, he thinks they're all the same. To him, Variants aren't human. They're like lab rats. Only there for the benefit of 'real' human beings."

"My God," Johnson exclaimed.

"As a matter of fact, the UCLA students we recruited were either pre-or post-manifested Variants. None of them were normal human beings."

"Excuse me, so Variants aren't 'normal human beings'?" De La Vega interrupted.

"I'm sorry, that's not what I meant…"

"You said the UCLA case wasn't the first," De La Vega said curtly, cutting Wu off.

"Yes, it's a little above my pay grade, but I know they've been doing augmentation experiments on Variants for a while. They use them to test out their latest bio-enhancing prosthetics."

"That makes sense," Johnson interjected. "His background with the SHARP program would put him at the forefront of augmentation design."

"What happened to those other Variants that were experimented on?" De La Vega demanded.

"I don't know all the details, but they had an international recruitment effort."

"Well, that's something we can't just let go."

"My supervisor would probably have more insight on that than I would. But I don't know if he'd be willing to talk."

"Don't worry," De La Vega said. "We have ways to make them talk."

Johnson turned to Wu. "So, how did you target recruits with your algorithm?"

"AlphA.I. has an extensive catalogue of apps, software, and programming. You know those terms of service you always have to sign?"

"Yeah."

"Well, tucked in there you give us permission to use your data," Wu said definitively. "After that, it was child's play to let the A.I. do its work to zero in on our recruits."

De La Vega scratched her head and looked in Johnson's direction. "My God, is there anything private anymore?" She then brought her gaze back to Wu. "Now, that you've seen the aftermath of this, what are you willing to do about it?"

Wu looked in De La Vega's direction. "I'm going to do what I didn't do the first time; the right thing."

CHAPTER TWENTY-SIX

KINSHIP CONNECTION

October 20th
Ritz Carlton
Tokyo, Japan

Arrowhawk heard two light knocks on his door. He quickly threw on his crisp, white dress shirt as he hurriedly went to answer the door.

"Who is it?" Arrowhawk asked as he peered through the peephole.

"It's me, John," Fighting Bull responded as she adjusted her fitted sport coat.

He grasped the door handle. Fighting Bull could see his shirt not fully buttoned, which exposed the many tattoos across his top of his chest as he eased the door open. She paused briefly.

"Eyes up here," Arrowhawk said with a smirk as he saw Fighting Bull checking him out.

"Uhm, are you ready?"

"Give me a second," Arrowhawk said as he began buttoning up his shirt. "Come in."

Fighting Bull closed the door behind her as she entered. Arrowhawk carefully placed his documents into his shoulder bag. Atop his desk, Fighting Bull saw a picture of his deceased cousin on his laptop. She looked away and shook her head.

"Sit down, John."

He turned toward her confused. "Why?"

Fighting Bull pointed in the direction of his bed. Arrowhawk smiled and plopped himself on the lush, queen-sized bed.

"You know, it's a little early for a daytime quickie, but if you insist," Arrowhawk replied with a smile.

"Please, don't flatter yourself," Fighting Bull said as she punched the side of his arm. She took a seat next to him and sat shoulder to shoulder to him.

"How are you feeling?"

He looked away with his lips curved into a smile. "I'm fine, seriously."

Fighting Bull cocked her head to catch his view. "No, you're not." She gently placed her hand on his thigh. "You just found out your cousin was killed. Believe me, you are not ok."

Arrowhawk patted the top pf her hand. "It's alright," he responded in a barely audible tone.

"Sit this one out. I'll meet up with Hamato," she said. "You need some time."

Arrowhawk looked down and nodded.

"Have you told your mom?"

Arrowhawk shook his head.

"I think it's time."

"What about the mission?"

"I can take it over from here. I'll let Alicia know. You need to head back home."

He stared into Fighting Bull's eyes and nodded once more.

Fighting Bull leaned in and kissed him on his right cheek. "I'm sorry." she said. She got up from the bed and headed for the door. Before she exited, she looked back at him. "I'm here if you need me."

He gave a broad smile. She did the same as she left.

It took a few moments for him to get off the bed. As he buttoned up his sleeves, they covered up the barbed wire and avian-themed tattoos on his forearms. He looked up in the mirror. His stomach tightened as he reached for his cellphone and dialed.

"Hi, Mom," Arrowhawk said as he heard his mother's voice on the other line.

"Hi, John John," Tanner Baisden said chipperly. There was a twelve-hour time difference, but one could hardly tell by her tone of voice.

"How is your novel coming along?" Arrowhawk asked.

"I'm actually working on it right now," she said as her voice lightened. "It's coming along ok. I mean, I feel like I should've done this way earlier in life."

"You're only sixty-two mom," Arrowhawk shot back. "You're not dead."

"I know, I know. But I think I let acting pour cold water on my other creative juices."

Arrowhawk gave a stilted smiled. "I see what you're saying."

"I can see the long face in your voice over the phone. Talk to me."

"You know me so well."

"Of course, I spent ten hours in labor with you! I better know you!"

Arrowhawk quickly countered, "But I wasn't as bad as Alan, though!"

Baisden paused briefly before she answered. "That boy gave me fits, during the entire pregnancy, and the twelve hours of labor I had to go through. Heck, he's still giving me ulcers now, with all of the craziness he's gotten in to."

"I know, Mom," Arrowhawk said reflectively. "He's always been a lot to handle."

"Hah! That's an understatement. It was hard enough being a single mom of two superpowered boys. Then, to have one go off and become an eco-terrorist? Yeah. That's, that's just a bit much."

"Believe me, Mom, I know. And to be the FBI brother of the eco-terrorist? It's overwhelming, to say the least."

Baisden cupped her cell phone between her right shoulder and cheek as she continued to type. "You know, after your father and I got divorced, I did my best. I know I couldn't fill the shoes of your dad—especially when it came to teaching you about your Lakota heritage—but I tried where I could."

"Believe me, Mom, you don't have to feel bad about anything." His eyes started to redden as tears began to well up in his eyes.

"But-but I do. I had acting gigs that took me away from you boys. I hated, *just hated* leaving you both in the hands of some immature nannies and au pairs." Baisden paused again. "I'm just, I'm sorry."

"Really, Mom, it's OK. What's going on? I thought I was the one who was feeling down."

"I don't know," Baisden said as she sniffled. "Maybe I'm just getting emotional in my old age."

Arrowhawk's vision started to blur slightly, as the tears began to stream down his face. "Well, mom, I just wanted to tell you that you did your best. I never held anything against you. Know this."

"Thanks, honey," Baisden said as she wiped away her tears. "So, enough of my over-emotional nonsense. How are you doing? What's got you calling at this hour?"

"Well, I..." he stumbled slightly before he continued, "I have some bad news."

Baisden straightened up in her desk chair. "What is it? What's wrong?"

"I wanted you to hear it from me before anyone else." Arrowhawk looked down as he clutched the phone to his ear. "Coryn's dead."

"Oh my God, no!" Baisden cried out. "How did it happen?"

"We don't know exactly, but we believe she was killed by some sort of virus."

"What? Oh my God!"

"Yeah, it's like nothing we've seen before," Arrowhawk said. "I've reached out to my teammate whose ex-wife is a specialist in this stuff. He's already reached out to her for help."

"Ok, has she said anything. Or found out anything?"

"Not yet. We're hoping to find out something soon."

"Ok," Baisden said as her voice shrunk.

"But my friends at the FBI are digging into this as well," Arrowhawk said.

There was a three-minute pause before Baisden responded. "Th-Thanks, hon. I appreciate you letting me know."

"And I also wanted you to know I'm coming home to find her killer."

* * *

One hour later
Surveillance Records Room
PSIA Headquarters
Chiyoda City
Tokyo, Japan

Fighting Bull sat back in a deluxe, swiveling, task chair, as she reviewed the records on Kaori Fujihara's capture. The surveillance footage was grainy, but she was able to run the film through Vigil's remote video enhancement program she downloaded to her computer terminal. The Saisentan / AlphA.I. merger documents were tucked nicely under the computer monitor. Agent Hamato barely made a sound as she walked into the room.

"Hello, Agent Fighting Bull."

"Oh, I didn't hear you," she said as she turned her chair around to look at Hamato.

"I didn't mean to startle you."

"No, it's ok."

Hamato took a seat next to her.

"What are you looking at?"

Fighting Bull pointed to the computer screen. "You see those guys chasing after her. I've run a facial recognition sequence on them, and I can't seem to get a solid match."

"Yes, we tried the same thing before you came," Hamato said as she nodded. "We ran it through our records and Interpol's, but there were no positive matches."

"My teammates back home encountered men who had the same profile," Fighting Bull said as she looked at Hamato. "The ones that Vigil encountered were former U.S. military special forces who all later went to work for PMCs in the U.S."

"Private Military Contractors?" Hamato asked as she leaned forward.

"Yes, do you know of any operations your government is running with any PMC's?"

Hamato shook her head. "We don't use contractors to the extent that America does. They must be extensively vetted before they can operate on Japanese soil. Also, we would never sanction a kidnapping."

Fighting Bull gently rested her chin between the webbing of her right thumb and forefinger. "Point taken, but these men must've been in the country previously to have tracked her down like this."

"Or they may have had someone already here in Japan to do the work beforehand," Hamato said as she nodded at the documents on Fighting Bull's desk. "What have you learned so far?"

"I learned a lot," Fighting Bull said as she swiveled slightly in her chair. "During the mergers and acquisition process it seems they do a thorough background check of all senior level officers in the company."

"On the acquired business or both?" Hamato questioned.

"Both, and as a matter of fact they run through all family contacts as well as associates." Fighting Bull paused briefly with a contemplative look on her face. "That's it!"

Hamato straightened up in her chair. "What?"

"Venturepointe," Fighting Bull said as she quickly grabbed the documents from underneath the computer monitor. "They were the company managing the M&A process. They used their own investigators to vet Fujihara." Fighting Bull carefully thumbed through the document pages. Multiple headings with titles such as: *Investigative Testing*. She came upon the page she was looking for.

"Here she is."

Fighting Bull lifted a page in Hamato's view. A picture of a young woman was paperclipped to it, with the name, Sato Ashido, written underneath it.

CHAPTER TWENTY-SEVEN

FOLLOW THROUGH

Two Hours Later
Shibuya District
Tokyo, Japan

"So, John's back stateside," Conrad said over Fighting Bull's phone.

"Yeah, his head's not in this," Fighting Bull responded as she viewed Conrad's image over the phone. "His cousin was killed. He needs to be with his family."

"And thereby disobeying my direct order."

"Seriously, Alicia, we're back on that again?" Fighting Bull answered from the back seat of the autonomous Lexus sedan she was driving in.

"There's a reason I do things, Cynthia. This is a two-person mission."

Fighting Bull's eyes narrowed. "I can handle this on my own, Alicia. Besides, the PSIA has been more than helpful."

Conrad shook her head. "I don't like it."

"Like I said, Captain, John's head was not in this mission. He wouldn't have been any good to me anyway."

"That's cold, Cynthia."

Fighting Bull recoiled slightly. "I'm not trying to be. It's just, I need him to be on his A-game. If not, then our mission's compromised. Which is something I know you don't want to happen."

"Is that a jab at me, Agent Fighting Bull?"

"No. Never that," Fighting Bull smiled back.

"Anyway," Conrad replied as she tapped on her holo-tab, "tell me a bit more this investigator you're going to see."

"Sato Ashido. Head of Venturepointe's Mergers and Acquisitions investigative division here in Japan. Based on what we've found, she knows the ins and outs of the AlphA.I. / Saisentan merger better than anyone."

"You think she'll talk?"

"We'll see."

Fighting Bull's vehicle pulls up to the Excel hotel's valet station.

"Gotta go, Alicia, I'll update you when I am done."

"Roger that."

Fighting Bull was helped out of the vehicle by the valet as she ended her call. She nodded to the Bell Hops as they opened the doors for her. Fighting Bull eyed the large bank of glass elevators as she entered the hotel's opulent lobby. Within moments she made her way into the elevator and ascended to Ashido's floor.

As the elevator doors opened, she could hear the staccato crackle of energy weapons fire from Ashido's hotel room. Fighting Bull instinctively unholstered her Sig Sauer Pistol from her rear waistband. Her mind raced as much as her body as she sprinted toward Ashido's room. She fired two shots at the handle and lowered her shoulder into the door. Fighting Bull's momentum thrusts the door open. She did a rolling somersault and recovered in a crouched position with her weapon in a high ready position.

Fighting Bull was welcomed by what appeared to be two individuals. Both looked to be no older than twenty-years old. Metallic limbs with unique wiring replaced their arms and parts of their torso. One of the attackers emitted a pulsed energy blast from his hand. The blast grazed Ashido's upended dining table, as she cowered behind it. Fighting Bull cut a glance to the second attacker as sharp spikes began protruding out of the skin of her fingertips. Fighting Bull's eyes widened as she witnessed the attacker's skin spikes fly like projectiles at Ashido's dining table. The spikes tore through Ashido's dining table, grazing Ashido's shoulder.

"Hey!" Fighting Bull shouted at the attacker, temporarily distracting them.

Two bullets from Fighting Bull's Sig Sauer ripped through the attacker's cybernetic trapezius and rhomboids. The attacker screamed and swiveled her body around as she grabbed her back. Fighting Bull quickly leaped out of the way of the spike projectiles that the second attacker launched at her. She struggled to get her footing after slamming into the vertical light fixture next to Ashido's coat closet.

"Dammit," Fighting Bull said to herself as she barely looked up to see a hailstorm of the skin projectiles flying toward her. Three spikes hit Fighting Bull in her right shoulder and arm as she tried to do a left side roll to avoid the projectiles. Thankfully, her Duritium/biosteel microweave clothes absorbed the brunt of the projectiles' impact.

Fighting Bull returned fire on the second attacker. The first attacker shielded the second one with a plasma energy shield that emanated from his cybernetic forearm. The first attacker then released an energy blast with his other hand toward Fighting Bull. As she hurled her body out of the way of the blast, Fighting Bull eyed Ashido trying her best to make her way to the door. The second attacker saw this and fired three skin spikes in Ashido's leg.

"Aaaaagh," Ashido screamed as she toppled to the ground. Sweat beaded up on Ashido's forehead as her attacker raised their hand to fire another round of projectiles at her. She closed her eyes. A loud thump was heard as the second attacker landed to the ground with a bullet wound to the head. The attacker's lifeless body collapsed on Ashido's wounded leg. She quickly used her good leg to kick the dead attacker off of her. Ashido looked up to see Fighting Bull firing her weapon on the first attacker.

Fighting Bull emptied the clip of her Sig Sauer on the first attacker. Her bullets melted as the attacker maintained his plasma shield. Fighting Bull reached into her side pocket for another clip. She looked up to see an elaborate chandelier above the attacker.

"Let's see if this works," Fighting Bull said to herself as she fired at the chandelier above the attacker. The crystalline structure crashed into the attacker. The attacker screamed as pieces of glasses embedded into his ear and next to the cybernetic implants on his temples. As he writhed in pain, the attacker's eyes began to glow.

Fighting Bull saw this and quickly reached for a metal serving tray that fell from Ashido's dinner table. Swiftly, she lifted the tray up to deflect the beams that emitted from the attacker. The energy beams ripped through the attacker's torso as they deflected off the tray. The attacker plummeted to the ground. Fighting Bull, after getting up from a crouched position, walked toward the attacker's body to assure he was dead. After confirming the kill, she walked toward Ashido.

"Stay away!" Ashido screamed.

Fighting Bull motioned her hands in a calming fashion. "It's okay, I'm here to help. My name is Cynthia."

"I know who you are. Just stay away."

Fighting Bull kneeled to tend to Ashido's wound. She pulled a piece of cloth from the damaged dining table to create a makeshift tourniquet. As she applied the tourniquet, Ashido screamed.

"I am so sorry, Ms. Ashido, but this should help slow the bleeding."

After a few moments, Ashido began to relax. "Thank you."

"Please, don't mention it. Do you know who these people are?" Fighting Bull asked, as she motioned to the newly deceased attackers.

"Yes," Ashido replied. "they were sent by AlphA.I."

CHAPTER TWENTY-EIGHT

INTERCONNECTION

October 21st
Office of Senator Matrice Malveux
Hart Senate Office Building
Washington, DC

"What've you got for me, Max?" Malveux asked as she leaned forward against her desk.

"I think we hit the motherlode of data privacy violations with AlphA.I," Golding said as he laid his holotab on her desk. Immediately, a holographic image of documents popped up.

Malveux put on her glasses. "What am I looking at here?"

"These are thousands of consumer complaints of AlphA.I. products violating personal privacy. We've retrieved complaints of peoples' information being used for unwanted targeted advertising."

"It happens all the time. The big tech companies have been doing that for decades. Why is that a big deal?"

Golding pulled his Tactile Holographic Interface Gloves from his briefcase to widen the image. "Difference is that those companies would base it on search query habits. Basically, their algorithms surmised what a person wanted based on how they searched—either through voice or typed prompts. This is different; these consumers didn't even search for the items that they were targeted for."

"So, how did they target them then?"

"Many of the complaints said the advertising that targeted them was based on things they thought about. Even in passing."

Malveux's eyebrows furrowed. "Are you telling me these devices are what? Reading peoples' minds?"

"Yes and no. Kind of," Golding responded. He manipulated the holographic image again to convert it to a slate of various mobile devices. "AlphA.I.'s product development process is held tightly to the vest. Mainly due to proprietary concerns. But it's believed their tech incorporates micronized EEG-like hardware."

"Like what neurologists use?"

Golding's eyes widened. "Yes, but specifically these look at something called Event Related Brain Potentials."

"Speak to me in English," Malveux said as she smiled back at Golding.

"I'm sorry," he responded. "ERBPs are a tool used to measure cognition, perception and attention."

Malveux pointed at the hologram. "Ok, so they're using this tech to read peoples' minds."

"On its own, ERPs can't read peoples' minds, but if tweaked, can essentially track peoples' cognitive centers."

"And read peoples' minds," Malveux responded, completing Golding's thought. "So, how come no one at the FTC or FBI has ever gone after them?"

Golding shrugged his shoulders. "Because there's been no hard evidence. It's all supposition."

Malveux clasped her hands together. "Well, it's a start." She leaned over to her left desk drawer and pulled out a manila folder brimming with papers. "It'll give us something for the CTIT committee."

"Hopefully," Golding responded as he put away the holo-tab and THiGs. "You want to go over the new data privacy legislation now, Senator?"

"Why else do you think I pulled out this massive folder? To work on my biceps?"

Golding eased back in his chair and smiled as Malveux slid over a packet of papers from the folder.

"This legislation is going to ruffle some feathers, Senator."

Malveux nodded. "That's the point. From what you're telling me, AlphA.I. is virtually peering into peoples' minds. And how they've basically taken over our country's technological infrastructure?" She removed her glasses and rested its temple tip against her mouth. "Something needs to be done."

Golding flipped through the documents. "What do you think about us copying the European Union's old General Data Protection Regulation law? Maybe we're being copycats."

"Well, it is the sincerest form of flattery, isn't it?" Malveux said as she pointed to him.

Golding nodded. "That's true."

"Besides, it's way past time we reigned in these companies."

Unbeknownst to them, Golding's holo-tab was transmitting audio data from their conversation to a non-descript van parked a few blocks away in which Stiles listened closely.

CHAPTER TWENTY-NINE

FEEDBACK

October 23rd
Vigil Headquarters
The Mirador
Washington, DC

An incessant buzzing erupted from Conrad's pants pocket as she silently, reviewed the after-action report documents on the Jones family extraction.

She pulled the phone out to see Fighting Bull calling. Conrad laid her phone against the briefing table and Fighting Bull's image projected up from the table's center holographic projector.

"Hey, Cynthia, what's going on?"

"Just wanted to check in so you know I'm not sleeping on the job," Fighting Bull replied with a smile.

Conrad shook her head and smiled. "You know I never have to worry about."

"Appreciate the vote of confidence, Alicia. Well, I've found some more interesting intel."

Conrad cocked her head to the side. "Interesting how?"

"Remember our Venturepointe investigator, Sato Ashido?"

"Yeah, what about her?"

"She was attacked by a bunch of, what appeared to be cybernetically enhanced superhumans. The PSIA's medical examiner's looking into their power origins, but it's believed they're Variants."

"Any idea as to motive?"

"Ashido, and this is according to her, thinks they were sent by AlphA.I. to silence her investigation."

Conrad scratched her head and leaned back in her chair. "But I thought she was the one giving intel to AlphA.I. on Fujihara's daughter?"

"It was part of a comprehensive investigation. As one of the merger partners, AlphA.I. provided strict guidance on how information they required on Saisentan would be provided in order for the deal to move forward. She thought it was just part of the detailed background check. "

"So, she didn't stop to think it was a little odd for them to want such a detailed family history of one of the chief officers of Saisentan?"

Fighting Bull shrugged her shoulders. "I agree. Kind of naïve on her part. But I actually believe her story."

"What else did she tell you?"

"Well, she was looking into both sides' dealings and found some disturbing info on AlphA.I.'s dealings. She eyed a number of transactions going to shell companies that funded unsanctioned research on Variants. Some other ones were involved in illegal surveillance tactics as well."

"So, she was getting too close and that's why she thinks they were after her?"

Fighting Bull nodded.

"Get as much info as you can from Ashido and the PSIA investigation as possible," Conrad said.

"Already working on it. As a matter of fact, Ashido mentioned one of the shell companies is based in Fukuoka—a drone manufacturer. I was planning on checking it out unless you need me back home?"

"No, go for it. We're good here stateside."

"Thanks." Fighting Bull paused for a moment. "Pendleton sent be the after action on the Jones family rescue mission. I'm sorry about what happened."

Conrad shook her head. "Yeah, me too. The only good thing to come out of it was that we were able to extract officer Morial. But we're going to find out who was behind it."

Suddenly, Fighting Bull's holographic image was interrupted by an incoming call. Conrad looked down at her cellphone screen.

"Cynthia, I gotta go, it's my grandmother calling. "

"Ok. I'll talk to you later."

Fighting Bull's holographic image disappeared as Conrad lifted her phone off the table.

"Hi grandma," she answered, as she pulled the phone to her ear. "How are you doing?"

"I had a little break and I just wanted to check on you, my dear," Phyllis Mensah said.

"That's sweet grandma, I appreciate it."

"And" Mensah said, getting ready to make her request known, "I wanted to see how it went with Hanahan."

"I came away with more questions than answers. He said he believed Harold Baltimore was behind my parents' death."

"Eh, I see. Do you believe him?"

"Grandma, I…I honestly don't know what to believe. I went back through the police reports from that day and there was some material that was questionable. I believe that some vital information, like eyewitness reports and salvage reports from the crash site were missing."

"I see," Mensah replied musingly. "What do you plan to do about it?"

"I'm gonna get some answers."

"And he mentioned Harold Baltimore. I remember when your mother introduced me to him. He was not the most pleasant of individuals."

"I agree. But I've also been looking into his company, CoBALT's, activities." Conrad cupped her chin in her hand. "Reviewing my shareholder reports. I believe that they've been into some dirty dealings, but I don't have any hard facts to back it up yet."

"I am certain you will, my dear." Mensah's tone had an unmistakable certainty to it.

"Hah, thanks grandma."

"Have you heard from the twins yet?"

Conrad looked down. "No, no I haven't."

"Don't worry about it Afua, they will call. You are their sister, and in many ways, you have had to be their parent. It's a responsibility I never would wish on you, especially at that young age."

"Huh," Conrad said as she reminisced. "I was just seventeen when they died." She looked down at the papers that were strewn across the briefing table. Her eyes caught a photo of Itrish. "Just like Itrish."

"Who?" Mensah asked.

"She's a young girl who we rescued from a kidnapping but," Conrad paused for a moment, "her would-be kidnappers also took her family and requested a swap."

"And what happened?"

"It all went to hell. They essentially ambushed us and killed her mother."

"Oh, *Awurade*! That's horrible," Mensah replied, with some of her native Akan language spilling into her English.

"Yes, it is." Conrad paused before continuing. "I was thinking about going to the funeral."

"Good, you should go. Have you talked to her since her mother was killed?"

Conrad laughed. "Are you kidding me; that girl has hated my guts ever since I met her."

"Why?"

"Because she thinks I failed her; or better yet failed everyone."

"How so?"

"She said that she saw me, she was excited because there was a black woman with superpowers just like her out in the public."

Mensah nodded her head. "She's right. Being in the public eye, especially in America, you have no choice. You are a symbol to many people Afua, like it or not. Yes, it is unfair, but your nation's history—to some, the few represent the whole."

Conrad tapped on the briefing table before she responded, "But, that's a burden I never asked for."

"It's one you have to accept. No matter whether you want it or not."

CHAPTER THIRTY

THEY REMINISCE OVER YOU

October 25th
Ebenezer Missionary Baptist Church
Chicago, Illinois

The sound of tambourines and drums filled the cavernous sanctuary as the congregation celebrated the life of Clarice Jones. Itrish and her family sat in the front pew as Reverend Ernest Holiday delivered his opening prayer. Her older brother, Magnus, pulled her close to his side. He gave her a tight squeeze.

"You alright?"

"Yeah," Itrish said as she tried to fight back tears. "I'm fine."

Magnus smiled. "Stop lying, I know you, Itrish, and you are not OK."

She glanced up at her brother's warm eyes and was reminded of her mother's own. Itrish could no longer hold herself and began to sob.

Magnus had no other response but to hold his sister closer as tears started streaming down his face as well. Their other sister, Laurel, sat on the other side of Itrish rubbing her back in an attempt to console her.

After Reverend Holiday's prayer, the musical selection, *Going Up Yonder*, was sung by one of the church's choristers. Her rich thunderous voice emanated through the sanctuary. The words of one of the last verses hit Itrish to her core: "I'm going up yonder to be with my Lord." That was it. The impact of the words was too much for her. She excused herself from the rest of the family.

Itrish rushed to the bathroom to try and get her bearings. Her father eyed his daughter as she headed toward the bathroom. He motioned to Laurel.

"Go check on your sister," he said as he tried his best to keep his voice down.

Laurel nodded and got up and quickly made her way past her uncles and aunts at the far end of the pew to go check on her sister.

Itrish grabbed a few tissues from the tissue box centered in the middle of the bathroom counter. She dabbed her eyes dry. Itrish thought about how much she missed her mother, how this did not have to happen. Suddenly, her flood of thoughts was interrupted as the bathroom door flung open. Itrish looked up in the bathroom mirror to see a face she didn't expect to see.

"Hi, Itrish," Conrad said, as she entered the room. She wore a dark skirt dress and black heels to fit the occasion. Her dreadlocks were pinned back to accommodate her wide brimmed Fascinator hat.

Itrish gripped the edge of the counter. "What are you doing here?"

"I came to pay my respects."

"I know that. I saw you in the back." Itrish turned to face Conrad. "I want to know what you're doing here when you know you were the one who killed my mother."

The pain in Itrish's voice was clear to Conrad. She tried her best not to retaliate with a harsh response. "I am so sorry about your mother, Itrish. We did everything we could to get all of your family out safe."

"Well, you didn't try hard enough!" she screamed back at Conrad.

"I understand how you feel, Itrish. But believe me, if I could do things differently, I would have. They had the area outfitted with some Variant power canceling field.

"But what about you? Your abilities still worked, didn't they?"

"Yes," Conrad said contritely.

Itrish pointed her index finger right in the center of Conrad's chest. "Then why the hell didn't you use them?! Don't you have that enhanced mental perception? You could have used that to spot the shooter and stop them!"

The full scope of Conrad's abilities had been kept away from the public's eye.

With the exception of her physical enhancements, no one outside of classified personnel, was supposed to be aware of her Enhanced Mental Perception, which allowed her to have a mental three-hundred-and-sixty-degree view of the field of combat. In essence it allowed her to "see" things behind her and around her up to approximately one hundred yards. All this information was still top secret and only those with access would be aware of this particular ability.

"What? How do you know—"

"I hacked into your headquarters' computer system," Itrish retorted matter-of-factly.

Conrad saw Itrish's eyes beginning to pulsate with a whitish glow. "Look, just calm down, I know you're upset, and I get it." She reached over to pat Itrish on the shoulder, but before she could, her hand started to freeze up. Suddenly Conrad felt lancinating pain course through her body. It was as if someone lit a match in her bloodstream. The pain was unlike anything she had experienced since being augmented. Previous bullet wounds, laser fire, and knife injuries she suffered couldn't match the level of anguish she felt. Immediately Conrad gripped her stomach and dropped to the floor writhing in pain. As she collapsed to the ground Itrish loomed over her with eyes set aglow.

"Wha-what are you doing?" Conrad asked.

"I'm turning all those nanites in your body against you," Itrish said angrily. "I want you to know how I feel right now."

Before Conrad could reach for Itrish, Laurel pushed open the bathroom doors. Itrish, surprised by her sister's sudden appearance, suddenly dropped her control over Conrad's nanites.

"Oh my God, Itrish! What are you doing?" Laurel demanded as she ran to help Conrad. "Are you ok?" she asked Conrad.

The pain Conrad experienced began to subside. She slowly pushed up off the floor, as Laurel grabbed her right arm to help her up.

"I'm better now," Conrad responded.

Laurel glared at her younger sister. "What the hell were you doing, Itrish?"

Itrish started to slink back as her older sister castigated her. "I don't know. I guess I got upset and lost control."

Laurel looked back at Conrad. "Look, I'm sorry miss." She then took a better look and recognized that it was Conrad. "Oh, my goodness, you, you're Captain Conrad."

Conrad nodded. Laurel's response at that point then shocked Conrad. She gave Conrad an overwhelming hug. Initially Conrad recoiled a little bit but then relaxed.

"I can't thank you enough," Laurel said with tears in her eyes.

"Really? But your mother—"

Laurel waved her hand to interrupt Conrad. "My dad told me what happened. You saved him and my little brother and for that I will always be grateful. I know you did your best to save my mom."

"I don't know what to say," Conrad replied.

"Look it wasn't you who pulled the trigger. It was those monsters who captured my family."

Conrad looked away from Laurel for a moment before she locked her gaze back on her. "Thank you. Thank you for understanding."

Laurel gently patted Conrad on her shoulder. "No, it's you that we have to thank." She then turned to grab Itrish's arm. "Come on, let's go."

As they left, Laurel waved back at Conrad while Itrish looked away. The bathroom was once again quiet as Conrad was left alone.

CHAPTER THIRTY-ONE

OFFICE SPACES

Fukuoka Tower
Fukuoka, Japan

Fighting Bull scaled the side of the Fukuoka Tower in the dark of night with the aid of the adherens points on her uniform's gloves and boots. Its electrostatic contact points allowed her to scale the building like an arachnid. It was retrofitted to fill in actual office space into the originally designed glass façade. She adjusted her modified PVS 7-2-night vision goggles as she inched closer to the AlphA.I. front company's office floor.

Fighting Bull tapped the side of her goggles to switch to pure infrared vision. As she scanned the area, her thermal scans came up with nothing. She gently pulled a laser glasscutter from the tactical webbing vest and used it to cut out a hole just big enough for her to slide through. Just before the cut-out piece of glass hit the floor, Fighting Bull quickly snagged it with her finger pads. A slight spark was emitted from her fingers as the adherens points' electrostatic charge kicked in to make the glass stick to her fingers like glue.

She slid her body through the glass opening and quickly rolled onto the carpeted floor below. Fighting Bull quickly threw a metallic disc at the motion sensor just above her. On contact the disc released an epoxy resin that engulfed the sensor, rendering it useless. Her feet barely made a sound as she moved from the office's open foyer into the CEO suite in the back of the office. Little did she know the visible motion sensor was not the only one present.

"What have we got here?" Fighting Bull said as she entered the CEO suite. In front of her was an array of LCD screens, holographic monitors, and a computer console at the center of the office. She walked over to the console and typed on its touchscreen keyboard. She reached into her webbing to retrieve a sleek, silver jump-drive device and plugged it into a USB port embedded within the console.

"Thank you, Aaron, for the tech," she said to herself as the device started to break down the computer system's firewalls. Rapid images appeared both on the multiple screens and in holographic images. It was almost impossible for Fighting Bull to process everything she saw until something flashed by that caught her eye.

"The fuck?!" she blurted out. She tapped the console's touchscreen keyboard to pause the image. Fighting Bull scrolled through the personal data---her personal data. As both a member of Vigil and a CIA agent, her personal information was highly classified. What she witnessed was explosive because her whole life story seemed to be streaming on screen. Everything from her blood type, family medical history, to even her most frequented websites were clearly there on display. Not only that, but she saw physical and capability assessments that were done when she is originally assessed to be part of the team. Curious as to how much more data AlphA.I. had, she slid her fingers across the keyboard and pulled up data on other members of Vigil.

As she continued searching the files, she came across the schematic of a global satellite array. She saw the word, *Tessellation,* above the image. Her eyes darted across the text next to the schematic. What she saw gave her pause. The beeping sound of the jump drive snapped her back into focus. As Fighting Bull pulled the device out of the USB port, she heard a whirring sound behind her. She yoked her head around to see a sextuplet of weaponized sentinel drones inches away from her. Immediately she ducked underneath the computer console as the drones opened fire.

She was pinned behind the console and the large glass window in front of her. As automatic bullets continued firing on her, Fighting Bull knew she had only seconds at best until the billets tore the desk to shreds and her along with it. Fighting Bull fired her Sig Sauer pistol at the glass window. The glass shattered and Fighting Bull hurled herself out of the building like a rocket. The drones quickly followed her as she hurtled to the ground from nearly 500 feet in the air.

Fighting Bull felt the bullets whiz past her ear as she frantically reached into her tactical webbing to retrieve her grappling gun. She twisted her body to aim the gun at the side of the building. As the compressed air grappling disc exploded, it landed at her intended target—a glass window façade on the fortieth floor. Fighting Bull crashed through the glass as the grappling rope retracted. She bounced into the lower-level office lobby and into a fountain pool.

The drones' buzzing sound was heard as they entered the office space after her. They scoured the area, trying to pick up Fighting Bull's thermal signature. Her heart was beating rapidly as she struggled to hold her breath in the fountain pool. After hovering around the expanse of the office, they came up empty and began to turn back to go to their point of origin. Suddenly, Fighting Bull emerged from the fountain pool and unleashed a salvo of bullets that tore through the drones, leaving nothing but metal and plastic in her wake.

CHAPTER THIRTY-TWO

TECHNICAL MALFUNCTIONS

October 26th
Silver Line Train
McLean, Virginia

"Senator Daniels, I wish we had taken ground transport instead of the Metro," Paul Ornette said to the junior senator from Florida.

"Are you kidding me, Paul?" Nicolette Daniels retorted with a smile at her head of security. "This is the best way to get to work. Besides, it beats getting stuck in traffic on the Washington Parkway."

Ornette glanced around as more people hopped on at the West Falls Church Metro—creating a tight squeeze within the train car. His eyes caught a digital ad above his handrail that read: *WMATA now runs on CYBRA.*

"It's just that it's hard to ensure your safety in places as like this." Ornette then nodded at one of the other members of Daniels' security detail. He in turn wove through the crowd, trying to eye any suspicious people.

"Look, I love mingling with the people," Daniels replied as she patted Ornette on his shoulder. "We don't have anything like this in Tampa, so it's nice to ride around with real Americans."

"Yeah, real Americans who can also pose a threat. You know what happened in early 2021."

"How could anyone forget? But that's why we passed legislation to fund personal security for members of congress for that exact reason. Besides, I have your team protecting me. What do I have to worry about?"

The train quickly departed the West Falls station. As the train barreled along its tracks, it started to accelerate to such a speed it jostled all the occupants within Daniels' train car. Ornette quickly grabbed Daniels by her shoulders to keep her from falling to the ground.

"Thanks, Paul," Daniels said as she settled herself. "What is going on with this thing?"

"I'm not sure, Senator," Ornette replied. He pressed his earpiece. "Does anyone have eyes on the train operator?"

Within seconds, another security agent responded. "This is Reece, I'm on it, Paul."

The security agent moved swiftly to the lead train car. He tapped on the operator's door and it quickly opened.

"What's going on here?" Reece asked the operator.

"I don't know. The ATP sub-system started to act up. Usually I can manually over-ride it, but it's not responding."

"ATP? What are you talking about?"

"It's the train's Automatic Train Protection system—basically controls the trains speed and keeps in running the way it's supposed to. But it just started going haywire."

"There's no kill switch on this thing?"

Just as those words left the operator's mouth, the train derailed, spilling over into the Metro Center platform, killing the throng of people on the platform as well as those aboard the train. Their blood curdling screams reverberated throughout the cold concrete walls of the underground station.

* * *

The Harlem Community Townhall
Harlem, New York

Senator Bryan Bence's back stiffened up as he listened to one of his constituents detailing her concerns.

"Senator, I've been a truck driver for over twenty-five years. About a year ago, when the new self-driving grid was put up, I was excited. Thought it could cut down on accidents and get rid of all the idiot drivers on the road. Little did I know I would be one of those drivers taken off the road because of the automated trucks my company put in place thanks to AlphA.I."

Bence put his head down. "I'm so sorry, Ms. Charles. I don't know what to say."

"Tell us you'll do something," another man with graying hair blurted out. "Since AlphA.I. took over, we've lost a lot of jobs in our community."

"I understand, Mr. Langston," Bence responded. "Since we've started the autonomous grid nationwide, there've been a lot of drivers' jobs lost."

Langston put up his right hand defiantly. "No, it's not just that. Grocery clerks, fast food, and even warehouse workers have been taking a hit ever since AlphA.I.'s autonomous robots have taken over."

"I know," Bence replied as he walked toward Langston. "That's why my colleagues and I are investigating their practices."

"Good," Langston retorted. "Because all this automation is killing us."

Bence's assistant then whispered in his ear. He nodded. His assistant then turned to address the audience.

"Thanks everyone for coming out, but the Senator has another engagement he has to get to."

Bence and his assistant bid farewell to the moderator and Bence waved to the crowd as he was escorted out of the room.

As they exited the building, Bence's black sedan automatically drove up. His assistant walked over to the driver's side window and immediately his face was scanned by the car's facial recognition program. Initially nothing happened, then the assistant leaned in closer. Three of the four passenger doors opened.

"They have a point," Bence said to his assistant as he made himself comfortable in the backseat.

Bence's assistant nodded as he sat in the front driver's seat. "I agree, looking at the stats, this district's been hit hard. "The assistant retrieved a holo-tab from his briefcase and passed it back to Bence. "The unemployment rate jumped from 15 to 35% after AlphA.I.'s New Road Initiative was implemented."

"I see," Bence responded as he saw the holographic states. "Mostly blue collar and service workers took the biggest hit. "

Their car's navigation sensors then picked up worsening traffic patterns on 125th street and eased them on to an alternate route.

"That's why they're all upset," his assistant said. Hopefully, we can provide them with some relief."

"There will be relief," Bence said with a hint of fatigue. As he said these words, he could feel the tires accelerating and the car swerving.

"What the hell is going on?"

Bence's assistant frantically tapped on the dashboard touchscreen to try and over-ride the driver-less function. Suddenly, the screen went black, while the driver's side telemetry showed the speed picking up rapidly.

"I don't know, Senator! I'm trying to over-ride it, but nothing's happening."

Before Bence could respond, their vehicle veered head-on into an oncoming semi-truck.

Meanwhile, miles away, Huntley looked on her computer screen at the closed-circuit video of the mangled remnants of Bence's vehicle. She tapped on her cellphone and instantly Stroud's image appeared onscreen.

"Sir, Daniels and Lance are off the board," she said with a macabre smile.

CHAPTER THIRTY-THREE

ASSET PROTECTION

October 30th
AlphA.I. Research Facility
Los Alamos, New Mexico

The New Mexico sun shone brightly through the large office windows of AlphA.I.'s director of DNA technologies, Dr. Brian Breckenridge. He wore a polished, tailored, deep blue colored suit with pristine wing tipped dress shoes. Breckenridge was about 5'7" with a slight paunch in his stomach. His wood-grained walls were aligned with his multiple framed degrees: Bachelor's and master's degrees from Boston College, an MD from Harvard, and a PhD from MIT.

Breckenridge sat back in his chair, looking through the large window, transfixed on the natural beauty of the mountainous region just outside. Suddenly, his meditative nature reflection was interrupted by a holographic alert on his computer.

"Breckenridge," he answered.

"Sir, Mr. Stroud is here," his assistant responded.

"Ok, bring him in." He could feel his stomach tighten.

Within moments, Stroud was ushered into Breckenridge's office.

"Welcome, Dennis," Breckenridge said as he offered Stroud a seat.

"Brian," Stroud responded as he stiffly took his seat. "I'll get to the point.

The viral delivery system is garbage."

"Dennis, I'm sorry about what happened with those kids. That version of the virus was cytocidal—killing off the cells instead of producing mechanized cell conversion." He paused then started again, "That's why I need the Adept. She's the missing piece to make successful widespread conversion possible."

"I know. With her ability to digitize organic material for radio wave dispersal, she was the last piece that we needed."

Breckenridge tapped on the surface of his smart desk and immediately a holographic image of a constellation of low earth orbit satellites popped up. "Yes, that was the original plan. The Tessellation satellites would have broadcast the digitized virus. The Adept would've been the perfect vector to deliver the Singularis virus worldwide—even in those not in a contact with an AlphA.I. product. But since we couldn't acquire her, we have to cut our loses and look for an alternative."

"We still have the secondary options in play."

"True. But those are secondary, Dennis. I thought we had broader ambitions?"

"We do," Stroud said as he leaned forward. "Not just with Singularis but also with the Backdoor Protocol."

"Indeed," Breckenridge said with a smile.

"Anyway, that's not why I'm here. I wanted to check on our Asset."

"Yes, I understand." Breckenridge said. "As a matter of fact, one member of my team was about to brief me right now."

Two knocks were heard at the door. Both men turned to see lead research assistant, Kacey Sullivan, standing in the doorway.

"Come in, Kacey," Breckenridge said as he waved her in.

She entered the room gingerly. Breckenridge got up from his chair and walked toward her as he motioned toward Stroud.

"Kacey, I think you know our CEO, Mr. Stroud."

"Of course!" Sullivan replied as she reached out her right hand to greet Stroud. "It's an honor to meet you, sir."

"Pleasure is all mine," Stroud responded politely.

"You had something to show me?" Breckenridge asked as he walked back to his seat.

"Yes, of course."

Sullivan moved quickly in Breckenridge's direction. She removed a 9 x 11-inch touchscreen tablet tucked underneath her right shoulder and placed it on Breckenridge's desk. The device tapped lightly on top of his smart desk. The desk's glass surface immediately lit up as it interfaced with the tablet. The desk's embedded holographic projectors came alive and a schematic of the CYBRA network came up in view of Sullivan and Breckenridge.

"Sir, the network roll-out has been going well overall. Especially the nationwide autonomous driving grid. So far we haven't had any push back from NHTSA or local governments."

"We have to thank Mr. Stroud for that," Breckenridge said, nodding in Stroud's direction.

"Thank you for that, sir," Sullivan said as she turned in Stroud's direction.

"No problem," Stroud replied with a smile.

Breckenridge tapped on his smart desk and suddenly the CYBRA network schematic changed to an aerial map of Washington D.C. with strategically placed large red 'X' marks throughout. "Tell me about D.C. It seems like we've been having a lot of issues with the roll out there."

"We've also, had reports of the CYBRA telecommunications and wireless nodes malfunctioning, with some customers stating that they heard an audible scream from their devices before they malfunctioned."

"Any unplanned fatalities from this?" Stroud asked.

"Thankfully, none reported so far. But there were serious injuries," Sullivan responded.

Breckenridge shook his head sadly. "What has initial analysis shown about the malfunctions?"

"We've run a thorough system-wide diagnostic, and nothing has come up. The software is not the problem." Sullivan looked down. "It was an outside threat."

"Was it a breach by Blackhats?" Stroud asked as he sat up in his chair.

Sullivan shook her head. "No, we've ruled that out. Plus, there have been no ransom demands. From our analysis, the program is being affected by random code alterations."

"But you said this was coming from an outside threat," Breckenridge said. "Only one of our technicians could do something like that!"

"Yes, sir, you're right," Sullivan responded as she raised up her hands palm side out. "We've gone through everyone's system activity and they're all clean. The only person who could do this is the Asset."

"Damn!" Breckenridge slammed his right hand against his smart desk. He turned away from Sullivan and began to pace with his arms folded behind him. "I thought she was heavily sedated, damn near comatose. How was she able to over-ride our system?"

Sullivan shrugged her shoulders. "Honestly, sir, I don't know. We've had the medical staff increase her propofol drip, but we have to be careful."

"But we planned for this, Kacey. The neural interface was supposed to keep her from taking over control of CYBRA while still operating it. That was the whole point—we need her abilities to work under our command."

"Well," Stroud said, finally interjecting. "This seems to be as good a time to check on our Asset."

"Definitely," Breckenridge said. "You can follow me, Dennis."

* * *

Sublevel Seven
AlphA.I. Research Facility
Los Alamos, New Mexico

AlphA.I.'s facility transport system was one of the most state of the art—utilizing advanced magnetic levitation tracks. The system encompassed an intricate tube system with enclosed passenger transport carriages. It took only three minutes for the pair to get from the third level of the expansive facility to the lower sublevel. Breckenridge and Stroud exited the transport carriage. They were met by a ruddy faced man with long sideburns, unkempt, sandy brown hair, a wrinkled button-down shirt, and a just as wrinkled lab coat. The rims of his wire-framed glasses fit him so poorly he constantly had to push them back over the bridge of his nose. The man's eyes widened as he saw both men exit the transport carriage.

"Hi, Morton," Breckenridge said as he firmly grasped Morton Stanwell's hand. Stanwell shook Breckenridge's hand and swiftly turned to Stroud.

"Mr. Stroud! It's a pleasure to meet you," Stanwell said as he reached to shake Stroud's hand.

"Pleasure's all mine," Stroud said.

Dr. Stanwell had been the oversight director of the CYBRA program. Where Breckenridge provided the overall guidance, Stanwell provided the execution. His appearance could fool anyone into thinking he was the messy, disorganized, nerd stereotype, but that was far from the truth. Stanwell had multiple PhD's in bioengineering and biomechanics along with an MD from Harvard. In fact, had been a practicing neurosurgeon, years prior.

"Hey, Brian," Stanwell replied in his chipper Midwest accent. "What brings you both to my neck of the woods?"

"We're being sabotaged, and we need to see what's going on with the Asset." Breckenridge said bluntly as he buttoned up his sport coat.

Stanwell motioned behind him, in the direction of an oval, stainless-steel sliding door with large, rectangular windows. Beyond the oval door was the hub of CYBRA network operations, a large workspace with multiple clinicians and technicians working on various computers, touchscreens, and holographic interface devices. The exterior was deceptive because one could not tell how deep the hub went. In the middle of the workspace was a spiraling stairwell that the trio took down to a lower level to see the Asset. Upon their arrival, Stanwell walked to a frosted glass door with a biometric scanner embedded where the door handle was supposed to be. He pressed his right hand on the scanner and a brief beep was heard. A slight hissing sound was emitted as the glass door slid open.

Two vertical glass tanks were apparent as the door opened. The one to the right was empty and the one on the left held a young woman adorned in a sleeveless bodysuit. The tank she was suspended in was filled with a hazy, yellowish liquid. Multiple wires and IV lines coursed in and out of her body. Her mouth and nose were covered with a mask that resembled something similar to a CPAP mask. She had what appeared to be hundreds of thin filament wires entering the base of her skull, funneling into an oval, robotic device above the tank that resembled the many-headed Hydra of Greek mythology. To the left of the tank was a raised control panel that jutted approximately three feet from the ground. It had a screen with scrolling data points as well as a touchscreen keyboard with keys shaped like puzzle pieces. The lettering on the keys transitioned from English to Japanese.

"How has she been doing so far?" Stroud asked as he walked to the control panel. He hovered over the control panel; and looked on the screen to see the name, "Kaori Fujihara, subject one."

"She's been doing ok," Stanwell said, as he walked over to the glass containment unit. "With the exception of the intermittent delta spike in her brain patterns, she's been pretty much stable."

"And nutrition-wise?" Breckenridge asked.

"We have her on TPN and we've been running regular labs daily. She's fine."

"Call Augustus, we may have to transition her to a G-tube in order to get her gut working again."

"Got it," Stanwell answered.

"Kacey tells me our Asset's breached the CYBRA system multiple times," Breckenridge said.

Stanwell looked away briefly. He loosened his collar before responding, "That's right. We've been trying to up her sedation to counter this, but if we overdo it, we could actually inhibit her technopathic abilities. Even worse, could kill her."

Stroud folded his arms and lifted one hand up to his chin, ponderously. "And the neural-interface's protocols were working appropriately?"

"That's the thing, sir," Stanwell began to say. "She has been able to figure out ways to rewrite the protocols, so we are constantly updating them. It's a twenty-four hour a day job just to keep up."

"Ok," Stroud said as he looked up at the young woman suspended in the liquid. "This electrolyte bath facilitates the data transference to CYBRA, correct?"

"Yes, and that's not a problem at all," Stanwell said. "We just have to make sure the solution is refreshed every twelve hours."

Stroud turned to Breckenridge. "How do we get her to…cooperate?"

"We can ramp up the data transference rate and cut back on the sedation," Breckenridge replied.

Stanwell pushed his glasses back over the bridge of his nose. "But sir, doing that could cause severe amount of pain for the Asset."

"It's a necessary evil," Stroud said as he looked the young woman up and down in the suspension tank. "I've been soft on her out of deference to Saro Fujihara. But we are on a schedule, and there are things way more important than this young woman's comfort."

Stroud glanced over to the empty containment tank next to Fujihara's. "Plus, the Adept won't be joining us anytime soon. So, the Asset is all we've got right now."

"Yes, sir," Stanwell said, as he bowed his head slightly.

Breckenridge and Stroud turned to walk out of the room. Stanwell turned to look at the suspension tank and lowered his head before he filed out of the room as well. Within the tank, Kaori Fujihara's eyes cracked open sluggishly. They scanned the expanse of the room through the haze of the electrolyte solution to see that she was alone. She glanced over to the empty containment tank next to hers. Kaori's eyes emitted a cool, azure glow before she faded out of consciousness once more.

CHAPTER THIRTY-FOUR

KINDRED

November 1st
Jones Household
Hyde Park
Chicago, Illinois

Itrish stared out the window at the police cruisers just outside her door and wondered if her life would ever get back to normal. She had been spending a lot of time in her room lately. Principal Gowan had given her bereavement time off from class. Several weeks had passed since her mother's death, but to her it seemed like yesterday.

Her phone buzzed. She picked it up off her nightstand and saw it was Malik Anderson. She cancelled the call. Anderson had been trying to contact her daily, but she could not bring herself to answer. Itrish pulled her comforter over herself and curled up in her bed like a hermit. Before she could comfortable, her father knocked on her door.

"Hey, can I come in?" John Jones asked with a warm smile.

"Yeah," Itrish said as she peaked her head over her blanket.

"It looks like this place has been hit with a hurricane now, child," he said as he took notice of how unkempt her room was.

Itrish shrugged her shoulders as she slid through the content on her touchscreen phone, without using her fingers. Her father removed the phone from the top of her blanket, where it was nestled comfortably.

"Look, Itrish, we need to talk," he said as he moved her phone to her bedstand.

She sat up more attentively as her father took a seat at the edge of the bed. "What did you want to talk about?"

Jones sighed. "We haven't really talked since your mom's funeral. With all the busyness of arranging the funeral and out of town visitors and whatnot, I haven't gotten the chance to really talk to you."

Itrish folded her arms across her chest as she listened. She curved her back against her headboard.

"I know you and your mom were really close," Jones paused to gather himself, "And I know how much you miss her. Believe me darlin,' I miss your mother so much."

Itrish looked at her father with tears welling up. "Dad, I don't know what I'm going to—" she could barely complete her sentence before the tears started to stream down her face. Her father reached over to hug her. He squeezed her so tight it felt like she would burst. Itrish didn't care though, she was in the loving embrace of her father, and in that moment, it was all she needed.

"I know my little Trish, I know," Jones whispered as he comforted her.

"It's like she was just here and now she's…she's just gone," Itrish said as she started to ease herself from her father's embrace. "This was never supposed to happen, not because of me."

"Now, now, don't go blaming yourself, Trish," her father said in an assuring tone. "This is no parts your fault."

"But it is!" Itrish exclaimed as she spread her hands out. "If it weren't for me, those guys—whoever they are—wouldn't have gone after you." Itrish curled her knees up to her chest.

John Jones lovingly patted his daughter's bent knees. "You don't know that."

Itrish encircled her curled knees with her arms. "Sometimes I hate having these powers dad. I wish I was just like everybody else in this family."

"Stop that now," her father said as he quickly rebuked her. "I don't ever want to hear that type of talk ever come out of your mouth." Jones pointed his right forefinger sternly at Itrish. "What you can do is a blessing from God up above. I know that in my heart of hearts. The Lord gave you to us for a reason. And he gave you these gifts for a reason."

Itrish acquiesced politely, although not thoroughly convinced of her father's pronouncements.

"Now, that's why your mother and I wanted you to go to that VERGE academy. It's not that we didn't want you living with us during the work week, but we knew that school would help you best use your gifts."

"I know, Dad," Itrish said. "But it can be a bit too much. Like, I don't want to be me anymore. Or at least that part of me with powers."

Jones nodded slightly and placed his hands in his lap. "I appreciate that, but your powers are part of what make you, uniquely you. There's no one else in the world with all the personality and whit like you. And what does the Good Book say? 'My yoke is easy and my burden light.' He's never going to leave you with more than you can bear."

She wiped away some tears. "That's funny, that's what mom would say."

"Where do you think I got it from darlin'?"

Itrish smiled at her father's statement. "But I wish Vigil had gotten you all out safely. They have a part to blame in mom's death."

Jones shook his head from side to side. "No, they don't at all. I saw firsthand how brave they were trying to save us. They did their best."

"Well, I still think they could have saved her." Itrish adjusted her Pandora bracelet as she continued, "At least Captain Conrad could have saved her."

"Is that why you darn near killed the woman during the funeral?"

"You knew?!" Itrish said with wide, sad eyes.

"Of course, Laurel told me everything."

"Sorry," Itrish said plainly as she looked down. "I was wrong. And I shouldn't have done what I did. But I was pissed, Dad."

"You're darn right, you shouldn't have," Jones said with earnestness. "They are heroes and deserve to be respected."

"But Dad, they're fascist. They have cameras and drones all over the place. They feel like they have the all-seeing eye! Like they're God or something."

"And that's why you broke into their satellite, hmm?" Jones gave her the look that a father gives a child when they know what they have been up to. "C'mon now, I wasn't born yesterday, my love. And you will be getting a punishment by the way, I just haven't thought about what yet."

"I know what you're saying, Dad, but I'm not sure," Itrish said as she looked down in her lap.

"And I know," Jones started to say, "that Vigil is trying to make things right to track down your mother's killers."

"That's their job."

"That's true, but if they didn't do their job, your brother and I wouldn't be with you today."

Itrish nodded.

Jones looked at his *Fossil* wristwatch, a gift from his late wife. "Wow, it's already two. I'm almost late for my meeting with your uncle." He leaned over to kiss his daughter on her forehead. "I have to go; I'll see you a little bit later." Jones stopped by the doorway and looked back before leaving his daughter's room. "Remember, I love you very much."

Itrish looked up and responded, "Thanks, Dad. I love you too."

As he left, she contemplated what he said about Vigil being heroes. She initially thought the same thing about the team, but lost faith.

Itrish reached for her phone, which her father had placed on her bedstand and began scrolling through hands free. As she scrolled through, a text message from an unfamiliar number came through that read: "35.8800 °N, 106.3031 °W."

"What in the world?" Itrish exclaimed to herself.

The text kept repeating itself multiple times.

"Ok, I've about had enough of this." Itrish placed her fingers on the phone's screen. The contact points of her fingers on the screen along with her eyes emitted a white glow. She tried to go into the code to find out from where the repeated texts were coming from. Her mind was plunged into a world full of numerous data points and binary code. This was the Cyberscape—the space where all data, communications, and electronics traveled. She frequently did this when she wanted to back track to see the source of various programming code.

As her mind sifted through the random number sequences, she came across a code sequence that was unlike anything she had seen before. It was as if the code itself was alive, constantly shifting and adapting, not static like most other code she had interactions with. Itrish reached out to try and alter the code but instead the alternating zeroes and ones in the code assemble themselves into the shape of a woman. Itrish never saw code act like this before in her life. Itrish started to pull herself out, but before she could, the coded woman reached out to touched Itrish's forehead. Itrish's mind was instantly filled with digitized images of the AlphA.I. headquarters in Los Alamos, Kaori Fujihara's profile, the containment tank of the electrolyte bath, and Breckenridge. She was overwhelmed to the point where she felt like her head was about to explode. Before she reached her breaking point, she was released from the grip of the coded woman.

"Oh my God!" Itrish yelled as she pulled herself out of the Cyberscape and back into the real world. As her heartrate started to slow down, she collected herself. She then looked at her phone and said to herself, "I know what I need to do now."

PART FOUR

DILIGENCE

(OWO: ADINKRA SYMBOL OF DILIGENCE)

CHAPTER THIRTY-FIVE

LOOK SHARP

November 5th
Office of the Director of Security
Presidential Palace
Delohar, Lemalia

Terrell Morrison's face was weary with exhaustion. His wood finished; metal reinforced desk was clogged with papers. The dim overhead light illuminating the photos made it harder for him to fight off the heaviness he felt on his eyelids.

"A penny for your thoughts, Agent Morrison," Legaud said as he knocked on the partially opened office door.

"Oh yeah, I'm sorry Mr. President I didn't see you come in," Morrison said as he tried to fight off a yawn. "I was just running through some potential candidates for your new security detail."

"And how is it coming along?" Legaud asked after closing the door behind him to take a seat across from Morrison. He sat in an opulent looking brown leather chair with Duritium coated armrests.

Morrison lifted the photos in Legaud's direction. Legaud pulled out his glasses from his inner right chest pocket and placed them squarely over the bridge of his flat nose. Morrison noticed Legaud's hands were sparsely covered with age spots as he reached for the photos. He brought the photos closer to his field of view.

"I think these are some of the top ones," Morrison said as he reached over the top of the photos arranged in Legaud's hands.

"I see," Legaud acknowledged as he shuffled through the photos. "Have these men all gone through the background check?"

Morrison nodded. "They've gone through the whole review process. I even ran them through our personal Vigil database, and they were all cleared."

"Yes, your team does have extensive surveillance and data resources," Legaud replied. He then leaned back in his chair and rested his hands lightly on the armrests. "I have to thank you Agent Morrison, for your willingness to help my country rebuild."

"Not a problem at all, Mr. President," Morrison replied as he leaned forward.

"I'm glad you're able to do this before your deployment with us ends. When is Captain Conrad expecting you back?"

"Just over three weeks from now. I would've stayed longer but there are some things brewing stateside she needs me back for."

Legaud nodded and slid his right forefinger and thumb underneath his glasses and pressed against the bridge of his nose.

"Are you ok, Mr. President?"

Legaud waved his hand. "I am alright. Thank you for your concern. I am just tired, that's all." He placed his glasses back into his front chest pocket and rubbed his eyes. "I've always wanted this, but I never thought I would face this much opposition."

Morrison nodded in agreement. "Yes sir, especially with rebuilding a country and assassination attempts left and right."

"You also forgot," Legaud said as he pointed in Morrison's direction, "having the United Nations playing overseer during this whole process."

"Yes, you're right!" Morrison laughed.

"I've always just wanted my country to be its own," Legaud said as he sat up in his chair. "No outside interference from greedy international corporations with their own self-interest in mind, nor from an international community with its own ideas of what Lemalia should be."

"I understand, sir, but you have to admit sometimes you need help," Morrison said. "Look at what's going on with us."

"This is a special case, Agent Morrison. It was a heavily funded group who aimed to dominate our natural resources. If your team had not discovered their intent, they would have duped you all into fighting against us as opposed to for us."

"That's true," Morrison replied as he stroked his chin. "But you can't shut yourself from the world completely, Mr. President. Or else you turn yourself into another North Korea."

Legaud crossed his legs in a figure four shape as he leaned back in his chair. "Come now, Agent Morrison. We would never do that. All I want is for Lemalia to control its own destiny."

"I can't disagree at all," Morrison replied.

"We have seen," Legaud began to say as he looked out at the sunset through the clear glass office window, "many other countries, mostly African ones, that were taken advantage of by outside forces. And their destiny is not their own." Legaud paused to look at Morrison. "Many of my very own people hail from across the African continent."

"That's right," Morrison said. "I read that many Lemalians' ancestors originated from parts of Africa."

"That is correct," Legaud said with a head nod. "To me, what's happened on the continent is a cautionary tale."

As Morrison and Legaud continued their conversation, two armed Lemalian security officers walked toward Morrison's office. They nodded in the direction of the guards that were stationed there to signal that they were ready to relieve post.

After the original guards cleared the area, the new guards unscrewed the ends of their rifle buttstocks. They remove foldable breathing masks from the hollowed-out buttstocks. The guards then removed four small metallic balls with side ports, from the thigh pockets of their tactical pants. The pair placed their breathing masks on and took a half kneeling position. They aimed their weapons at Morrison's door—firing four rounds into the door handle. One of the guards kicked it open and flung the metallic balls into the room. They bounced three times before they emitted teargas from the side ports.

Morrison's Secret Service instincts kicked in. As he hurled himself in Legaud's direction as the molecular structure of his cells altered into the density of titanium. Bullets deflected off Morrison's body as the attackers fired off their weapons in Legaud's direction. Morrison reached over with his free hand, while still covering Legaud, to grab Legaud's chair. He hurled the chair in the direction of one of the guards. The chair's impact sent the guard through the damaged doorframe and onto the floor just outside of the doorway.

Morrison's eyes burnt from the teargas. He could barely see the second attacker reload his rifle with a new magazine. The second attacker trained his rifle in Morrison's chest.

Morrison yelled as the bullet hit him squarely in the chest. "Aaaaagh!" The bullet's impact sent him hurling into the adjacent wall. Thinking quickly, he grabbed the edge of his toppled over desk to shield himself from more bullets. The desk's reinforced frame helped to blunt the impact of the weapons fire. Bullets grazed Morrison's forearms as he covered himself with the table. The attacker then turned his rifle in Legaud's direction. Seeing this, Morrison lifted the table and rushed toward the attacker. The attacker's eyes widened as he tried to furiously fire off his weapon in Morrison's direction. It was too late. Morrison slammed the attacker against the side of the wall with the table, squashing him like a pancake. The attacker collapsed to the ground unconscious.

Morrison ripped the gas mask off the unconscious attacker and turned to Legaud. He carefully placed the mask on Legaud's face, as he himself choked on the fumes. After Legaud was fitted with the mask, Morrison slung him over his shoulder As they made a hasty exit out of the office. Once safely out of the smoke-filled office, Morrison gently placed Legaud against the wall that faced his office.

"Are you ok, sir? Have you been hurt?" Morrison asked Legaud as he checked him for any wounds.

Legaud shook his head.

"Good, I'll need to borrow this." Morrison then took the mask off Legaud and placed it on himself. He then walked back into his gas filled office. He checked the area once more to make sure there were no other attackers. A quick scan of the area showed there were none. Morrison leaned over the unconscious body of one of the attacking guards. He carefully examined the serial numbers and manufacturer engravings on the rifle and magazines to see the name, *Cygnus Weapons*.

CHAPTER THIRTY-SIX

CONFRONTATIONS

Capitol Rotunda
Capitol Building
Washington, DC

Senator Malveux gazed over the closed caskets of her colleagues. She lingered by Bence's casket and traced her hand across its brass exterior. As she pressed her hand against the casket her mind shifted back to the image of her old friend, Constance Akosua Conrad. Malveux's mind suddenly flashed back to the mangled car that her best friend's body was found in after the horrendous accident that took her and her husband's life. Malveux was startled by a sudden light hand on her left shoulder. She quickly turned to see senator Royce. The latter removed her hand as she saw Malveux glaring down at the appendage.

"Hey, Matrice."

"Sylvia," Malveux replied in a monotone.

Royce glanced down at Bence's casket and then her eyes cut away to Daniels,' which was right next to it. "It's sad what happened to Bryan and Nicolette."

"Yes," Malveux nodded. "Yes, it is."

"I'm sure this must be awfully hard for you. I know you and Bryan were awfully close."

Malveux fanned her fingers over Bence's casket. "You know, Pat and I were in the same freshman class."

"I've heard," Royce replied. "They called your class the gifted ones. Passed some of the most consequential legislation of the past decade."

"That's right," Malveux responded. "And don't you forget it."

"I won't." Royce moved in closer to Malveux's ear. "Look, I know this might not be the best time, but I have to ask. Have you thought about dropping this privacy legislation?"

Malveux flinched back with furrowed eyebrows. "Excuse me?"

"Look, we've lost two of our own. Is it really worth it to move this out of committee where it might not have a chance?"

"So, essentially you want to give AlphA.I. a free pass?"

Royce backed away and shook her head. "No, that's not what I'm saying. I'm just thinking that we're grieving right now and maybe we should put this on the backburner for a while."

Malveux's back stiffened. "Drop DEPA? Hell no! That's not what Nicki or Bryan would've wanted. They would've wanted us to pursue the best interest of the American people."

"Matrice, I'm just making a suggestion."

"Do me a favor. Don't."

Royce's face began to get flush. Suddenly, Malveux's assistant, Golding, walked in behind the two women.

"Excuse me, senator."

Both women turned to Golding.

"May I speak with you, senator?" Golding asked as he nodded in Malveux's direction.

"Sure," Malveux replied.

"Well, I'll let you two talk. I have some things I have to attend to," Royce said as she slinked away.

Malveux glared at her as she walked off.

"Don't stare too hard, senator," Golding said. "You may burn a whole in the back of her head."

"If only I had that superpower," Malveux shot back playfully. "What've you got for me?"

Golding pulled his holo-tab from under his arm. "I've had some of my team look into the NTSB investigations into Bence and Daniels' accidents."

Malveux grabbed the holo-tab. "From initial reports they said they were all related to system malfunctions within the CYBRA operating system."

"Right, but we've been able to uncover more about what's going on."

Golding reached over to the holo-tab and tapped the screen. "The CYBRA system had a brief glitch in the autonomous grid running the New York traffic system as well as the one controlling the DC Metro. But prior to Senators Bence and Daniels' accidents, CYBRA'S autonomous grid had a malfunction rate of zero percent."

Malveux shook her head. "I knew there was something going on." She cut her eyes to Golding. "Get me everything you can find beyond the NTSB investigations. I want interviews with engineers, programmers, whoever. We are going to find out who killed my friends."

CHAPTER THIRTY-SEVEN

ALLIANT

November 16th
Vigil Headquarters
The Mirador
Washington, DC

"First of all, I want to apologize," Itrish Jones said quietly, in display of her father, as well as Vigil and their support staff. The young woman sat at the head of the large meeting table. Itrish brushed her braids off her shoulder and continued. "For breaking into your satellite system and then for…" her eyes locked in on Conrad, "…for rejecting your help."

John Jones patted his daughter on her shoulder. "My daughter and I came back to formally thank you for your help. For saving my boy and myself." He looked in his daughter's direction and wrapped his right arm around her. "My Itrish and I were talking, and she told me she found out something that may be important to you." Jones looked at his daughter with a smile.

"I think I know what those guys who were after me wanted," Itrish cleared her throat before continuing, "A few days ago I thought my phone was being hacked, and God knows I wasn't having that," she said with a smile as she looked around the table. "So, I tapped into the Cyberscape."

"The what?" Pendleton asked as he sat up in his chair.

"Cyberscape. It's kind of like cyberspace but can only be tapped by certain individuals," Blankenchip said in response.

"Hold it there infobot," Itrish said as she raised her hand in Blankenchip's direction. This noticeably annoyed him.

"It's a little more than that," Itrish said. "Besides, the term cyberspace came from a sci fi writer, not a scientist." She shifted back to her chair. "Most of our communications run through fiber optic wires, servers, wireless routers, cable cords and internet-enabled devices. But that information gets filtered into the Cyberscape. It's where all the code and quantum digits come together to translate into usable data. It's also how, according to my teachers, I access integrated communications networks."

"Ok," Conrad said, as she inched forward in her chair. "So, what did you find?"

Itrish looked in Conrad's direction. "Another technopath, like me." Her eyes drifted down at the table. "May I?"

"Sure," Conrad responded.

Itrish placed her right hand on the table, light emitted from the contact point between her hand and the surface of the table. A glowing circuit-like design emanated from her hand as she interfaced with its elaborate electronic system. Immediately, an elaborate holographic display of the Los Alamos landscape popped up right above the center of the table. She stood up from her chair and reached into the image with both hands and extended the image out like one would expand the image on a touchscreen phone. She manipulated the image down to a multi-building compound nestled in the midst of a thicket of foliage.

"These coordinates were sent to my phone." A digital image of the numeric latitude and longitude appeared above the image as she spoke. "And the message was sent from within this building." As Itrish continued to manipulate the image, and the marquee on the building read, *AlphA.I. Research Center.*

"It was an SOS message from a girl---what I could tell from the data stream was projected into the Cyberscape---she's being held hostage somewhere in that building."

Conrad turned to Pendleton, "I need specs on that building right away." She then turned her gaze in Itrish's direction. "Who's this girl?"

"Her name is, Kaori—I think I'm pronouncing it right—Kaori Fujihara."

Pendleton's eyes caught Conrad's. "There's our missing girl." He turned in Itrish's direction. "Can you tell us anymore about who captured her?"

"The data stream wasn't completely linear. She was processing all this to me..." Itrish rubbed her hands forcefully. She looked remorseful as she continued speaking, "and she was in pain—like she was being tortured."

The team members took pause on this somber news. Conrad tapped hand on the table. "All right ladies and gents, we know what we need to do." She looked behind her to one of the support staff and motioned with her right hand.

"Please escort Ms. Jones and her father to the waiting lounge so we can discuss next steps."

"No! I want to help," Itrish shouted in protest.

"That's out of the question," Conrad said. "It's too risky and I damn sure am not going to risk another innocent life in the field."

"Then don't put me out in the field. I can help you guys remotely. All I need is access to your tech."

Conrad shook her head. "I can't."

"Yes, you can! Please, I need to do this," Itrish said adamantly.

Conrad rested her chin on her clasped hands and sighed. "I will need your dad's permission."

"What about security clearances, Alicia?" Pendleton noted.

"This is an emergency situation so I'm sure that can be expedited."

"Ok we'll see what we can do," Pendleton said in a skeptical tone. He pointed in Itrish and her father's direction. "You two can come with me, please."

As they were being ushered out, Itrish paused and looked in Conrad's direction. "Can I talk to you for a second?"

Conrad nodded and got up from her chair. The two of them separated themselves from the rest of the team.

Itrish clapped her hands in front of her as she began speaking. "I wanted to speak to you directly. Because I wanted to apologize to you specifically."

Conrad shook her head slowly. "No need, Itrish."

"No, I have to. There was no excuse for what I said to you." She paused and looked down. "And what I did to you."

"It's ok," Conrad's eyes looked away briefly. "I know how it is to lose my mom, too."

"But I want you to know I'm doing this because of this girl. And that's all."

Conrad nodded. "Understood."

CHAPTER THIRTY-EIGHT

LINKS IN THE CHAIN

November 18th
FBI Field Office
Los Angeles, California

Johnson pulled out his holo-tab and placed on his THiGs. "This is what we have so far." Johnson expanded the holographic image that emanated from the holo-tab to reveal various images of the mangled, metallic bodies of Arrowhawk's cousin as well as the other UCLA beta testers.

Arrowhawk flinched at what he saw.

"We've gotten intelligence from our informant regarding AlphA.I.'s experimentation on Variants."

Arrowhawk threw up his hands. "Excuse me, I thought this was about Coryn's killers."

Johnson looked at De La Vega before manipulating the image again. This time, the images of the dead students transitioned into a picture of Coryn along with bulleted text. Arrowhawk saw that Coryn's image appeared partially faded out.

"What's wrong with the resolution on your holo-tab. Coryn's image is washed out."

"She's not washed out," De La Vega responded, "she's manifesting."

"Really?" Arrowhawk responded.

Johnson nodded. "She was a spectral cloaker. Basically, able to manipulate light waves so that they pass through her."

"Essentially making her invisible, "Arrowhawk said, completing Johnson's thought. "She never told me."

"You and I both know how it is to manifest," De La Vega responded. "Maybe she wanted to keep it a secret."

Arrowhawk turned to look back at his colleagues. "So, what's the plan?"

Johnson pulled out three manila folders from his desk drawer and laid them atop his desk. "Our informant also provided us with intel regarding not only AlphA.I.'s recruitment of Variants but also their experimentation on them."

"Why? What've we done to them?"

Johnson looked up. "We? I don't follow."

Arrowhawk shook his head. "Sorry, I'm talking about us Variants."

"Excuse me, just a resident normal human being here," Johnson said with a smile.

De La Vega patted him on the back. "It's ok, we'll make you an honorary member of the club."

"I appreciate that," Johnson chuckled. He then used his THiGs to manipulate the Coryn's holographic image to that of Stroud's. "To go back to your question John, it's because they think—specifically Stroud thinks—that Variants are an ungodly aberration. Only useful for the advancement of 'real' human beings. Good for nothing more than labor or experimentation." Johnson said as he pointed at Stroud's image.

"Asshole," Arrowhawk mumbled as his balled fist crackled with energy.

"Well, he blames us Variants—all of us—for what happened to his family during the Minneapolis event," De La Vega responded.

"Right, and it doesn't hurt that they've invested in all of the VERGE schools across the country. They have access to almost every young Variant in America."

De La Vega pointed to Arrowhawk. "Exactly." She then pulled a sheet of paper from one of the manila folders on the able. "We've tracked a lot of the missing Variants in the greater L.A. area and cross-referenced them with

VERGE academy rosters. About ninety percent of those missing were former VERGE students."

"Ok, so not only are they killing us, but their kidnapping us as well," Arrowhawk responded.

"Well, that's where our informant came through," De La Vega responded. "She provided us with a list of AlphA.I.-run sites where we suspect they've housed some of those captured Variants."

Johnson turned in Arrowhawk's direction. "We've just got a search warrant approved for one of their sites."

"What are we waiting for?" Arrowhawk asked excitedly.

* * *

Three hours later
El Canyon Industrial Park
7306 Laurel Canyon Boulevard
Los Angeles, California

A large team of FBI agents surrounded Cameron Conductors, a front company for AlphA.I. The strike team leader motioned for his team to be silent as he reached for the doorhandle. As soon as the strike team leader's hand touched the doorhandle, the door and front façade exploded. Flames and debris eviscerate the agents closest to the agents nearest to the explosion. Arrowhawk's eyes lit up and he quickly erected an alternating hot-cold energy shield.

Two individuals emerged from the facility as the smoke began to clear. They appeared to have what appeared to be cybernetic appendages. One of the individuals immediately crouched and laid her hand to the ground. Immediately, the ground underneath the FBI agents began to collapse around them. Thinking quickly, Arrowhawk expanded his energy field to create a protective cocoon. He then shifted the orientation of the cocoon to move the agents out of the way of the collapsing ground beneath them.

The second individual raised up his cybernetically enhanced arms to release a salvo of direct energy fire at Arrowhawk's cocoon. He cringed as he felt the attacker's energy blasts pummeling his force field.

De La Vega tapped her earpiece. "John, let me out."

Suddenly a space in the energy cocoon opened and De La Vega landed hard on the crumpled concrete below her. Seeing the second cybernetic attacker turning in her direction to fire, De La Vega's right hand immediately became coated with a film of ice. Shards of crystalline ice projected from her fingers and lodged into the attacker's cybernetic arm. The attacker screamed as he retracted her damaged arm. De La Vega's lower eyelids developed an icy film as she looked at the first attacker. As if on cue, streams of ice crept up the attackers' legs and moved up so fast they couldn't move. Within what seemed like seconds, the first attacker was encased in ice.

Meanwhile, the second attacker struggled to remove the ice shards from her cybernetic hand. Just as he's able to pull the shards out, she felt a cold sensation rapidly moving up his legs and toward her torso. The attacker was in shock as he saw De La Vega shooting a cold blast at her. Before he could move another inch, he was encased in ice.

Arrowhawk released the cocoon and the rest of the FBI agents, after they gathered their bearings, moved to secure the site. The fires were easily doused by De La Vega.

As the agents entered the facility, they saw multiple bodies in containment units. Most of them looked to be those in their teens and early twenties.

"My God," Arrowhawk said in exasperation as his eyes traipsed across the rows and rows of bodies.

De La Vega walked toward one of the agents rummaging through the vast amount of hardware and computers.

"You find anything good, Martinez?"

"From what it looks like, cybernetics is on a level we've never seen. It also looks like they had a failsafe protocol that activated these sentry Variants and triggered the wired explosives at the entrance."

"And from the wreckage it looks like they also wired the area with explosives," De La Vega added.

"John, Cristina come over here," Johnson shouted from the head office in the facility. The pair quickly came to Johnson's side.

"What've you got?" De La Vega asked as she quickly entered the room. Johnson was in front of a partially damaged computer with an eighty-inch screen mounted against the back wall.

"I think we've hit on what AlphA.I.'s been purposing for these Variants," Johnson responded. "These are the programming protocols built into their cybernetic neural implants." Johnson clicked on a folder on the large screen. The screen shifted to black initially. After a few seconds, images began to crystallize onscreen. All three of them looked up in trepidation as the images fully formed.

"*Jesucristo*," De La Vega blurted out.

CHAPTER THIRTY-NINE

SECURITY BREACHES

November 19th
Office of the Director of Security
Presidential Palace
Delohar, Lemalia

The bright sunlight beamed through Morrison's office window and reflected off his new computer screen. He felt a brief tinge of pain in the center of his chest where he was hit with the armor-piercing round. Even though altered to a titanium density, the bullet might have killed him had he not worn his Duritium biosteel microweave uniform.

"Hello, Terrell."

Morrison looked up to see a familiar face knocking on his temporary door.

"Do you have time to speak?" Minister Prashad asked.

"Of course, I do," he said as he waved her into the room. "Please take a seat." He offered her a hard-plastic porch chair that he had to make do with temporarily, and placed it right beside his desk. "It's always nice to see you, but to be honest I thought one of your assistants would have come down."

Prashad gave a warm smile as she leaned toward Morrison. "I don't mind it at all."

She took a seat and lightly placed the manila folder tucked under her arm, on to her lap. She sat up formally in the uncomfortable plastic chair. Prashad surveyed the yellow caution tape and evidence markers that still arrayed Morrison's office.

"Are you comfortable working in an active crime scene?" Prashad asked.

"You know what, I didn't even notice. I've been so busy trying to nail down who's behind these attacks."

"Well, I have retrieved the files that you requested," Prashad said as she placed the manila folder on the desk, next to Morrison's bent right elbow. He angled his chair toward her and flipped open the folder.

"I believe all the details of the opposition fighters are in there," Prashad said as she pointed to the pages in Morrison's hand. "What are you thinking so far?"

"Hmmph?" he said looking up at Prashad, "Oh, I'm sorry. I was trying to see the connection between one of the men who attacked my office and the rest of the UPF resistance fighters." Morrison turned to his computer keyboard and started typing in the name at the top of the page, 'Mycran Stocault.' As he cross-referenced the name across Vigil's database, Prashad leaned over to see that was on his screen.

"Did you get him into interrogation after he was captured?" Morrison asked as he turned to Prashad.

She nodded. "We did. He admitted involvement with the UPF."

"But my question is, who is supplying their equipment? They specifically targeted me with armor piercing rounds. They knew what they were doing."

"I agree," Prashad responded. "We've traced some of their funding sources." She reached over Morrison's arm and pulled a form from the manila folder. "They trace back to multiple shell companies."

"Any common thread with the previous attackers?"

"Yes, their funds were routed through the same network of banks." Prashad smoothed out the side of her skirt as she reached into her side pocket to retrieve her phone. "We have looked into many of the customers who bank with these institutions. There was a pattern of a few common players." She tapped on her phone screen and lifted it up to Morrison's view.

He cocked his head to the side. "Oh, that's interesting. What about the UPF's trainers? Since we shut down the Network, their training through Dankwah's people was cut off. So, I'm wondering who has taken over that function."

"That part is almost as interesting as the funding pattern. We have found that some rogue UN peacekeepers have been providing training to the UPF resistance."

Morrison's eyes widened. "What? Are you serious?!"

"Yes, Terrell," Prashad said with a stern voice. "There have been links between a dozen UN soldiers and the UPF resistance cells." She looked down and tapped on her phone screen. "In fact, these UN soldiers have been supplying weapons to these UPF cells."

"And let me guess, Cygnus weapons were the ones they were using."

"Yes, how do you know?"

"They used Cygnus weapons to attack the president and I," Morrison said as he folded the manila folder closed.

CHAPTER FORTY

ESCAPE PLAN

November 24th
AlphA.I. Research Facility
Los Alamos, New Mexico

Bledsoe was welcomed by a deluge of technological wonders as she stepped through the lobby entrance. A vast array of holographic monitors, mini transport drones and individuals with model BCI headpieces surrounded her. One of the mini drones buzzed up to her and flashed a cascading light across her face.

"Welcome, Dr. Moore, our staff will be with you shortly," an automated voice said from the drone.

The lower hub of the drone had an opening that resembled a disc drive. Out of it came an ID tag. Bledsoe grabbed it.

"OK, thank you."

She made her way to a circular sectional couch just a few feet away. She carefully scanned the area before tugging her right earlobe.

"Captain, do you hear me on this line?" she asked over her nearly invisible earpiece.

"You're loud and clear Karen," Conrad replied 30,000 feet above, in the Avian.

"I think Cynthia's facial prosthetics did the trick. It fooled their biometric scan."

Indeed, Bledsoe spoke the truth. Fighting Bull came through once again with updated facial prosthetics from the CIA stockroom. These were improved from the ones that team used over a year and a half ago when they infiltrated the NSA. These new prosthetics incorporated Duritium-based peripheral particles which not only molded to the face perfectly, but also threw off any deep mind powered facial recognition devices.

"You're right. Even thousands of miles away, she's still helpful," Conrad said with a smile.

Bledsoe looked at the ID tag. "'Dr. Louisa Moore?' Who came up with that alias?"

Conrad looked to Blankenchip to her left. "Your knight in shining armor."

"Shut the hell up, Alicia," Blankenchip retorted as he reviewed the schematics of the facility on a holotab.

"Well, I like it," Bledsoe said with a sweet voice over her earpiece.

Blankenchip shot a mean look over to Conrad. "Thanks babe. I figured a Louisa Moore, a former research PhD in integrative artificial intelligence was a great cover."

Conrad walked up to the pilot's cockpit. "Hey Regent, how soon until we are at the drop point?"

Chiu reviewed his telemetry and turned to Conrad. "We should hit the HALO drop window in five minutes."

Conrad nodded. "Perfect. Gives me time to deploy the drones."

She tapped on her wristwatch. The drones immediately deployed from the Vigil SDS. As the drones entered the atmosphere, Conrad put on her interactive glasses. With them, she saw the aerial footage in picture-in-picture-like fashion from the drones as they entered earth's atmosphere.

Meanwhile, Bledsoe waited quietly in the main lobby. It didn't take long before a young woman wearing a pencil skirt and conservative blouse, emerged from the main elevator.

"Good morning, Dr. Moore," she said as she extended her hand to Bledsoe. "I'm Mr. Breckenridge's assistant, Lanette. He's been looking forward to meeting you. Follow me, please."

She ushered Bledsoe into the elevator. As they walked through the sliding doors, Bledsoe was surprised to see they were entering a transport carriage with a clear glass exterior. The carriage immediately shot through a winding array of magnetic levitation tracks.

After a few moments, Bledsoe was guided into Breckenridge's office.

"Dr. Breckenridge will be with you shortly," his assistant said.

"Thank you," Bledsoe responded.

Bledsoe's eyes scanned Breckenridge's office as she sat down. Her phone beeped. She pulled it from her suit's jacket pocket. When Bledsoe lifted the phone's screen close to her face, she was met with infrared and structural schematics of Breckenridge's office from the recently deployed reconnaissance drones. The information keyed on his smart desk as the system access point.

Breckenridge walked in from his side office door to meet Bledsoe. After greeting pleasantries, Breckenridge got down to business.

"So, I must say I am impressed with your credentials," Breckenridge said as he scrolled through Bledsoe's information on his holotab. "So, what can I do for you?"

"Well," Bledsoe said, "Dr. Breckenridge, I am interested in getting out of academia and more into the commercial arena."

"I see," Breckenridge replied. "As someone who was formerly in academia, I know how unfulfilling it can be sometimes."

"That's right. Plus, I have heard such great things about your company's pioneering work with brain computer interfaces," Bledsoe said as she leaned forward to rest her right arm on Breckenridge's smart desk.

His ears perked up. "Well, I appreciate the compliment, but I wouldn't say we were pioneering—more like revolutionary." As Breckenridge continued to speak, he failed to observe that Bledsoe slipped a small circular disc underneath his smart desk.

Meanwhile, high above Bledsoe and Breckenridge, Conrad and Blankenchip made their HALO jump. As they tumbled through the air, Conrad received the streaming data from Breckenridge's office on her glasses. The data detailed the location of each lab and facility. Within seconds she had a lock on Fujihara's location.

After they descended, they quickly dispatched their parachutes. Conrad and Blankenchip made their way to a large exterior cooling fan at the base of the facility. Conrad saw a service entrance next to the fans. She pulled a small acetylene torch from her tactical webbing to cut through the doorhandle.

As they entered, Conrad's interactive glasses picked up Fujihara's location close to a half a mile down. Blankenchip tapped her shoulder. He pointed to her glasses and then to his helmet. She nodded and tapped the side of her glasses to immediately transfer the data from them to Blankenchip's HUD.

As they moved in formation, they saw four security guards in the bisecting hallway. The guards were relatively underwhelming—wearing blue polo shirts with the AlphA.I. logo on it, and khakis. Their only offensive threat were the Sig Sauer P-225s pistols in their thigh holsters. The only peculiar thing about them were dermal neural monitors affixed to their foreheads.

Conrad peaked her head around the corner where the guards walked, she noticed surveillance cameras. She looked back at Blankenchip who was behind her and motioned at his left forearm gauntlet. Without hesitation, he removed a black metallic disc from his gauntlet and placed it against the wall.

"You're up, kid," Blankenchip whispered over his armor's communications system.

Hundreds of miles away, in Vigil's Satellite Command and Control Center, Itrish sat in Director Davis's control chair with the headpiece firmly attached to her head. Davis stood next to her and a detailed visual of Conrad and Blankenchip's location popped up on screen.

"Gotcha, grandpa," Itrish responded.

"Why you little—" Blankenchip started to protest before he was cut off.

"Uh-uh uh, watch the language around minors," she responded smartly.

Itrish's eyes let off a whitish glow. Immediately all of AlphA.I.'s surveillance cameras and sensors went blank.

"You guys are clear."

"Thanks, Itrish," Conrad whispered. She motioned with her two fingers to Blankenchip for him to take the two guards on the left and she would take the two on the right. He nodded.

With an unbelievable speed, Conrad ran up behind the guard on the right and grabbed him by the neck with her right hand. With the left she struck him behind his right knee. The man collapsed awkwardly on his back. She finished the combination with a quick punch to the face which took him out of action. His partner barely moved fast enough to reach for his pistol. Conrad's right boot connected with the second guard's jaw with a round house kick. The man swiveled around and hit his head against the adjacent wall. He was left with a huge gash on his forehead and without consciousness. Unnoticed was the blinking light on the guard's neural monitor.

Meanwhile, Blankenchip's approach was more direct. He fired two tranquilizer rounds into the necks of the two guards on the left side of the hallway. Both guards slumped hard to the ground.

"You know," Blankenchip said as he holstered his rifle, "that girl has some mouth on her."

Conrad smiled. "Did she bruise your ego, Aaron?"

"She didn't bruise nothing. I ain't old, that little girl is just being a brat."

"You know I can hear you," Itrish interjected over the communications line.

Conrad smiled at the remark and then motioned for Blankenchip to follow her.

The pair made their way to the back entrance of Fujihara's holding cell. They saw a small touchpad next to the small, oval, stainless-steel door. Conrad attached a disc to the touchpad. A small beep and a hissing sound were heard as the doors opened.

Before them was Kaori suspended in the containment unit. Conrad's eyebrows furrowed as she saw how frail Kaori looked in the containment unit.

"Stop looking mad, we have a job to do," Blankenchip said. He quickly rushed to the control panel next to her containment unit. His armor's glove released a small wire into the panel's USB port. The glass cover of Kaori's containment unit opened up and released a small flood of the electrolyte bath that she was suspended in. Conrad grabbed the head gear and facial mask that encumbered Kaori as the latter collapsed in her arms. Conrad cradled Kaori's bald head that was littered with insertion ports.

Conrad then affixed a dermal translator on her neck before asking Kaori, "Are you alright?"

"Yes," she responded slowly in English.

Conrad ripped the translator off her neck and continued to remove the IV lines and wiring that ran through Kaori's body. She took a small, thin poncho packaged in a three by three-inch plastic sleeve from her tactical webbing. Conrad unfolded it and draped it over Kaori.

Blankenchip looked over to Conrad. "I've uploaded all of the info to our server."

"Ok let's get out of here," Conrad said as she draped Kaori's arm around her neck.

As the trio turned to exit through the back entrance that they came from, they encountered six more security guards. These guards were better equipped than the initial ones they first encountered. These guards wore silver exoskeletal harnesses and carried directed energy weapons.

"Halt!" the lead security guard said, with his weapon pointed inches from Conrad and Fujihara. Conrad mulled which of the many ways she could take the man out. Before she could react, Fujihara grabbed the guard's firearm. It immediately stacked around her arm like construction equipment. The weapon's barrel immediately shifted positions from pointing in Conrad and Kaori's direction, to the guard's.

The pupils of Kaori's eyes came alive with an azure glow as she fired the weapon into the guard's chest. The blast thrusted him back ten feet. She then turned her attention to the other guards. They were too slow to react before Kaori completely dismantled their exoskeletal armors. Piece by piece, their armors started to pop off as they short-circuited. The resulting short-circuiting of the armors electrically shocked the guards into unconsciousness.

Blankenchip glanced around at the felled guards and back at Conrad.

Conrad raised her eyebrows and tapped her earpiece. "Regent, we've acquired Fujihara. We'll meet you at the rendezvous point."

CHAPTER FORTY-ONE

PINPOINT

November 25th
Evidence Room
FBI Field Office
Los Angeles, California

"John, do you have everything you need?" De La Vega asked over the phone.

"Yeah, I do Tina. The info we found at the El Canyon raid was game-changing."

"I agree. And time sensitive. They've already deployed their programed Variants."

"Have you sent out teams to go after them?"

"We did but got there too late. They've pretty much vanished without a digital trace."

"Which makes sense when you have the number one tech company in the world covering your tracks," Arrowhawk acknowledged.

"Did you already send the info to your team?"

Arrowhawk nodded as he rode in the back of the autonomous car taking him to the airport. "I did."

"Well, please be safe."

"Will do. What are you and Lee doing?"

De La Vega looked at her partner as he tapped away on his keyboard.

"Working on tracking Lawson's killer."

"Good luck. I'll be talking to you soon."

"Take care, John."

De La Vega clicked her phone off and plopped it on the table that was loaded with mounds of information they had gathered on the Lawson family's killing, along with the UCLA student murders. She took a seat in front of her laptop.

"How does this all fit?" Johnson muttered to himself within earshot of his partner. They had been wading through the mounds of info on the Lawson case for hours. His voice clearly echoed his fatigue.

"That's what we're here to find right, Lee," De La Vega replied as she peered from behind her laptop.

"We have the Palo Alto PD's info on Doug Lawson and his family," Johnson said as he lifted a thick manila folder jam-packed with paper. "But we don't have any DNA from the killer, clothing fiber samples are non-existent, and their home surveillance records were wiped."

De La Vega scratched her head. "Did we ever find out from the home security company how that happened?"

"They said it was done on-site, but they believe whoever did this used a layered hacking approach to break into their servers and erase the evidence."

De La Vega pointed at the manila folder. "Can I take a look at that?"

"Sure," Lee responded as he handed over the folder.

De La Vega opened the folder and carefully scrutinized every sheet and photograph within. Her eyes settled upon the letterhead of the home security company. She guided her left forefinger down the contents of the document.

"Do we know who supplies their servers?"

"Wait a sec," Johnson typed away on the computer. "I had Martinez and her team look into it. She uploaded pics of their findings onto the database." Johnson paused again for a second. "Ah, here it is."

He turned his laptop around in De La Vega's full view. The pictures of the manufacturer and serial numbers of the servers were visible. De La Vega tapped on the screen.

"Who own's this company, 'SynchronServ'?"

Johnson slid the laptop back around. "Give me a sec, Cristina," he said as he typed on his keyboard. "You're not gonna believe this."

De La Vega leaned in. "What is it?"

"It's a subsidiary of AlphA.I."

De La Vega nodded her head in response. "Why am I not surprised? They would know exactly how to break into one of their own systems." She looked on to her screen, "And from what we gathered from that Joyce Wu girl, AlphA.I. would certainly have a hand in making sure any whistle blower would be dealt with—even killed if necessary."

"We have an association but no evidence of a direct killer," Johnson exhaled in frustration as his red hair spilled over his forehead.

"Not quite," De La Vega replied. "There was a forward-thinking Palo Alto police detective who canvassed the neighborhood to request video footage from the Lawson's neighbors' security systems. Their department was gracious enough to send it over."

Her heart raced in anticipation as she tapped on her keyboard. She pulled a piece of grainy footage.

"You see that, through the back door," De La Vega said to Johnson as she turned her laptop around to him.

"Yeah, it's hard to tell but by the body frame it looks like a female. Can you image enhance it?"

De La Vega obliged. "I can't get a good look at her face. It looks like some awkwardly shaped mask."

Johnson pointed to the image, "Yeah, looks a little disfigured. Run it through Ultima and see if you can get a three-sixty-degree extrapolation."

After the image rotated around, they could see that mask resembled a ski-mask.

"What's that?" Johnson asked as he pointed to the dark blue sedan feet away from the assailant.

"It's not parked in the usual spaces, and they only had two cars, which were parked in the garage," De La Vega said as she folded her arms and leaned back in her chair. "That's got to be the killer's vehicle."

De La Vega tapped on her keyboard to enlarge the image of the vehicle. "Looks like a late model Ford sedan—definitely fake plates but there's a locator sticker in the bottom corner of the windshield."

She enhanced the image of the sticker. "Bingo, the car was a rental, through Intrepid Rental Car, in Oakland."

* * *

November 26th
Intrepid Rental Car
Oakland, California

"This is the transaction record from the blue Ford Focus you asked about," the rental car manager said as he looked on his computer screen. De La Vega and Johnson stood behind him as they looked on at his screen.

"May I?" De La Vega asked as she reached for the desktop computer's mouse.

"Sure," the manager stated as he rolled his chair out of her way.

She scrolled through the transaction record. "It shows a company card from Aegis Parts was used?"

"Yes, that's the card that was used to secure the rental," the manager replied.

Johnson, who stood behind De La Vega, asked, "Now who picked it up?"

"Oh, we delivered to their location. They never came in."

"Where was it?" Johnson asked.

"A place in the waterfront warehouse district. My employee said he handed the keys off to a security guard at the fence and left."

De La Vega and Johnson looked at each other with knowing looks.

"Let's see who owns Aegis Parts," De La Vega said as he nodded at Johnson.

He pulled out a small laptop from his shoulder bag and ran the name 'Aegis Parts.' Within a few seconds his screen illuminated with one name, AlphA.I.

PART FIVE

SINGULARITY WAVE

(NKONSONKONSON: ADINKRA SYMBOL FOR CHAIN-LINK)

CHAPTER FORTY-TWO

CELL INFILTRATION

November 30th
UPF Safehouse
Ansora, Lemalia

Under the cover of darkness, the Lemalian Tactical Action Group moved silently on approach to their target. The UPF rebel safehouse was nestled within the lowly populated mountainous Ansora region. It made for an ideal hideaway from which they could launch attacks. TAG leader, Denevan Esaal, took point for the ten-man team, which included Morrison.

They positioned themselves in the surrounding thicket of brush just outside of the safehouse. The TAG leader surveyed the building's exterior with his tactical night vision goggles. Its perimeter was lined with multiple Jeeps and bastardized cybernetic armors left over from the civil war. Just outside of the dilapidated garage, adjacent to the safehouse were three tactical Hummers with the white logo of the United Nations emblazoned on them. Two pairings of the TAG split off from the main group.

Esaal observed the sentries stationed at the safehouse entrance. He radioed the rest of his team. "Team one is in position. Team two are you in position?"

"Yes," the second team leader responded.

Esaal tapped his earpiece once more. "Team three are you in position?"

"Yes sir," the third team leader responded.

Esaal glanced over to Morrison to his right. He nodded back at Esaal. Esaal put up his right fist. Immediately, all the men on their team firmly placed on their gas masks. As he emerged from the brush, Esaal hurled three flash bang grenades in the direction of the building entrance.

The loud explosion of flash bang grenades confused the gaggle of UPF sentries. As the rebel insurgents tried to recover, they fired their weapons haphazardly, in a vain attempt to counter their attackers. The action was ultimately fruitless as they were cut down by a hail of bullets from the Lemalian Security Forces' assault weapons.

After clearing the sentries, Esaal motioned at the front door. Within seconds, two men with a battering ram emerged from the group. They moved in quickly after crashing through the door. Meanwhile, the second TAG unit moved in from the rear of the building, while the third team approached from the western side.

Seeing that they were overwhelmed, a quadruplet of UPF insurgents retreated further into the safehouse. Morrison, along with the forward TAG unit, advanced into the building. They quickly followed the insurgents through the poorly lit hallway. The insurgents promptly turned the corner at the end of the hallway. As the TAG unit made the turn as well, they were welcomed by an onslaught of armor piercing high caliber bullets. Thankfully, Morrison wore a specialized reinforced tactical jacket on top of his Duritium/biosteel microweave uniform. He easily shielded his men with his molecularly altered, titanium body.

Morrison punched the lead rebel through the side of the wooden doorframe that led to a second side room. He turned to the rebel to his right and grabbed his rifle. Morrison flipped the barrel of the rifle around and swatted the rebel in the face with it. One could hear the blood curdling sound of his jaw cracking as the rifle's buttstock connected with his face. The blow's impact sent the second rebel into the side of an adjacent wall lined with weapons.

The last two rebels quickly pulled the pins off the grenades they had hidden in their tactical vests and flung them. Morrison slapped one of the grenades back in the direction of the rebels. The resulting blast sent them through the adjacent wall. The second grenade landed just feet in front of Esaal. Morrison twisted his body around and hurled himself on top of the explosive. The blast elicited a horrible booming sound. Surprisingly, Morrison's body and layered outer garments absorbed a majority of the impact. He was left with a scorched, but intact, tactical jacket.

Morrison dusted himself off as he got up. He and the rest of the TAG unit scoured the remainder of the room. He tapped his earpiece to radio the other members of the team: "Team two have you secured your area?"

"Yes, the western sector of the building is clear," responded the second team leader.

"How about you, team three?"

"We have secured the rear section of the building," the third team leader answered.

"Ok, any signs of the UN trainers?" Just as Morrison asked the question, two men emerged from a hidden trapped door adjacent to him and his unit. Catching the TAG unit off guard, these men fired their semi-automatic weapons at them. Two TAG unit members were instantly struck down by the weapons fire. Morrison immediately reached for a long, wooden support beam from the remains of the damaged wall. The beam struck both men cross wise and sent them tumbling to the ground. Swiftly, the two remaining TAG members aimed their weapons down at these men. Both men lifted their hands up in surrender. As they were lifted from the ground and handcuffed, Morrison noticed the UN insignia emblazoned on one man's flak jacket. He pulled the man toward him and ripped open his collar to reveal a dog tag with the name Jason Reis.

Morrison hoisted the man up in the air. "How long have you been training and arming these rebels?"

"That's way above your pay grade, my friend!" Reis responded.

"Oh really?" Morrison said with a smile of his own. He flipped Reis face down and rammed his head into the wooden floor. Embedded wood splinters bloodied his face as Morrison lifted him back up. He readied himself to slam Reis back into the ground.

"Ok, ok!" Reis squealed as he pleaded with Morrison. "We've been helping them ever since the UN was brought in to help with the post war transition."

"Why?"

"We were doing what we were told to do. We contracted with the UN to provide security. But our boss had other ideas."

"Who do you work for?"

Reis shook his head rapidly from side to side. Morrison gritted his teeth as he cocked his fist back. Reis's eyes widened as soon as he saw Morrison's arm take on the density of diamond.

"CoBALT. CoBALT Securities," he blurted out.

* * *

Two hours later
Presidential Palace
Delohar, Lemalia

"Mr. President, you're being undermined by rogue UN security contractors," Morrison said to Legaud as he handed him a large folder.

Legaud put aside what he was reading and reached for the manila folder. Carefully thumbing through the file, Legaud raised his eyebrows at what he came across.

"These men have been running weapons and tech to the UPF rebels.

"Yes, they were contractors with CoBALT. The same company that provided security to Analaise's intended cabinet during the civil war."

Legaud's countenance darkened. "They have been playing both sides."

"Whoever pays is all that matters."

"So, where do we stand so far with the UPF insurgents?" Legaud asked as he sat up in his executive leather chair.

Morrison nodded his head. "Our coordinated strikes against the UPF strongholds were successful. Almost ninety percent were killed or captured."

"That is encouraging. Now, I need to find out who approved those contractors," Legaud responded, as he slammed the folder down on his desk.

"Lirwa and her team are already on that, sir."

"'Lirwa'?" Legaud said as he raised his right eyebrow with a smile. "I didn't know you two were on a first name basis."

Morrison gave a small smile. "My mistake, I meant Minister Prashad. I would recommend you also have your UN representative reach out on the diplomatic front as well."

"I agree," Legaud said as he reclined back in his chair. "This goes back to what I was saying before. I want my country free from foreign rabble-rousers."

"I understand, sir," Morrison answered, as he glanced down at the document that Legaud just previously put to the side. The title on the cover caught his eye: *Security Pact*. "Is that from the UN too?" Morrison asked as he pointed down at the document.

Legaud turned to look at the document. "You don't know what this is? This is your team's agreement with us."

"The memorandum of agreement from last year?"

"No, it is updated. Take a look." Legaud handed the document over to Morrison.

Morrison thumbed through the first few pages. He then came across the financial agreement section. Morrison's heart started to beat faster.

"What's this?!" Morrison shoved the financial agreement sheet in Legaud's direction.

"Exactly what it looks like, Agent Morrison," he said as he clasped his fingers. "Our financial agreement to supply ten percent of Duritium export sales to Vigil as recompense for the cost of securing our nation."

"I can't believe this," Morrison said as he re-examined the page, as if to confirm what he initially read. "No one ever told me!"

"Maybe someone thought it best you didn't know."

CHAPTER FORTY-THREE

STRATEGIC AIMS

December 2nd
Corner of Second Street and C Street NE
Washington, DC

"Dwayne, take me back home, the scenic route," Malveux said from the backseat of her automated Lincoln Town Car.

"Yes ma'am," her driver, Dwayne Jenkins, responded. He typed in the Malveux household's location data on to the navigation panel. The car's artificial intelligence interface routed Malveux's preference into its driverless system. Within seconds, the steering wheel began to turn as the car hummed to life.

Malveux brought her phone to her face, but it failed to unlock.

"So, you're going to do me like that, huh?" Malveux mumbled to her phone as if it were a real person. She then typed in her passcode. Immediately, the phone's screen came alive.

"Get me Stansfield," Malveux mouthed into her phone.

After a few rings, she heard the FBI Director's voice on the line.

"This is Stansfield."

"Martin, it's Matrice."

Stansfield gave a broad smile. "What can I do for you, senator?"

"Oh, a lot."

"Heh, start with the most important."

Malveux reached into her shoulder bag and retrieved a few folders she received earlier from Golding.

"I had some of my aids do some digging with NTSB about the accidents that killed senators Daniels and Bence. It seems like, or at least on the surface, that it was pure coincidence. When they looked into it further, it seemed like there may have been some foul play. Have your boys in the bureau looked into this?"

"As a matter of fact, NTSB reached out to take lead on the case, as you probably already know, because of what seemed to be intentional sabotage."

Malveux pressed her phone closer to her ear. "What've you found? Anything?"

"As of now, we may have a lead on some possible Kremlin-backed hackers interfering with our autonomous grids."

"But why would they target Nicki and Bryan? They're not even on any foreign relations or intelligence subcommittees."

Stansfield shrugged. "My guess is to set an example; that they can collapse our infrastructure anytime."

"I'm still not buying it," Malveux said, shaking her head.

"That's just one of the leads we have. There are several others we have in the works."

"What about an inside job? Possibly someone within AlphA.I.?"

"It's a possibility but it wouldn't make sense that they'd ruin their reputation since they designed this country's autonomous grid."

A large sigh emanated from Malveux. "Ok, let me know what you find."

"Will do."

After Malveux hung up on Stansfield, she noticed her car's wheels started to squeal. Her body slammed hard against the back passenger door. Her shoulder bag exploded open with papers that peppered the back seat.

"What the hell was that, Dwayne?"

"I don't know ma'am. The autonomous driving function went crazy all of a sudden."

"Switch to manual goddammit!"

"I'm trying but it's not responding," Jenkins shouted back.

The Lincoln Town Car began to swerve into adjacent lanes. Her vehicle side-swiped a heavy-duty truck and then rear-ended a large SUV. Malveux's head slammed against the back of the front passenger seat. She felt a trickle of blood flow down her nose. The car then reversed and slammed into another SUV in the adjacent lane. Malveux's neck snapped back violently from the impact.

Jenkins, desperate to bring an end to the destructive ride, popped off a panel from the steering column and reached into the wiring inside. Thinking little of himself, he grabbed the wires and tore them out with reckless abandon. The front end of the car crumpled as it made impact with the broadside of a pick-up truck.

As people stopped to assist, a silver sedan slowed down as it passed by the scene. The driver's side window rolled down to allow Stiles a closer view of her handiwork.

CHAPTER FORTY-FOUR

CLANDESTINE OPERATIONS

December 3rd
Fujihara Household
Shibuya Prefecture
Tokyo, Japan

Fighting Bull and Kaori Fujihara stood outside of her parent's modest home. After Kaori gave three quick rapping motions at the door, it opened. The light from the overhead fixture almost blinded Kaori as the door flung open. After spending months in a dark containment tank, her eyes were still adjusting to her environment.

"Kaori!" Saro Fujihara shouted as he saw his daughter's face. She adjusted the wig on her head as her father tightly embraced her.

Fighting Bull's face lightened as she saw the long-awaited reunion. "As promised, Mr. Fujihara."

Saro looked up from his daughter. "Thank you so much. I can never thank you enough, Agent Fighting Bull. Come in, come in!"

The trio stepped into the home's small vestibule. Within moments, they were welcomed by Kaori's family and friends. The group ushered Kaori in the direction of the dining room. Fighting Bull stayed in the background as love was heaped on the young woman.

"Agent Fighting Bull?" Mariko, Kaori's mother, asked from behind her.

She turned around. "Yes, Mrs. Fujihara." Fighting Bull extended her hand. "Great to meet you."

"The pleasure is all mine. Thank you for letting us know you were bringing Kaori home ahead of time." She gestured in the direction of the kitchen, "Please, join us for dinner."

"I really should be going, I'm on a tight schedule."

"I insist," Mariko responded with a friendly but stern look.

Fighting Bull nodded and obliged. Upon entering the dining room, she was inundated with a table full of the best cuisine. The whole table was filled with just one spot open for Fighting Bull. After taking her seat, she was helped to many of the dishes that were passed her way.

About two hours passed as well-wishers eventually left the house; only the Fujihara family and Fighting Bull remained.

"Well, it's getting late, I better head back to my hotel," Fighting Bull said as she pushed away from the table.

Kaori raised her hand. "No, please don't go quite yet."

Her parents looked back at her and to themselves with slightly confused looks. Kaori looked back at her parents.

"Mom and dad, can I speak to you privately?"

Her parents nodded. Kaori looked in her younger brother's direction. "Why don't you show Agent Fighting Bull your new gaming console?"

"Yes!" Yuuto said. He quickly grabbed Fighting Bull by the hand and drug her to his room to play on his new Sony PlayStation.

Kaori's countenance darkened a bit after the pair left.

"What is it?" Saro asked his daughter.

Kaori looked at her parents with eyes almost filled with tears. Her father quickly moved over to hug his daughter.

"I just have missed so much," Kaori responded as tears flowed down her cheeks.

"I know, I know," Saro responded as he held his daughter close. "Agent Fighting Bull told me they are moving to arrest those behind your kidnapping.

And I have made the CEO cancel the merger agreement with AlphA.I."

Mariko also walked over and gently patted her daughter on the back of her head. "We never gave up getting you back, my dear. Now that you are home, we can get back to how things were."

Kaori's head shot up as she briefly broke from her father's embrace. "No."

She lifted her wig to display all of the scars on her bald head from the neural interface ports that were placed in her skull.

Her mother gasped at the sight.

"I will never be the same," Kaori responded defiantly with her arms spread wide. "They made me do things…" her voice cracked. "They used me like I was some type of animal."

Saro eased his way toward his daughter. "Kaori, I know, and I am furious," he turned to look at his wife, "we are furious. But we caught them---they can't do anything to you anymore."

He reached over, but she immediately pushed away.

"No!" she yelled.

"Kaori, show some respect to your father," Mariko shouted.

The young woman backed away from both of her parents. "You don't understand, they took so much away from me." She turned to look away from her parents briefly. "I cannot let this go."

Saro's brows furrowed as he responded. "What do you want to do?"

CHAPTER FORTY-FIVE

REUNION

December 4th
George Washington University Medical Center

Conrad looked down at Malveux's still body as she laid in her hospital bed. The thought of someone attacking one of the few links to her mother roiled her. Her nares flared as she thought back to getting the call from Malveux's husband about the accident. She gripped the side of Malveux's bed railing so hard it cracked its plastic casing. That cracking noise woke Malveux back to consciousness.

"Hey," Malveux 's raspy voice whispered.

"Hey yourself, Aunt Mattie," Conrad replied with a stilted smile.

"How long was I out for?"

Conrad looked down at the digital readout on her watch. "About two days."

"My God."

"You suffered some minor head trauma, but thankfully the CT scan didn't show any brain bleed."

Malveux sat up in her bed, leaning her back against the headboard.

"Well, I guess God's not ready for me yet."

"Or the devil?"

"Hey!"

Conrad smiled and put up her hands. "Kidding."

Malveux eased back in her bed. "Where are Perry and Justin?"

Conrad pulled the chair from the corner of the room and closer to Malveux's bed. "They came through already, along with Uncle Malcolm. They had been here for a couple of hours, but I decided to take over the night shift."

Malveux coughed. "I'm glad they decided to check in on their dear mom."

"C'mon now, Aunt Mattie," Conrad said. "You've got two amazing sons and a husband who loves you."

"I'm glad someone loves me," Malveux said as she folded her arms in her lap. "More than I can say for whoever sabotaged my car."

Conrad reached into her breast pocket to retrieve her phone. "I've looked into that." The screen illuminated and a holographic image popped up. "The car's navigation system was remotely tampered with. We narrowed it down to a local transmitter."

Malveux pointed at the holographic image. "Any leads?"

"We've gotten it down to a few actors."

"Don't bother. I know who it was," Malveux said shaking her head. She looked up and pointed at the mounted television behind Conrad. Conrad turned her head to look at the screen and saw Stroud's image.

"Stroud?"

"Yes, him or more accurately, AlphA.I."

"I can't say I'm surprised but why you?"

"C'mon Alicia, look it's all there. I'm moving legislation forward that will unravel their complete control of our entire technological infrastructure."

"I see," Conrad said as she eased back in her chair. "I know your legislation has already gotten out of committee and is headed for a full vote."

Malveux nodded. "And there's a similar bill passed on the House side. We have the votes."

"So, you figure they're out to shut this down."

Malveux nodded. "By taking me out and everyone else associated with the bill."

"Well, we have people moving on them as we speak."

CHAPTER FORTY-SIX

CONTAGION

December 10th
AlphA.I. Research Facility
Los Alamos, New Mexico

"Look Bridgette, I'll take full responsibility for the Asset's escape," Breckenridge said contritely while speaking to Huntley on the other line. He fiddled with his tie as he nervously listened to Huntley's response.

"Brian, I understand," Huntley responded in a surprisingly calm voice, "I don't blame you. Did Stanwell's team give you a full report?"

"Yes, he did. We lost video surveillance, so we have no record of who broke the Asset out of her containment unit. The guards said they thought they were superhuman infiltrators."

Huntley put her head in her hand and sighed. "Where do we stand now with Singularis?"

Breckenridge tapped on the surface of his smart desk and a hologram of the molecular structure of the Singularis virus popped up. "The embedded viruses are ready."

"Go ahead and activate then."

"Are you sure? Did Dennis sign off on this?" Breckenridge asked hesitantly.

"Yes," Huntley said as she looked down at her desk. "To be honest, after he gave me the go-ahead, he cut off his phone and all tracking."

"Well, we expected that it might come to this."

"True. With the virus coupled to the nanites embedded in every AlphA.I. product, we should be able to get partial global exposure. Not quite what we had hoped but it's close."

Breckenridge tapped on his smart desk. A few levels down Stanwell received the signal on his computer. He paused and stared at his screen. His hands shook as he reached for his desk telephone. Stanwell's voice cracked as he started to speak.

"We are a go for Singularis activation."

"Yes sir," the technician responded.

The satellite technician hung up and pressed the button on his elaborate computer keyboard. Immediately their radio base station's large satellite array shifted toward the sky. Within seconds a radio signal was sent out to AlphA.I.'s low earth orbit satellites.

After Stanwell hung up, he motioned the sign of the cross across his forehead and chest. He tapped on his keyboard. Immediately, Breckenridge received the confirmation that the radio signal was sent out.

"It's done, Bridgette," Breckenridge said to Huntley.

"Brian, you have just participated in changing the course of mankind," Huntley said as she looked up at her front door and saw her assistant flanked by four individuals with dark blue coats adorned with the FBI initials. "Brian, I have to go."

* * *

Bridgette Huntley's Office
AlphA.I. Headquarters
Palo Alto, California

"May I help you?" Huntley asked as she ended her call. Four FBI agents walked past Huntley's assistant, among them was De La Vega. She flashed her credentials.

"Agent De La Vega. Bridgette Huntley, you are under arrest for the murder of Doug Lawson."

Huntley gave a slight smirk with a hint of inevitability. She stood up from her chair and stretched her hands out. A junior FBI agent instead brought Huntley's arms around her back and clasped metallic handcuffs on.

As Huntley was walked out, she smiled and said, "You all are too late. The singularity is already upon us."

* * *

Southern Arizona VA Health Center
Tucson, Arizona

An army veteran moved slowly as he balanced on parallel bars. He gripped the parallel bars gingerly as he moved along. His fingers traversed the AlphA.I. logo on the parallel bars.

"You're doing good," his physical therapist said, encouraging him.

"I'm trying," the veteran replied.

As he looked down at the stump that used to be his left leg, tears started to well up in his eyes as he lamented his loss. Then as he continued to move, he felt pain in his lower leg—a kind he had not experienced since he lost his leg. As he looked down, he could see a metallic stream of tissue emanating from his stump. Within moments his lower left leg started to form, in a metallic, circuit-laden limb.

The veteran's eyes widened as he started to see a new leg form. He began to smile, but his happy smile was interrupted by the scream of his Physical Therapist. He looked at her in horror as he saw her body overtaken by metallic strands and circuitry.

* * *

Independence Hall
Philadelphia, Pennsylvania

A trio of tourists in front of the notable site where America's founding documents were signed writhed in pain. The horror of their human flesh transforming into a grotesque, metallic, wiry mass was overwhelming to observe. Just a few moments ago they were enjoying a pleasant day, taking pictures with their *Turing Two* phones when they were suddenly overtaken by gleaming metallic tendrils emanating from the charging ports and earplug jacks.

Other tourists ran hysterically outside of the storied building as not only their limbs but also their midsections and face took on a metallic texture with circuitry overlain upon it. During the mayhem around, a police officer tried to get the affected individuals to safety but was herself affected upon contacting the virus afflicted individuals. She looked at her hands as they were eaten away by silicon wafers, circuitry, and metal. She screamed in disbelief as her flesh transformed into something far less than human.

* * *

National Institute of Allergy and Infectious Disease
National Institutes of Health
Bethesda, Maryland

The plasmapharesis machine's whirring sound almost lulled Itrish to sleep as the serum was extracted from her blood. The only thing keeping her from the precipice of sleep was the sound of 9th Wonders' beats playing through her headphones.

"Itrish?" Dani Morrison asked as she knocked on Itrish's patient room.

Itrish removed her headphones and sat up in her reclined chair. "Hi, Dr. Morrison, how are you?"

"I am well," Dani said as she shook Itrish's hand. She then looked over to the machine as the IV bag next to the machine filled with gold colored serum. "I want to say thank you for doing this."

Itrish waved her hand. "After I found out what those AlphA.I. jokers wanted me to do—digitizing their virus and sending it across the world, it's the least I could do."

"You're very brave, we tried to do this in the lab, but we came up empty. You allowing yourself to be exposed to a weakened form of the Singularis virus, not 100% assured of the outcome…all I can say is you got balls my friend," Dani said.

Itrish smiled again. "Yeah, it was pretty scary not knowing what was going to happen. But after talking to you and Principal Gowan, I was comfortable doing this." Itrish paused. "Besides it's what my mom would've wanted me to do, if she were here."

Dani nodded. "And it was worth the try. So far the samples of convalescent serum we've gotten from you has been 100% effective in neutralizing and reversing the effects of the virus."

Itrish nodded.

"The CDC and NIH are working on a plan to mass produce your serum and disseminate it to the public. We're also modeling a vaccine using components of your serum with a protein from the virus."

"That was a great idea. What made you come up with it?"

"I would love to take the credit, but it wasn't me. It was her." Dani turned in the directed of the doorway. Kaori immediately walked in.

"Kaori!" Itrish responded ecstatically.

"Hello," Kaori smiled. She leaned over to hug Itrish.

"My God how are you? I never got the chance to personally meet you after they rescued you from New Mexico."

"I am happy to finally meet you, too, Itrish. In person this time," Kaori laughed.

"I know, right," Itrish responded with a smile.

"I want to say thank you, Itrish for helping to save me."

Itrish waved her off. "It's not a big deal. I know you would've done the same for me. We technopaths have to stick together."

"Thank you."

"I thought you went back to your parents. What happened?"

Kaori paused and looked down. "You all helped me. Now it's time for me to help you."

CHAPTER FORTY-SEVEN

GLOBAL FREQUENCY

December 11th
The Mirador
Washington, DC

"Terrell, we're about to land," Chiu said over the Avian's radio.

"Copy that," Morrison responded over his seat's arm rest radio. He then turned his attention over to his laptop. His eyes scanned his mission report from his assignment in Lemalia. His brow furrowed as he came upon the section concerning CoBALT security's involvement in the insurgencies. Morrison's focus was broken as he felt the slight jolt of the Avian's wheels touching the airstrip.

As he gathered his things to deplane, the rear hatch opened. Beyond the entrance he could see Blankenchip waiting just outside sporting a Cheshire cat smile. Blankenchip greets Morrison with a bear hug.

"I coulda sworn you were going to buy a vacation home in Lemalia."

Morrison smiled. "Hardly, Aaron. You can't get rid of me that easily."

Blankenchip patted Morrison on the back. "I know, who would shoot the breeze with me if you were gone?"

"John."

"Get the hell outta here, man."

Morrison laughed. "You know I had to put that out there, right?"

"Yeah, I see you have a lot of fun just yanking my damn chain."

"Has Alicia started already?"

"Yeah, that's why the rest of the welcoming committee wasn't out to greet you," Blankenchip replied. "So let's get our asses in gear before she gives us the worse possible assignments."

* * *

The Briefing Room

As Blankenchip and Morrison walked into the room they could see a holographic display of a virus particle and an array of satellites emanating from the center of the briefing table. The rest of the team turned to look as they entered.

"Look who I found slumming in Lemalia?" Blankenchip said as he motioned to Morrison next to him.

Morrison was greeted with warm hugs and handshakes before he took his seat.

"Welcome back, Terrell," Conrad said as she stood at the head of the table. "How was the mission?"

Morrison paused briefly before answering. "Eye opening."

Conrad cocked her left eyebrow. "I see. I'm looking forward to your report."

Morrison nodded.

Conrad then turned her attention back to the meeting. "As you all know, AlphA.I. released the Singularis virus on the world yesterday." She rotated the holographic image. "It's essentially a novel techno-organic virus."

"What are its specs?" Pendleton asked.

Conrad tapped the control panel on the briefing room and the hologram transitioned to an animation of the virus fusing with a normal cell. "The virus causes rapid cell degradation. Basically, it transforms carbon-based tissue to metallic, almost robot-like material…"

"But why release a virus that could kill billions?"

"Because they're transhumanists—they believe humanity's next evolutionary step is through technological fusion."

"But based on the data you gathered back in New Mexico, it's mode of transmission is via radio waves," Pendleton responded.

"That's true, but that's just part of how it's transmitted."

"What do you mean?"

Conrad altered the holographic image again. "They originally planned on using Itrish as a vector to transmit the virus globally---hitting anything and everything with a human brain."

"But how?"

"Their CYBRA operating system was based off Kaori Fujihara's brain patterns. They found a way to reverse engineer her ability to mentally control machines to pick up on people's brain waves."

"Is that how they targeted the virus?"

"Partially," Conrad replied. "When we stopped them from capturing Itrish they moved on to their contingency plan."

"Which was?" Pendleton asked.

Before Conrad could respond, she was interrupted by Blankenchip.

"They coated every piece of their tech, from consumer goods to the CYBRA nodes with a version of the virus that was coupled to nanites. The virus is essentially dormant until it receives the radio signal."

"Almost everything we interact with now is AlphA.I.-based. How come none of us are affected?"

"Because it's also contact dependent," Conrad responded. "People have to be in physical contact with a device or someone in contact with an affected device at the time of the radio transmission. If you weren't using any of those devices at the initial transmission of the radio signal, then the virus won't affect you."

"So, what's the plan?" Morrison asked.

Conrad looked in Arrowhawk's direction. "John, go ahead."

Arrowhawk tapped on the control panel in front of him. Immediately the holographic image in the center of the table transformed into a display of Stroud along with cybernetically enhanced Variants.

"I've been tracking Stroud since the Bureau discovered he'd been kidnapping and augmenting Variants for his own ends."

"What've you found so far?" Morrison inquired.

The holographic image altered into a picture of the U.S. Capitol building. "He's been amassing an army of augmented Variants to launch an attack on Congress."

"The hell is his beef?" Blankenchip blurted out.

"Because of the privacy legislation that's about to be passed," Arrowhawk replied. "The Digital Emancipation and Privacy Act is essentially the kill shot to AlphA.I.'s control of America's tech infrastructure."

Arrowhawk then turned to look in Conrad's direction. "And he has one target in particular that he's after, the bill's lead sponsor, Senator Malveux."

"Damn," Blankenchip said as he looked at Conrad.

"When is he planning on unleashing this attack?" Pendleton asked.

"I'm not sure. From what I gathered from the raid on one of their depots, it may be during the joint session that's coming up."

"Yeah," Conrad responded. "So, we have our work cut out for us."

"Well, Alicia, that's going to be a little bit difficult," Fighting Bull said.

"The hell are you talking about, Cynthia?" Blankenchip asked.

"When I was in Japan, I discovered that AlphA.I.'s been running full data surveillance on us."

Conrad leaned back in her chair. "How, our system is virtually unhackable… well with the exception of what Itrish did."

"Exactly, proving that no system is unhackable. They've installed something called the Back Door protocols. Essentially a self-evolving program that can access and over-ride any piece of tech or A.I., from cybernetics, phones and super computers, anywhere in the world. With that program he was able to get into our personal data records---he knows everything from our weakness and strengths all the way down to the granular level." Fighting Bull then scanned the table. "Stroud's been planning for a potential conflict with us for a long time."

"Well, we'll just have to be a little more unpredictable then," Conrad replied.

Bledsoe looked down at the table and then in Conrad's direction. "What's the plan, Captain?"

"You, Aaron, and Regent are taking point and stopping this virus. I'll be working with you guys on the back end coordinating with Kaori and Itrish."

Conrad then turned to look at the rest of the team. "Terrell, you know Capitol security inside and out, so I need you to work with Capitol police to fortify the building against any attacks."

She then looked in Fighting Bull and Arrowhawk's directions. "John, I need you to work on getting a track on where Stroud is now. Based on the FBI reports you sent earlier it looks like he's fallen off the grid. And Cynthia, I need you to work on developing countermeasures to Stroud's attack plan against us."

Conrad then lightly tapped on the control panel in front of her. "The specs of your assignments have been uploaded to your holotabs."

The team members promptly dispersed with the exception of Morrison. He walked toward Conrad as she gathered her belongings.

"Alicia, can I talk to you?"

'Yeah, what's going on?"

"I wanted to talk to you about what I found in Lemalia."

Conrad put her hands up. "That can wait for our official debrief. Right now, the main priority is stopping this virus."

"This can't wait," Morrison responded with a firm tone.

Conrad's eyebrow's furrowed at the sudden change in Morrison's tone. "Ok what is it?"

"I found out what you did in that Lemalian security agreement."

Conrad froze. This was something that one almost never saw Conrad do. She slowly turned her body more toward Morrison.

"Terrell, I promise you, I will explain everything. But right now, we need to focus on the disaster at hand."

Morrison looked down and then back up to Conrad. "Fair enough, but we will have to deal with this."

* * *

December 12th
The Skies above the Pacific Ocean

"Karen, are you ready for the drop?" Chiu asked his teammate as she stood at the Avian's rear hatch.

She nodded. The wind rushed in her face as the hatch opened. She leaped out into the blistering wind. Immediately she generated a localized air pocket to keep her aloft. Her eyes began to glow, and her skin began to emanate particles into the atmosphere.

Meanwhile, Blankenchip radioed Bledsoe from the Avian's jump seat as she began creating a weather pattern above the wide-open ocean. "Can you hear me, honey?"

"Despite the windshear, loud and clear."

"I just want to say that you're brave to go along with this cockamamie scheme."

"Whatever needs to be done to save lives, Aaron."

As she spoke, a large cloud pattern began to cover the expanse of the ocean. As the clouds rapidly expanded, Bledsoe's nose began to bleed. She cringed. The ocean below began to darken as the clouds thickened.

The Avian ascended through the clouds. Hitched to the aircraft's underside was an atomizer coupled to a pyrotechnic dispenser. As the plane reached its maximal height above the clouds, it began to dispense atomized golden particles. The aircraft doubled back and made several passes over the cloud masses, dispensing the substance throughout.

Bledsoe's eyes began to glow brighter as she manipulated the clouds—separating them. The larger clouds began to disperse farther out to continental

Asia and the western coast of the Americas. Blankenchip watched onscreen at his tablet as it recorded the cloud saturation points. A reddish color overtook the areas onscreen that they had just seeded.

"We're at maximum saturation, Karen!" he shouted over his radio.

Taking it as her cue, Bledsoe triggered the clouds. Immediately, a golden shower of rain fell on the populace below. Many of those affected by the Singularis virus began to see their metallic skin and wiring revert back to flesh and blood. The vast majority of those affected no longer felt the cold metal trailing up their bodies and felt restored once again. Many in Japan, the Indonesian, and Malay Archipelago began to feel the virus's grip over their bodies fading.

Blankenchip eventually saw on his tablet the hot zones most affected by the Singularis virus gradually receding along the Asian continent and the western part of the Americas. He radioed Conrad.

"Alicia, your crazy cloud seeding idea worked!"

"Glad you're giving me credit, Aaron."

"Don't let it go to your head.".

Conrad laughed. "Believe me, I will."

Blankenchip shook his head. "And I'll always be there to bust your bubble." He looked at the number of infected and the corresponding recession of the hot zones. "Atomizing Itrish's convalescent serum helped. The fact the CDC and NIH were able to mass produce this thing is amazing."

"Yeah," Conrad began, "and how they were able to manipulate the serum for dermal absorption was a feat in itself. Karen just has to make sure she doesn't overdo it to avoid excessive flooding."

"So, now that phase one was a success, we move on to phase two?"

Conrad looked onscreen at the Satellite Control Center's main control hub. "Yep, the weather phenomenon Karen created will cover just part of the globe. We need the drones to help seed other parts and deliver to those indoors."

'And have the technopaths been able to intercept the radio signal?"

"We're working on that right now."

CHAPTER FORTY-EIGHT

PRIMACY

Director's Office
Vigil Satellite Control Center
Fort Meade, Maryland

"Kaori, Itrish, are you two ready?" Conrad asked in a reassuringly to the two young women through the PA system.

"Yes," Itrish responded.

"Yes, Captain," Kaori responded spritely.

Both young Variants sat in Neuro-Interface Control Units. One of the technicians placed the glass headgear on Fujihara's head.

Director Davis stood next to Conrad as they peered down to the hub below from her office. A bank of computers rested next to Itrish and Kaori's chairs. The technician manning the computers looked up to Director Davis. Behind the glass façade, she nodded. The technician pressed a large, red, circular button and immediately the headgear on both young women started to glimmer. A whitish aura emanated off Itrish and an azure one came off Kaori. Both young women grimaced at the strain of their task. On a large, LCD screen projected against the far end of the Director's office was a video feed of the Vigil SDS satellites coming to life. After a few minutes, the satellites realigned in an oval pattern that overlapped with AlphA.I.'s Tessellation satellites.

"We have satellite uplink established director," the technician said over his radio.

"Copy that." Davis replied. She turned to look in Conrad's direction.

"Do it," Conrad responded.

Davis nodded and replied back over the PA system. "Itrish and Kaori, it's your show."

Within an instant, multiple panels opened from the SDS satellites' side compartments and a rocket propelled drone swarm was unleashed. As these drones dispersed, they made their way down to low earth orbit, where the numerous Tessellation satellites resided. The drones attached to the underside of each of the satellites' antennae module. More and more the drones began to spread out, almost as a multiplying force for the Vigil SDS.

"Using the service drones was a great idea, Kellita," Conrad said to Davis.

"I figured it would be the best way to intercept the AlphA.I.'s sats. Easier to jam their radio signal."

As the drones continued to spread out amongst the numerous Tessellation satellites, a small grouping of these satellites' solar array panels began to glow.

"The hell is that?" Davis openly mused as she saw footage of what was going on.

Immediately, a dozen of the Tessellation solar array panels unleashed directed energy beams toward the Vigil drones.

"Kaori," Conrad began to say over the PA, "just like we talked about."

Even though she couldn't respond verbally, Kaori knew what was required. A side compartment of one of the larger SDS command module opened, releasing a suite of offensive drones equipped with mini-directed energy cannons. Swiftly, the drones fired upon the attacking Tessellation satellites, ripping through their solar arrays and main propulsion modules. Some of the Tessellation satellites were able to angle their arrays to fire upon the Vigil drones. The drones narrowly evaded attack and returned fire. Within seconds, the last offensive Tessellation satellite was rendered useless.

Conrad smiled as she observed the drones' triumph over AlphA.I.'s weaponized satellites.

"We're moving on to the next phase," she said as she looked in Davis' direction.

CHAPTER FORTY-NINE

CASCADING EFFECT

December 15th
Halcyon Studios
New York, New York

"The world is still in shock as it deals with the onslaught of a plague," anchor Spencer Benson said. "What authorities are describing as a techno organic virus has ravaged large parts of the world. We are receiving reports that it was activated via radio signals from satellites owned by AlphA.I. Thankfully, Vigil has been able to intercept the signal transmission and stop the continued spread of the virus."

"Although," his co-anchor Alita Ross began to say, "there are those in the international community who are upset with Vigil for violating international law, by distributing the anti-viral serum through drone payloads. Many object not just to the use of drones but also the use of climate manipulation to deliver the anti-viral serum to the global populace."

Benson nodded in Ross's direction, "That's right. There have been statements coming out of Moscow and Beijing to immediately arrest Vigil and even levy UN sanctions against the United States."

"Meanwhile back home, many of the AlphA.I.'s upper echelon has been arrested and indicted on multiple charges," Ross said. "Authorities have yet to apprehend CEO and founder Dennis Stroud. The biological attack has also prompted Congress to quickly approve new sweeping Privacy legislation that will strip AlphA.I. of its control of America's tech-infrastructure, as well as crack down on unchecked data collection. Both houses plan on a symbolic joint session to cast their final votes. The president is planned to sign it into law."

* * *

The Mall of America Memorial
Bloomington, Minnesota

Dennis Stroud sat solemnly amongst throngs of wilted flowers, photos and other mommentos to the Minneapolis event. The outdoor memorial was one of the few signs of life after the attack.

His eyes started to tear up as he looked down on a photo of his parents. The visor on Stroud's hazmat mask started to fog up. The residual radiation was still too much for anyone to venture around the state without protective gear. Suddenly, the rush of air from Stroud's automated jet landing bore down on him. As he entered the jet, he observed the replayed newscast regarding Vigil thwarting part of his plan. He shook his head as he began to remove his hazmat suit.

"I just wanted us to evolve as a species," Stroud muttered to himself.

Stroud tapped on the glass panel on his armrest. "It was supposed to be us, the real humans, not these God-forsaken Variant abominations."

A schematic of the Capitol Building popped up on his TV screen, supplanting the newscast.

"Thankfully Bridgette's mapping disc has been working well," Stroud said to himself. The TV screen then transitioned to images of the cybernetically augmented Variants.

"Well, at least these abominations will be good for something."

Stroud tapped on the glass paneling again and the screen changed. On the screen popped up the words, "Nullification Imperative Initiated."

CHAPTER FIFTY

CRESCENDO

December 18th
George Washington University Medical Center

"Here you go, honey," Malcolm Hudson said as he draped a blue overcoat over Malveux's shoulders.

"Thanks, babe," Malveux responded with a smile as her husband helped her adjust her overcoat.

"You ready for this big vote today?"

"As ready as I can be, babe. I only wish you were coming with me."

Hudson nodded. "I know, 'Trice, I wish I was there, too, but with all the safety concerns, you know your security detail didn't think it would be a good idea."

Hudson turned to look at the six large men with earpieces just outside of Malveux's hospital room door.

"As a matter of fact, you know you don't have to go, babe. You could always vote remotely."

"No," Malveux said. She laid her hand at the center of her husband's chest. "After that nightmare virus that AlphA.I. released and all the craziness we've experienced over the last few days, I have to take a stand in person. It's my duty."

"I married one of the most stubborn women in the world," Hudson said as he shook his head and smiled.

"That you did."

"Well, I'm glad you have one of the most dangerous women alive protecting you." Hudson turned around and motioned to Conrad as she walked into the room.

Conrad smiled as she walked toward Hudson. She gave him a kiss on the cheek. "Hey Uncle Malcolm, good to see you."

"Same here, Alicia." Hudson then turned to his wife. "Make sure you keep her safe for me."

"Always," Conrad responded.

Hudson gave Malveux a farewell kiss and walked out of the room. Three large guards flanked Hudson as he left.

Conrad looked at Malveux. "Ready to go?"

"Yeah."

As they exited, Conrad handed Malveux a phone.

"It's a secure line-linked straight to our satellite system."

"You're not worried that AlphA.I. won't be able to breach it."

Conrad turned to Malveux with a roguish smile. "We've already taken care of that."

Malveux gave Conrad a nonplussed look. "My dear goddaughter, what kind of scheme have you come up with now."

"Just trust me."

"Oh I do, but I worry sometimes," Malveux responded. "Where is the rest of your team?"

Conrad tapped her watch and a holographic image of the Capitol building and its surroundings appeared. Within the schematic were small red dots aligned outside of the building.

"Terrell and Aaron are stationed at the perimeter of the building. Capitol police and National guard are backing them. Cynthia and John are securing the Senate and House chambers respectively. They're being backed by National Guard and Capitol Police as well."

Marveling at the holographic display Malveux responded, "Damn, you have the place covered like Fort Knox. What about Bledsoe and your pilot?"

"Regent you mean?" Conrad asked to clarify.

Malveux nodded.

"They're still running operations over the African continent and southeast Asia. We're still trying to get the antiviral serum to the rest of the globe."

"From the intel you gathered, you still think Stroud would have the balls to still move on Congress. In the middle of a joint session that will have the eyes of the world on him?"

Conrad nodded adamantly. "Right now, he's a man with nothing left to lose."

* * *

One hour later
Outside the U.S. Capitol Building

Morrison looked up in the sky to see a flotilla of hi-tech gunships soaring above him. He saw the AlphA.I. logo on the tail of the ship. As these planes came just above him he saw the hull open up. Columns of augmented Variants descended upon them.

"Terrell, we got a whole bunch of company," Blankenchip said over Morrison's earpiece.

"I know," Morrison said as one of the Variants hurled themselves in his direction. He altered his body's molecular density to diamond. Morrison delivered a crushing blow to the Variant's jaw. The Variant's body flew into a gaggle of other Variants… One of the Variants from the felled group quickly got up and unleashed an energy bolt that hit Morrison squarely in the chest. He tumbled backward. Morrison shook his head and the impact of the blow; his ego was more bruised than his body. He pushed himself off the ground and leapt toward the Variant that attacked him. Within an instant, Morrison was hit with a circular disc that caused a coursing electrical pain to run down his body. His diamond density melted back to reveal his natural skin. Morrison landed awkwardly to the concrete pavement below. As he rolled over to recover, he saw just inches above him another augmented Variant with an energized fist about to bear down on him. Three bullets ripped through the Variants arm and stomach before Morrison could alter his density.

Blankenchip reached out his hand to Morrison.

"Thanks," Morrison said as Blankenchip gave him a hand up. Morrison looked down at the Variant below.

"I thought we were using non-lethal tactics?"

"Your ass was about to get smashed by that guy. So, excuse me for trying to save you."

Morrison shook his head. "No complaints. I appreciate the assist." Another Variant tried to run up behind them, but Morrison swatted him back with a titanium-dense back hand. Morrison then nodded in the direction of the Capitol building itself. "I wonder how they're doing on the inside?"

* * *

Underground Tunnels
Capitol Building

Arrowhawk tried his best to use nonlethal energy blasts against the attacking Variants. He remembered that his opponents were programmed and not in control of their actions. Looking at their faces, he was barely much older than they were. Arrowhawk was flanked by National Guardsmen and Capitol Police as they tried to fend off the attacking augmented Variants. In the corner of his eye, Arrowhawk saw one of the Variants raise up a cybernetic hand that appeared to be pulsating. Within seconds a group of police officers and guardsmen are knocked off their feet by the sonic blast emitted by the Variant.

Seeing his allies downed, Arrowhawk in turn countered with a broad band electrical burst. As the burst hit the attacking Variant and those in its group, it quickly dissipated--almost as if it had no impact.

"What the hell?" Arrowhawk wondered out loud.

As he mused about the ineffectiveness of his attack, the Variants began to advance. One of the Variants emitted a subzero cold blast to the ground that laced it with ice. Many of the officers and guardsmen lost their balance as they slipped on the icy surface below them. The attacking Variants fired bioenergy blasts and bullets at the vulnerable officers. Arrowhawk was too slow to erect an energy shield to protect many of the officers before they were killed.

"No!" Arrowhawk shouted as his eyes began to glow. Within seconds Arrowhawk began feeling energy pulsing within his chest. Electrical sparks emanated from his eyes and fingertips as he emitted an electromagnetic pulse that enveloped the Variants. Surprisingly, the pulse had no effect on the Variants. They advanced toward him, firing both derma-projectiles and directed energy at him. Arrowhawk erected an energy forcefield that deflected these attacks. Thinking back to the Lemalian war, he emitted a concentric electromagnetic wave pulse that covered the immediate area. The augmented Variants seemed to pause for a minute but continue to attack.

"The hell, that EMP should have shut them down," Arrowhawk said within earshot of the officers around him. He then quickly emitted a solid-state energy wall that pushed the augmented Variants back, giving them some breathing room.

* * *

The Senate Chamber

Fighting Bull and the surrounding police and guardsmen were trying their best to get the senators to safety as they were met with wave after wave of attacking Variants. One large augmented Variant leaped off the gallery balcony and landed on Fighting Bull on the senate floor below. She let out a grunt as her ribcage and spine were squeezed under the impact. Thankfully, her Duritium-biosteel weave uniform helped absorb a majority of the impact. The Variant tried to pin her to the ground facedown. She immediately swiveled her torso around and as she turned, she morphed into Arrowhawk. Her eyes glowed and she hit the Variant with a bioelectric blast that thrusted him off her and flat on his back. Fighting Bull righted herself and followed through with a directed energy blast to her attacker's chest—crashing him through five senate desks. She tapped her earpiece.

"Alicia, where are you?"

Conrad fired five rounds of SPLATT bullets at three Variants who were attacking Malveux's security detail before she responded.

"We're heading through the southeast chambers exit. We're moving to secure Senator Malveux in the saferoom."

After the insurrectionist attack on the U.S. Capitol in early 2021, Congress thought it wise to create fortified saferooms for legislators to escape to in the event that a similar attack happened again.

"Copy that, Alicia," Fighting Bull responded. "I'm headed your way now."

She quickly morphed into Morrison, assuming a titanium density, and barreled through a group of augmented Variants in her way. As Fighting Bull cleared the main chambers, she saw Conrad, Malveux, and the rest of the security detail rushing toward the basement. A Variant with a third cybernetic arm grabbed Malveux by the arm. Seeing this, Conrad shifted the setting on her rifle to fire a directed energy blast that severed the augmented Variants cybernetic limb. Sparks flew from the amputated limb as the Variant recoiled in pain.

"Thanks for the save, Alicia," Malveux said, looking up Conrad.

"Don't mention it." She turned to her left to see Fighting Bull running toward them. Just as she was feet away from them, more Variants began spilling in from the Senate chambers toward them. Conrad grabbed Malveux by the shoulder.

"Senator, we have to get you out of here fast."

* * *

Senate Saferoom

Malveux placed her hand on the entry door's biometric panel and the door began to slide open. Conrad and the security detail entered first. As the door opened, they could see the room littered with bodies of dead senators and staffers. Within seconds, three of Malveux's security detail were hit with directed energy blasts. Their bodies hit the ground with a thud. Conrad immediately raised her rifle to return fire, but she too was hit was a plasma blast that floored her. Thankfully, her body armor absorbed the brunt of the blast. Before she could get up, steel coils began covering her body. She looked up to see that one of the augmented Variants released the coils from ports in his cybernetic hands. Conrad took stock of the room as she tried to break free. There were three other Variants outside of the one that had entrapped her. At the center of the room stood Stroud. She could see that there was a briefcase atop the desk behind him. He pointed to one of the Variants and they forcefully grabbed Malveux and dragged her over to Stroud.

"What the hell are you doing, Stroud?" Conrad yelled as she laid incapacitated on the ground.

"What needs to be done, Captain," Stroud replied in his melodious voice. "These people don't get it; at least not like you and I do."

"These people?!"

"Bureaucrats—these senators. They don't know that before we get over-run with these abhorrent genetic accidents, Variants; true humans must evolve."

"That's rich, considering you're using Variants to do your dirty work."

"I never said they weren't useful. They have their place, but not over real humans like you and me, Captain." He glanced over at Malveux who struggled under the grip of the Variant holding her. "You of all people should know that, being you're one of the only successful products to come out of the SHARP program."

Conrad shook her head. "You're insane."

"Am I really? I was there when you told Dr. Cornelius that you wanted him to make you unstoppable. You saw the need to evolve back then. I'm just accelerating the process for everyone else."

It felt like a cut to her soul, hearing her words from so many years ago spoken back to her. "Last I checked you weren't God. Who gave you authority to decide how humanity will evolve?"

"I did. I gave myself authority when I saw a misbegotten Variant decimate my hometown."

"You can't blame a whole group just because of one man's actions."

"Please, spare me the speech," Stroud said as he turned to pop the latches on the briefcase behind him. He removed a syringe with a cloudy mixture that almost resembled mercury. "This legislation they're pushing will put an end to my work and I can't let that happen."

The Variant holding Malveux shoved her head against the table, right next to the briefcase. Without hesitation, Stroud plunged the syringe into Malveux's neck. She collapsed to the ground and writhed in pain. An interlacing network if of metallic tendrils began to creep up from the injection site down Malveux's neck and toward her chest.

"No!" Conrad screamed as she struggled to break free from the metallic coils that encumbered her.

"A concentrated form of the Singularis virus," Stroud said as he stood over Malveux. "Pretty soon senator Malveux will see what it's like to become an evolved human."

Conrad's eyes welled up with tears. She tried her best to break free from the metal coils, but they just seemed to clench tighter and tighter around her body. Ultimately her struggle was futile. Then, in the midst of her trying to break free, a voice came over her earpiece.

"Captain," Itrish said over her earpiece. "It's done."

"Then do it."

The augmented Variants around Stroud all began to go limp as they seemed to have been powered off. Stroud winced as he saw this. Conrad quickly freed herself from the metallic coils as the Variant who controlled them froze. She got up and lunged toward Stroud. He tried to hit her with his cybernetically enhanced arm as she lunged. Unfortunately for him, Conrad's enhanced reflexes were too fast for him. She easily ducked his attempted blow and connected with an uppercut to his jaw. The impact of the punch laid him flat on the top of the desk behind him. Conrad quickly pinned him against the wooden framed surface.

"How?" Stroud asked.

"You should know. The Back Door Protocols. You're Plan B to spread the virus through over-riding all tech. Those 'abhorrent Variants' were the ones who outsmarted you and gave control to us."

Stroud smirked. "You think you've won but you haven't. You've lost your beloved senator Malveux."

He turned his head to look at Malveux on the ground. Strangely the metallic tendrils that had been overtaking her body had begun to retract. Stroud saw a cylindrical auto-injector device in her hands as she got up from the ground. As Malveux began to straighten up, her skin and clothes melted away to reveal Fighting Bull's figure. Stroud's eyes widened at what he saw.

"You see, I never lost her because she was never here," Conrad said in response to the question that was clearly written on his face.

"Bait and switch? Clever," Stroud said as he tried to gain some leverage on Conrad's grip. "But my dream will never die."

Stroud twisted his right arm free of Conrad's grip and grabbed the unfinished syringe that he used and injected himself with it.

Conrad immediately pulled back from Stroud's body as it was rapidly overtaken by a cascade of metallic wiring and circuitry. Both Conrad and Fighting Bull could do nothing but watch as Stroud's body was eaten away from the inside out.

CHAPTER FIFTY-ONE

LOOSE ENDS

December 20th
Union Station
Washington, DC

"Alicia, we have to stop meeting like this," Malveux said as she gave Conrad a hug.

To Conrad's left stood Fighting Bull, whom Malveux extended her hand to. "Agent Fighting Bull it's great seeing you again."

"Pleasure is all mine, senator," she responded as she shook Malveux's hand.

"No, I owe you my life. If you hadn't taken my place back there I would be dead right now."

Fighting Bull waved deferentially. "That's what we do, senator. You can thank Alicia for coming up with the plan."

"Well, I want to thank you anyway," Malveux said as she took a seat. The other two followed suit. They sat in a booth just outside of the food court.

"So, I just wanted to let you know that since the president signed the Digital Emancipation and Privacy Act, the federal government's association with AlphA.I. has been completely dismantled."

"So, what's the plan moving forward," Conrad asked as she looked at Malveux intently.

"We've assumed control of the whole national tech infrastructure. The federal government is working with state and other localities to help them assume their parts of the grids." Malveux paused before continuing, "The only thing we need is access to the Tessellation satellites."

Conrad's eyes tracked back over to Fighting Bull and then back to Malveux. "We're working on it."

Malveux leaned in closer to Conrad. "Alicia, this is serious stuff. There's been international backlash over Vigil peeping into private communications. Even communications of both our foreign adversaries and allies."

"Doesn't the NSA already do that?"

"Stop being cute, Alicia."

Conrad's eyes narrowed. "In all seriousness though, I understand but it's more complicated than that. There are a lot of dangerous actors out there and we finally have access to intel we could've only dreamed of just a few months ago."

"But we also have to remember the importance of autonomy," Fighting Bull said, finally interjecting.

"I couldn't agree with you more, Agent Fighting Bull," Malveux said in response. She looked at her phone. "I have to go but I'll catch you soon."

Malveux stood up and shook Fighting Bull's hand and hugged Conrad. Before she released her embrace she said, "You and I need to talk some more, understood?"

Conrad smiled and bowed her head deferentially to Malveux.

As Malveux walked off, Fighting Bull tapped the table. "You know the senator is right."

"Cynthia, you know the challenges we face. What's wrong with having a heads up on any and everybody, so that what just happened, won't happen again?"

Fighting Bull's eyebrows furrowed. "Because we aren't tyrants, Alicia."

Conrad leaned back in her chair and looked off contemplatively. Fighting Bull waited a moment before continuing.

"And speaking of tyrannical things, I found out more about how complex AlphA.I.'s plans were."

"Well, considering they had all of our psychographics and data it doesn't surprise me. They had a countermeasure to almost everything we hit them with."

"Except," Fighting Bull said as she raised up her right forefinger, "they didn't count on us having Itrish and Kaori on our side."

"Exactly."

"It pays to have Variants on your team, doesn't it?"

Conrad gave a small smile. "Yes, it does, you smart ass."

Fighting Bull smirked. "Anyway, when I was in Japan, I found that Stroud was planning a major merger with a Chinese tech firm, Xiaobo Technologies."

"Really?"

"Yes, and they have strong ties to the politburo, and one minister in particular." Fighting Bull pulled her phone from her pants pocket to show Conrad.

"Weiping Pei," Conrad responded as he saw the man's image on Fighting Bull's phone.

"The last remaining members of the Network we haven't caught."

"Being the director of the Ministry of State Security, he's well-protected."

Fighting Bull tucked the phone back in her pocket. "There's something there, Alicia."

"Say no more. You have my permission to move on this."

"I thought you'd say that. And by the way, I wasn't asking permission, just wanted to give you a heads up."

* * *

December 26th
Holy Cross Cemetery
Los Angeles

The cool winter air embraced Arrowhawk and his mother, Tanner Baisden. He knelt to lay a wreath at his cousin Coryn Baisden's grave.

Arrowhawk covered his eyes as tears began to stream down. His mother gently patted him on the back to comfort him. As he rose, he hugged her with tear filled eyes.

"She didn't deserve this."

"You're right, John, none of us do but you found her killers and threw them behind bars."

"Well," Arrowhawk said sniffling. "We got most of them. Their boss, the crazy one was killed, apparently by a version of his own virus."

"Karma is a bitch, isn't it?" Baisden said.

* * *

December 28th
Jack Blankenchip's apartment
Manhattan, New York

"Hey, Dad," Jack said as he opened the door to let his father and Bledsoe in.

Blankenchip hugged his son before he entered the apartment.

"I'm glad your ass is ok, Jack."

"Same here," Jack responded with a smile. He then looked in Bledsoe's direction and extended his hand to greet her. She pushed his hand aside and instead gave him a hug.

"Please have a seat," Jack said as he motioned to the brown leather sectional in the living room.

"So, how have things been, Jack?" Blankenchip said as he made himself comfortable on the couch.

"Well, after all of the craziness with AlphA.I. I decided to resign from Venturepointe."

"I would call that a genius move."

"Please, Dad, I could do without the sarcasm."

"I'm serious though."

"How can you deal with this guy?" Jack said to Bledsoe as he pointed to Blankenchip.

Bledsoe smiled at Blankenchip, "A lot of tequila."

Jack chuckled. "I have to say, it was genius what you did to spread the antivirus worldwide."

"Thanks, Jack. It was a team effort. I know we kicked it off, but we needed the rest of the world to hop on board. Thankfully most of them have been able to distribute the antiviral serum."

"I agree," Jack said.

"It's just sad that so many people still were killed." Bledsoe paused and looked at her hands. "I just wish I could have done more."

"Babe don't be so hard on yourself," Blankenchip said as he rubbed Bledsoe's back. "Stroud and his whole psychopath tribe at AlphA.I. were the ones to blame. Granted he had noble ends but psycho means to that end."

Jack cocked his eyebrow. "Noble ends?"

"Look, Stroud wanted to help advance humanity, but he went about it the wrong way."

"Yeah, I would say," Jack said.

Bledsoe looked in Blankenchip's direction. "And he wanted to use Variants to accomplish that goal, remember?"

"Yeah, I remember that babe. And no offense but Stroud did have a vision to help maimed and disabled people. Even some of the ones who contracted the Singularis virus were able to regrow limbs."

"But at the cost of thousands of lives though, Aaron."

"I agree, babe," Blankenchip said contritely. "But like I said, the means were wrong even though his intent wasn't all that bad."

CHAPTER FIFTY-TWO
CONSEQUENTIAL DECISIONS

December 30th
The Mirador
Washington, DC

"It's time, Alicia," Pendleton said as he thrusted a tablet computer in Conrad's direction. On the active screen was an outline of a red handprint. Itrish and Kaori sat across the table as Pendleton spoke to Conrad.

"I'm not ready," Conrad said as she sat at the team's round briefing table.

Pendleton placed the tablet right in front of Conrad. "Alicia, I am sorry, but you don't have a choice."

"You are not God," Itrish interrupted. "We," Itrish said as she pointed over to Kaori, "created this protocol with our literal blood sweat and tears. We hoped that you would do the right thing."

Pendleton gently tapped Itrish's shoulder. "Look Alicia, if you don't relinquish control of the Tessellation sat system, you've essentially turned into a digital god. Every computer stroke, video chat, encrypted communication will be under your supervision. And you'll be no worse than any other dictator."

Conrad got up from her chair, looking at both Pendleton and Itrish. "But the world needs protection. You saw what we've just been through. And if it means giving up a little bit of privacy, then so be it."

"Listen to yourself," Itrish said as she shot up from her chair. "You sound like a demagogue. Can you imagine the headlines: 'Vigil has eyes on everyone?'"

Pendleton nodded in agreement. "There are countries ready to go to war over this, Alicia. Having complete control over every piece of tech on the planet is a weight that no one should bear."

Conrad saw the earnestness in Itrish's face. Once again, her eyes were so reminiscent of Conrad's sister's. She relented and slowly placed her hand on the tablet. A red flash emanated from the touchpoint between her hand and the tablet's screen. Immediately, the screen text changed to: "Overwatch protocols deactivated."

"You've done the right thing, Alicia," Pendleton said. Itrish smiled and nodded at Conrad as she walked out with Pendleton and Kaori. As they exited, they passed Morrison.

"When it rains it pours," Conrad said to herself under her breath as Morrison entered.

"We need to talk, Alicia?" Morrison said as he placed his leather brief case on the table.

She motioned to the chair next to her. "Be my guest."

"What is going on? You and I have had our disagreements in the past, but I never would have imagined you would force a protection racket on Lemalia."

Morrison removed the Lemalian agreement from his briefcase and handed it to Conrad. She looked at the document with raised eyebrows.

"Look, Terrell, it's not a racket." Conrad leaned forward, pressing her elbows against the table. "We don't have the funding that we had under the Network. Congress is by no means going to pony up the money and we don't have any other options to keep our team going. So, I made the decision that I thought was best."

"Without discussing it with the team?" Morrison asked.

"This was not a team decision." Conrad brought her hand to her chest. "I am ultimately responsible. No one else." Her voice got louder as she concluded her statement.

"That's the problem, you take it all on yourself. You've forgotten there is always a better way." He reached back into his briefcase to remove two folders—one thick and another thin. He laid the thick file in front of Conrad. "This is the final report on the Lemalian security situation and Harold Baltimore's involvement as you had asked for." He then laid the second folder down and flipped it open. "This is my signed resignation."

Conrad's eyes shot up. "What?! Terrell, you can't just…"

Before she could complete her thought, Morrison closed his briefcase, leaned over, and gave Conrad a hug.

"I pray that God give you peace, Alicia," Morrison said before he left.

CHAPTER FIFTY-THREE

RENDITION

December 31st
Federal Correctional Institute
Cumberland, Maryland

Hanahan's restful sleep was interrupted by the sound of bustling tactical boots and the clack of semi-automatic weapons. As he wiped away the crust from his eyes, he was nearly blinded by a piercing bright glow. Hanahan brought his right hand up to protect his face from the glaring luminescence emanating from the flashlight. He could barely make out the forms of the men who were just outside of his cell. As best as he could tell there were five silhouettes. The clinkering of keys was heard as his cell door slid open.

"Who the hell are you?" Hanahan demanded.

"That's none of your concern," the lead man in the group said. "The better question to ask is, why are we here?"

Hanahan's heart rate quickened. Instinctively, Hanahan swung at the lead man with a right cross and connected with his jaw—scraping his knuckles on the man's helmet chinstrap. The man dropped his flashlight.

Hanahan's fist throbbed, but he was not going to let that stop him. He reached for the flashlight the first man dropped and swung it in an upward arc---hitting a second man in the jaw. The man's head snapped back violently from the impact.

Hanahan suddenly felt a jolt of electricity course through his body. He looked down to see the cords of three taser guns attached to his torso. Hanahan tried to rip the cords off of himself, but instead felt the electrical intensity increase. His body shook violently as thousands of volts of electricity surged through every aspect of his person. Before he lost consciousness, he looked up to see the bloodied face of the first man that he struck.

"We're here to deliver justice," the man said as he wiped the blood from his nose.

THE VIGIL SAGA
WILL CONTINUE IN

BOOK 3:
FACE THE NATIONS

GLOSSARY OF TERMS AND ABBREVIATIONS

BCI- Brain Computer Interface

BDU- Battle Dress Uniform

CCS- Command and Control System

DARPA- Defense Advanced Research Projects Agency

DEPA- Digital Emancipation and Privacy Act

DoD- Department of Defense

DOJ- Department of Justice

ETA- Expected Time of Arrival

FAA- Federal Aviation Administration

FCC- Federal Communications Commission

HoST- Holographic Simulated Training Room

IARPA-Intelligence Advanced Research Projects Agency

IoT- Internet of Things

ICJ- International Court of Justice

ICC- International Criminal Court

MSS- Ministry of State Security

NHTSA- Nation Highway and Traffic Safety Administration

NRO-National Reconnaissance Office

NSA- National Security Agency

PMC- Private Military Contractor

PSIA- Public Security Intelligence Agency

OST-Outer Space Treaty of 1967

SBL- Space Based Laser

SDS- Satellite Defense System

SHAN- Superhuman Abilities Nullifier

SHARP- Superhuman Advanced Research Program

STARS- Surface to Air Retrieval System

THIG- Tactile Holographic Interface Gloves

TPN- Total Parenteral Nutrition

UPF-United Peoples Front

VERGE- Variant Encompassed Research & Group Education

VPN- Virtual Private Network

REFERENCES

Defense Intelligence Agency. "Challenges to security in space."
https://www.dia.mil/Military-Power-Publications.

Johnson, Bernadette. "How the Internet of Things Works."
https://computer.howstuffworks.com/internet-of-things.htm/printable

Leonhard, Gerd. *Technology vs. Humanity.*
United Kingdom: Fast Future Publishing Ltd, 2016.

Mitragotri, S. Immunization without needles. *Nature Reviews: Immunology.* 5.
905-916. (2005).

Rouhiainen, Lasse. *Artificial Intelligence: 101 Things You Must Know Today About Our Future.* Columbia: Self-Published, 2019.

Webb, Amy. *The Big Nine: How the Tech Titans & Their Thinking Machines Could Warp Humanity.* New York: Hachette Book Group, 2019.

SCAN THIS CODE TO BUY 'VIGIL'

ALSO BY P.B. OBENG

A POST-HUMAN ERA. POWER PLAYS DEEP WITHIN THE SHADOWS. A THREAT UNLIKE ANY THE WORLD HAS EVER KNOWN...

Captain Alicia Conrad worked hard to get herself back together. Weighed down by her father's military legacy, she accepts command of a team of superhumans protecting the U.S. from foreign threats.

But when their first mission turns out to be a cover for illegal operations, she vows to bring the villains to justice… no matter the cost.

With the world still rocked by the recent assassination of a small nation's president, Captain Conrad discovers a connection between her unit's target and the country's precious resource. And as she juggles a crew unsure about fighting this new enemy, she fears she might be steering them all into insurmountable peril.

Can Captain Conrad take down a sinister cabal bent on global domination?

Vigil, Book 1 of the Vigil Saga, is available now to *buy in paperback, hardback and Kindle from Amazon. (*You can scan the QR code opposite to do so).

Vigil Merch Available now on Teespring!

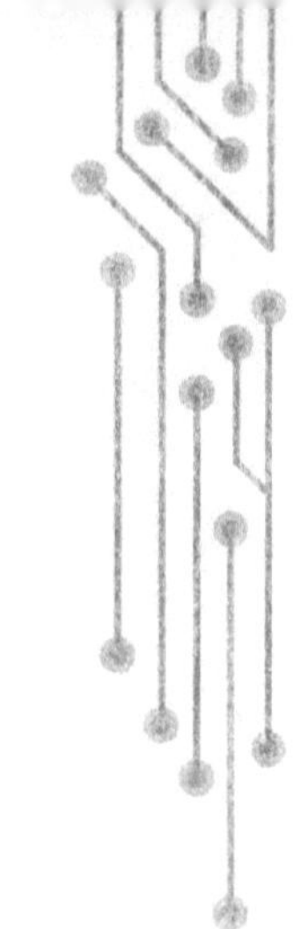

WWW.AUTHOR-PB-OBENG.CREATOR-SPRING.COM

ACKNOWLEDGEMENTS

This story in its current form could not have come about without the editorial guidance of Chinelo Onwualu who challenged me to dig a little deeper on my character development. I also want to thank Jaime Powell for her copyediting help.

ABOUT THE AUTHOR

Paa-Kofi B. Obeng is a full time internal medicine physician who lives in Virginia with his family.

Vigil is the first novel in series. The inspiration for his novel comes from his love of comics, family dramas as well as current events.

You can reach him at **www.pbobeng.com**.

You can also connect with him via the following social media:

www.facebook.com/authorpbobeng

www.instagram.com/author_pbobeng

www.ingramcontent.com/pod-product-compliance
Lightning Source LLC
Chambersburg PA
CBHW021810110726
47902CB00006B/1728